The Narcissist's Lover

N. I. Lockwood

DEDICATION

For my mum, the strongest woman I know – who endured too much abuse and kept quiet because in those days that's what women did. Your little girl was watching and this book is for all the women out there who have been or are trapped in an abusive, toxic, destructive, relationship. May this book help you to see the light and escape the madness. Live life by your design – no one else's.

ACKNOWLEDGMENTS

CM Taylor – my mentor and friend. Without your encouragement - this book would never have seen the light of day. Thank you for believing in my ability when I didn't believe in myself.

My Mum: Who taught me to face my fears and live my dreams – and that things are always brighter in the morning.

My Little Bee: Now you're the daughter watching her mum. Thank you for the cuddles – they get me through!

W.J.S: The love of my life who I am grateful for every day. You are amazing.

My friends: Who are the family I have chosen for myself, who continue to inspire and support me - no matter what – because that's what friends do.

1

One of my friends once told me I was a kind, loving, gentle soul. What that translates to is I'm plain-looking, but I have a good heart. It's ok, I'm a realist. I know how the world works. I look in the mirror, and do you know what I see? I see an obedient daughter, an abandoned sister, a tired mother, a devoted friend, but mostly I see someone who has the face for radio. If dating were like that, if you got to know the person before you saw what they looked like, then maybe people would fall in love with what's on the inside – with souls not faces. That said, I did believe in love at first sight. I didn't know I did. But I hadn't met Edward Coolidge then.

The first time I met Ed I was with my then boyfriend Daniel. We'd driven to Bristol so Daniel could introduce me to him and then we were going to a gig. I was so in love with Daniel then. Happy and excited that we were at the *introducing each other* to our friends' stage. Daniel parked outside the red-brick terraced house, we got out the car and, holding hands, walked up the path beside the neat hedge to the blue door complete with traditional brass knocker. I stood slightly behind Daniel. I was slim then. The door pulled open instantaneously and there he was. In that brief second, my heart called to me. It was as if my inner self recognised him from somewhere. I felt I knew him – maybe from another life? My heart said, *there you are – I've been looking for you!* I reached for Daniel's hand. Ed's smile wrapped around my heart and squeezed.

"All right dude!" he said to Daniel as they exchanged banter and a manly hug.

He pulled me in for a hug too and kissed my cheek.

"Hello darling, you must be Isobel."

"How'd you score her?" Ed said abruptly, turning to Daniel, who was still clinging onto my hand. I could feel my past rising up from my gut into my throat. *No,* it said. *No.* I knew the *no* was right. I had to learn from my mistakes. Never again. It had taken me seven years to find someone as wonderful as Daniel, and I wasn't going to lose him now. I'd push this feeling away, and I'd heed its warning.

That night we went to a gig at a local pub where Ed was singing. He had a spellbinding smile that my heart couldn't get enough off. My brain fell out with my heart that night. *You always get us into trouble!* said brain.

But look at him, he's so gorgeous, said heart. *Don't you just want to hold him and never let go…?*

Heart loved Daniel, but couldn't deny the feeling she got from looking at Edward. That night as I made love with Daniel on the lounge floor, flashes of Ed sneaked into my brain and my climax was so intense that the next day Ed asked me about it while I made Daniel breakfast.

"Did you have a good time last night?"

"Yeah, the gig was great!" I said.

"I was referring to the reason all those tissues are in the bin!" he said, laughing.

"Oh," I said, heat rising to my cheeks. I reached for a little more butter to spread on Daniel's toast. He liked that I always spread out the butter to all of the corners.

"Don't be embarrassed, it's just sex. How does Daniel take his tea again?" he asked, pouring the hot water into the mugs.

"White with one," I replied.

"And you?"

"The same please."

That was seven years ago. Daniel and I had three years together. The usual plans in place. We decided that with my biological clock ticking away we'd try for a baby before we got married. I got pregnant straight away. Daniel's face was a picture. I don't think he expected we'd get pregnant quite so soon. He had strong swimmers – the boy should be proud, eh? Our darling daughter Maddy was born, and my life became all about her. Somewhere along the line I lost sight of my relationship with Daniel, and then the weekends where Dan would work away seemed to roll on and on. We were never together as a family. He'd never help me with the baby. I had to beg him to have her for twenty minutes so I could take a bath, even then he'd go outside and make secret phone calls, leaving her crying in the house. I was so swollen from childbirth (no one tells you about that) I seemed to only be able to wee in the bath or shower. My ankles were rippled with the after-effects of a blood transfusion which caused water retention. My face grew fat and round. I hated how I looked. Dan didn't have to say it – I could see by the way he looked at me he did too. I looked disgusting to him

And he made me feel that way daily. Life became very hard. New Year's Eve of 2009, I decided this couldn't go on. I asked Dan what was wrong and how could we fix it. He said he didn't want this. He didn't want us. He couldn't do family. I think I already knew that, but I was still shocked that he didn't even want to try. That's when I looked in the mirror. That's when I saw the frumpy 35-year-old I'd become. My hair two days overdue a wash. My waist incapable of fitting into the size twelve jeans I used to wear pre baby. My face tired and withdrawn. I looked back at him.

"I don't blame you – I'm not what I said on the tin any more, am I?"

He simply shook his head and gave me a sympathetic smile.

It'd been four years since Dan and I broke up. Maddy was about to start school. Ironically the school that Daniel and I had picked out for our kids when we had first started dating. Family *had* been important to us. It was 2012, the year of the Olympics. The place I worked for decided to get some teams together to compete in the Virgin Triathlon in London. I was doing the swim leg. I completed 750m in 22 minutes 59 seconds. I was so proud! Naturally I had to brag about it on Facebook. I uploaded a picture of my medal and time. I got loads of likes and comments congratulating me - *well done Izzy!* My friends knew I didn't have an athletic figure so for me to do something like that was indeed an achievement. I felt so pleased with myself. Maddy enjoyed wearing my medal and took it to pre-school for show and tell. It was a happy time. Then one evening a message popped up on Facebook Messenger.

So, you competed in a triathlon – well bloody done!

My heart stopped. *I remember you,* it said. It was from Edward. I hadn't seen him since Dan and I broke up.

Thank you, I replied. His profile picture had him looking as dashing as ever. His short dark hair, cheeky smile and strong eyes. He replied straight away.

How's things with you – gotta boyfriend? Well, that was to the point I suppose. Not that I thought he'd ever be interested in me. I was Daniel's ex. There had to be some bro code that forbade that kind of thing. There certainly is in the sisterhood.

Things are good thanks. Maddy's about to start school soon. No, no boyfriend – no time for that! Lol. How's things with you?

He came back with: *Ella and I split up. About to go through a divorce. I'm ok. Ella's hurting.*

Hmm. I wasn't really sure how to respond to this. I never did much like Ella – I found her so negative. I went with, *I'm sorry to hear that mate.*

Thanks. So, what's next after your first triathlon?

Actually, I'm doing another one, a full one this time, on my own!

Wow – where you doing that?

Blenheim Palace. I think I'm gonna end up killing myself! Lol!

Edward asked what I was up to. Well, I was training like mad for the triathlon – a challenge to myself for my thirty-ninth birthday. Running was an issue for me; I just couldn't get the breathing right.

Let's meet up one night, we could go running together at the local track, always good to have someone to run with.

He wanted to see me!

Always good to have someone around to call the ambulance, I jested.

We planned to run 2.5K, which was half the distance I needed to cover in the triathlon

We agreed to meet up on Wednesday, after work, Maddy was with her dad that evening so it freed me up to go out. As I pulled into the car park, my stomach was doing somersaults. I walked through the park to the track and sat down on one of the benches. A voice came from behind.

"Are you warm?"

I looked around; Edward had run over and was staring down at me smiling. *I remember the feeling of that blanket* whispered heart. I stood up and greeted him with a kiss on the cheek.

"I did some stretches in the car park," I lied. He was jogging on the spot in front of me, he had on one of those vest tops, which showed off his guns. Man had he beefed out! He was definitely stockier than I remembered. I bit my lip to snap myself out of it. We had come running together because I had trouble with my breathing; I didn't feel that was going to improve by my running with Ed. That smile. Its effect on me. Seven years ago, I first saw that smile and my heart had never forgotten it. That didn't happen to me often. Actually, it had never happened to me before. But I didn't really know him. He was Daniel's friend. I remember

Daniel didn't like it that Ed and I used to share the same sense of humour. I got accused of flirting once. I wasn't – we were sharing *Star Wars* quotes is all. Ed and I bantered better than Daniel and I did. "You are going to kill me ya know; I'm not that good a runner." I said laughing.

"Well, that's why I'm here, my training is progressive, we'll take it gently, I like to go nice and slow. How does a 2k jog sound?"

I looked at the track. "How many laps is that?"

"About five."

My body felt defeated already. How was I going to drag my sorry arse around that massive 400m track, not once but five times! And he's let me off half a k already! "Yeah sure, why not," I said with a slight whimper.

"Come on then. No time for slacking, let's get to it."

I stood up, holding in my stomach and pushing my breasts out. I started off at a gentle pace. He was kind enough to run at my speed so we could at least run together for a little while. It was very uncomfortable running like this and I'd hardly gone anywhere.

"I just can't get my breathing right; I feel like I'm going to die!"

That's it – flab out, tits down it is – I can't run slim!

Not even 100 yards in and I was knackered.

"Take deep breaths, in through the nose, out through the mouth." He emphasised the point by demonstrating it to me.

Why did he have to keep standing in front of me for goodness' sake. I copied his technique. I felt like I could keel over, I was so unfit. Running was my weakest leg of the Triathlon.

"That's it, keep going, run through it, you are using muscles you haven't used for a long time, try and switch off from the pain," he said encouragingly.

He seriously had no idea of the pressure my abs were under right now. There's a reason men and women aren't supposed to run together. It isn't sexy.

Everything inside me was telling me to stop, my body was crying, it didn't understand what I was doing to it, I could feel my midriff bouncing around under my chest, but I kept going. I had to show him I could do this. I couldn't talk. I focused on the track ahead, the next bend, the straight, the bend after, how many laps I had left. *(Currently 4.5!)* Ed talking to me helped, but it was all I could do to breathe. I'm glad he understood I physically couldn't respond to him.

Noticing just how unfit I actually was he said, "Let's walk for a while."

I was so relieved; as I walked my breathing steadied and the power of speech returned to me. "I'm so unfit," I blurted out.

"It's all in the mind. Tell yourself to keep going, and you will," he said.

"What do you think about when you're running? What keeps you going?" I gasped, lifting up my top to wipe the sweat from my forehead.

"Targets are the one thing that drives me when I am running. I set myself a time of thirty to forty minutes, or a distance, and then I push harder to get there." He sounded so alluring when he spoke all confident like that. So forceful. My mind started to wonder again...

"Right, come on, let's jog now, until the end of the lap, then we can walk for a minute again," he ordered. I must admit, he made sense, walk for a bit then jog, then walk then jog, it was the progression I needed, it needed to be achievable for me to do it. If we had been running straight off the bat, I'd have sat down defeated by now. This was painful but manageable, I could do this, three more laps.

Ed kept talking to me every now and then. All I could do was give a nod or a semi- smile, but he got the picture that I was ok, and was intent to carry on. On our penultimate lap he slowed to a walk and I kept going, if I stopped it would be harder to start again, and I could feel my legs starting to seize from the punishment they were receiving.

"Well done," Ed said as he came up behind me. I smiled. I had both needed and wanted his praise and recognition, I wanted him to be proud of me.

On the last lap he moved from beside me to out in front. As I followed him around the last bend, exhausted, I wanted to drop down on the floor then and there. I could hardly breathe. Listening to myself, I sounded like I was having some sort of attack. I reached Ed and stopped, standing bent over, my hands on my knees, gasping for life like a fish out of water trying to catch my breath. I could feel the sweat dripping from my forehead; I watched it hit the ground like rain.

Well, this is attractive.

When I stood back up, Edward was looking at me.

"You did well," he said, throwing a towel at me.

Great, he's noticed my dripping sweat!

He continued, "It'll get easier, it's just practice."

I nodded; I was too exhausted for conversation.

"It's important to stretch out, I'm going to hit the shower," he said, turning and heading inside.

I followed him. "Yeah, me too."

As I stood in the shower, the warm water massaged my aching muscles. I shouldn't have lied about having warmed up. I placed my hands against the wall and pushed my left leg back and let the water rush over me.

It had, I reflected, been nice to be out with a guy. I hadn't been in male company for a while. It was fun. Especially with Ed – he was cheeky and made me laugh. I couldn't help but wonder if we'd meet up again. It was a nice feeling to think we might. I stepped out the shower and walked over to the locker, taking my clothes out.

"Are you ready yet?" shouted Ed.

I looked toward the door; he was holding it open. "I thought we could go for a drink."

"Lucky I had my towel on Ed, for goodness sake!" I said.

"It wasn't lucky for me," he said, giving me a flash of that smile.

I could feel my cheeks redden. "You charmer!"

"What? Just saying, you look sexy in that towel."

I could feel my face glowing from the heat of embarrassment.

"A drink sounds good, I need to cool down, give me five and I'll be right out."

"Made you feel hot, have I?"

"I was hot anyway!" I said laughing.

"Really? Good to know…" He smiled and allowed the door to close.

Oh my God, he wants to go for a drink and I look like shit. He thinks I look sexy. And he wants to go for a drink. Hang on Izzy, lets assess the situation.

I looked in the mirror. My face had run off me forty minutes ago. I had no make-up. The sexiest guy alive wanted to go out for a drink with me in five minutes. He asked me out while seeing me looking like this. I didn't look much different to when Daniel left me. But to Ed, maybe I was a new tin, with a new label, and so far, he seemed to like me – wobbly bits and all. Maybe he saw what was underneath. He made me feel like I didn't need to be anyone else. Maybe, just maybe, I was enough.

2

Before I met up again with Edward, life had been simple. When I say simple, I mean boring, but it was simple, and without the heartache. I'd mostly lived a single life. For some reason my relationships just hadn't seemed to work out. Someone once said to me, if everywhere you go people tell you it stinks of farts, sooner or later you have to ask yourself, was it me that farted?

My friends were accepting of my singledom. They said things like, *well at least if you're coming you won't need a plus one*. Ouch. It stung when people made comments like that. I wanted the Disney ending I was promised back in the 1970s. I played up to social perceptions. I said, I'm happy on my own, I don't need a man to make me happy. I didn't mean it though. I didn't believe it. It was just easier to say to people that the reason you didn't have the thing you wanted the most in all the world was because you didn't want it. Far easier to say, *my single status is my choice.* If only.

As soon as I left the gym I reached for my phone and without thinking had already started texting Edward, it was as if a bigger force was in control of my actions. I couldn't help myself. I knew what I was doing was dangerous, yet here I was doing it anyway.

Evening, was wondering if you fancied coming over for dinner one night this week? Send.

My heart was in my mouth. Already I was interpreting what it would mean if he did reply, if he didn't reply, and potentially what he would say. Thank goodness I didn't have long to wait, almost immediately I received a text saying, *Dinner eh?* I smiled to myself. As I was contemplating a reply, I received another text. *That'd be lovely.* I stamped my feet and did a little dance. He was going to come to dinner! I couldn't wipe the grin from my face as I drove home.

As I got in the front door, my phone beeped, the tone I had given to Edward's number. *What's on the menu then?*

I paused before replying. *Anything your heart desires. What do you fancy?*

Are you still talking about food?

I was feeling devilish. *Maybe.*

Be careful Miss Burnell, you'll get me chasing you, and if that's a game you want to dare to play…

I could feel the excitement in the pit of my stomach. Edward Coolidge was telling me outright that he wanted me. Without hesitation I wrote back,

Double dare you.

Get ready.

Huh?

You have 40 minutes. You better be ready for me or else there'll be consequences.

What?

I expect you to be clean shaven and wearing something black and sexy. Now go and get ready. I'm coming for you.

Standing in my lounge, gym bag at my feet, I looked into the kitchen, looked back at the front door, looked down at my phone, my brain was catching up, we'd skipped dinner and moved straight to dessert. I didn't have time to be standing here, shit I had to get ready!!

"Are you really coming over? You're joking right? Lol"

"35 minutes, stop wasting time."

Holy shit, he was serious. Adrenaline started pumping, excitement ricocheted through my body. I felt scared, promiscuous. Oh my gosh, thirty-five minutes, I had to shave, do my hair, have a bath, what was I going to wear? Arrghh! This wasn't enough time, I had to get moving.

I ran a bath, realising I could panic about what I was wearing while it ran. Everything I needed to do pumped through my head, shave my foo fee and moustache, pluck my chin hairs. (Dark haired girls get a bad deal I'm telling ya.) I think I had a black basque, hopefully I had stockings? Maybe I could wear my lace nightie over the top? I had to do my hair and make-up; I was never gonna be ready at this rate.

Beep from phone. *I've left the house. 25 minutes.*

Who put him in charge? Although I must admit it was very erotic being told what to do and when, more so with the knowledge that the guy I'd fancied for seven years had as good as said he wanted to fuck me. I found a short black skirt and a lace shirt. I'd wear that over the top of my underwear.

I was ready just as his car pulled up outside on my driveway. The car door opened, there was a slight pause and then it slammed shut. Hesitation consumed my throat as my ears waited for the knock at the door. My heart fell silent with the sound of *knock, knock, knock.* My feet carried my arms towards the porch, my hand reached out to pull open the door, and there he was. Standing there smiling at me with that boyish smile of his and suddenly I wasn't scared any more.

"Hello," he said, as I stepped back and let him in.

"Hello," I replied. I knew my face was beaming. I swear if it had been raining, there would have been a rainbow with the glow I was giving off. He was wearing a chocolate- brown polo shirt; it matched his eyes.

He came in and sat next to me on the couch and we just talked for a while. I wanted to be sure things were over with his wife before we did anything that might compromise that. He assured me it was over, he said she thought they were trying because he didn't have the strength to end it properly, but in his mind, it was over and had been months ago. Suddenly he stopped talking and moved closer to me. Oh God he was going to kiss me. I wasn't as slim as I was when I first met him, but that didn't seem to worry him. He'd seen me at my worst when we went running. He'd seen I'd gained weight and he hadn't changed his mind.

"Look at you all dressed to impress," he said. And he leant in and pushed his lips against mine. I was filled with a deep, wanton longing for him. It was as if I was dreaming. This was the guy I'd fantasised over for years and here he was, right now, in my living room. And he was expressing the same feelings I'd been carrying for him the instant I met him back at the blue door with the brass knocker. Maybe it simply wasn't our time then — was now our time? I couldn't wait to find out. The air fell still as his eyes searched mine for permission. His lips met mine lightly at first, causing me to gasp inside; then moved to kiss around my neck, sucking up into my ear, whilst his fingers set to undoing my blouse with minimal effort. I thought of Daniel and for a brief second doubted what I was doing. But we'd been split for four years. I couldn't stop myself now even if I wanted to. I was already in too deep. I wanted this and I was fully committed to the cause of fucking Edward Coolidge. I started at unbuttoning his top, pulling it up and over his head, I wanted to feel his skin against me. He had a full chest of dark hair; I couldn't wait to run my fingers through it. He undid his belt, I moved my hand down to unbutton his jeans, gravity took them to the floor and he stepped out of them, holding me close to his body as he continued to kiss me with those soft gentle lips. My eyes glanced down at his black boxers. His thighs were thick and sturdy, his arse firm. He wrapped his arms around me and for the first time in a long time, I felt safe.

Looking down at me he slowly unzipped my skirt and it fell to the floor. He picked me up, my legs wrapped around his waist as he lowered me to the sofa. His lips kissed down my neck, across my breast, stopping to gently nibble at my nipples, before giving them a gentle lick. I ran my hands through his hair as he pushed his crutch into mine. My nails gently pulled over his arse cheeks and slid off his boxers.

"Don't mark me," he said, pushing his cock into me. I could feel every bit of his length as he pushed deep inside me. "Do you like that?" he whispered.

"Yes," I said rising my body up to meet his thrust. He brushed my hair away from my eyes with his palm. I could feel he was examining me.

"Look at me," he commanded. I opened my eyes. He looked so

hot. His deep brown eyes sank through me. I was in total awe of him: from this moment, I was forever his. Of all the women in the entire world, why the hell was he here with me? I pushed the thought from my mind as he started to pump me harder, making me scream out in pleasure.

"Oh Ed, oh my God, don't stop, please don't stop." His thrusts became more targeted and powerful and I almost yelped in delight as he pleasured me.

"You look very sexy, I like you in this, you'll wear this again for me."

Wear it again, bloody heck, he wants me again and we haven't finished this time yet.

He pulled me in to meet his face, kissing me firmly on the mouth, I searched for his tongue but it was a no-go zone to me. His hands caressed my breasts, I felt so aroused, a wetness I'd never experienced. My hands gripped into the couch, my arse pushing my vagina up to meet his cock. It suddenly hit me I wasn't on birth control, and he wasn't wearing a condom.

"You can't come inside me," I blurted out.

"Yes, I can..." he said sternly, thrusting himself deeper inside me.

I was so aroused I didn't care. I'd get the morning after pill.

"I'll always come inside you, Izzy." He moved his hands to hold onto my wrists, my arms above my head and then came in me whilst looking deep into my eyes. "That was just as good as I imagined it would be, you were worth the wait," he said, moving his lips down to kiss me.

"So were you, Edward." He smiled at me as he pulled out of me and went off to the toilet.

I grabbed the opportunity to tidy myself up. He returned still fully naked; he was so confident in his perfect body. His chest was well defined and muscle-toned. His arms were strong, they screamed: *These guns will protect you, baby.*

"Come here," he said gently, as he lay down on the sofa. I moved over to snuggle into his chest and he held me close to his heart for a while.

I knew I likely meant nothing to him. I had to confess to myself though, I enjoyed cuddling up to him all the same.

If only for tonight, maybe I did mean something.

The deafening sound of my alarm clock woke me. Six am. Flashes of the night before ran through my mind. His flesh on my flesh. A wetness started to develop between my legs. I jumped out of bed, I had to shake thoughts of last night from my head. I'd probably never hear from him again. I couldn't allow my head to go all fuzzy. A shower would cool me down. I had to shake this feeling from me. My body has been awakened to sex and now it was as if it had realised how starved it had been – I could feel myself wanting to stock up for the next famine!

I stepped out of the shower feeling frustrated and angry at myself. I wasn't going to call him. As I toweled myself down, I kept glancing at my phone. I'd dry my hair off first then I'd check my messages. *Nope, best to check now – you never know!* I lurched across my bed and grabbed my phone. Nothing. Hmm. Well, it had only been last night. I wouldn't allow myself to obsess over this. I had to get my head together. I had an important seminar today, I needed to be professional. I dressed, and as I looked in the mirror, no amount of showering and make up could remove that expression. I was going to be walking around all day with that *I've been fucked* look on my face.

I entered the seminar and sat down next to my colleague Sam who had grabbed me a coffee. Damn it, she picked up on my happiness straight away. What lie could I come up with to cover this? As I sat there trying to think of a good enough story, the speaker started.

"Thank you for coming along today to this talk about the duty of care in the workplace, and how protected your organisation is…" Laughter started to enter my right ear. I turned to look at my colleague who was almost crying with silent laughter. I looked at the guy presenting, his flies weren't undone, he looked normal… Looking at her, I mouthed "What?"

She shook her head, unable to speak. Instead, she pointed at me and then her own neck. I didn't get it.

"What?" I mouthed again.

"Love bite on your neck," she mouthed back. Oh my God! How embarrassing, and here I was trying to be someone. I slowly removed the pin from my hair and pulled my hair down around my shoulders. I wanted to disappear into the chair. I was sat in a seminar with a hickey! It was disgraceful. I tried desperately to concentrate on what the speaker was saying. I was aware of Sam who was still sniggering to herself. Half time came and I raced to the toilet for a look. How the hell had I missed this before I left the house? Thank goodness I had long hair I could wrap around me. When I joined Sam, she pulled me to the side of the room, she had already got me a drink so there was no escape.

"Well, you had a passionate evening, Miss Burnell! Come on then, spill." Sam looked at me, as only a woman can, with enough of a pregnant pause, that makes you tell her everything. I decided I'd go for factually correct as opposed for recounting every fine detail. I figured offering the facts might just keep questioning to a minimum.

"I did go to the gym and then a friend came around unexpectedly."

"You mean a friend unexpectedly came in you more like!" she said laughing.

"Ladies and gentlemen. Please take your seats; our next speaker will shortly be telling us all about the latest legislation."

I tried to take notes and listen, but my mind kept wandering off to images of last night. His chest, the touch of his lips on my skin, his fingers causing little rushes of excitement across my body. The chemistry between us. It was hard to concentrate. Least of all on the latest legalities.

There is something about being sat in the dentist waiting room that fills you with anticipation and dread. The *will I or won't I get a filling today, and if I do, could I still give good head?* I pondered on it, as a beep from my phone disturbed my thoughts. My fanny was alerted and promptly woke up.

I had fun last night, you're bad, I like it. I'm feeling horny Iz.

A smile beamed across my face, completely not understood by anyone else in the waiting room at the dentist's.

"Miss Burnell?" I was awoken by the dental nurse. As I entered the dentist's room, I calmed myself with the knowledge it was just a check-up.

3

As he walked through the door in his army uniform, I could have easily

fallen at his feet. Instead, I stepped forward into him, looking up at him –

at six foot one he towered over me. We paused for a few seconds, before

throwing our arms around each other and pulling our lips together. Our

hands were wild, grabbing and fondling each other's bodies like they were

on an SAS raid. He hoisted my right leg up to his crotch as he kissed into

the left side my neck, then he pushed me back against the wall, holding my

shoulders with his hands, and whispered, "Drop down and take my

temperature." Easing myself down to the floor, my eyes had line of sight of

his fly and a very complicated-looking belt. *Hmm I'll leave that for him to do*

and just move in for the blow job like I was told.

    The sound of his zipper was intense. It held with it all his pent-up

desire, desire for me to suck him dry on my lounge floor. As I untucked his penis from his boxers, I looked up at him just as I wrapped my lips around his cock. He leant against the wall, exhaling a gasp of satisfaction, his left hand lightly stroking my hair. I could feel the wetness start to run from between my legs. I wanted him to be thrusting inside me. He started to let out moans of delight, inspiring me to suck him further. I moved my mouth along his length, taking one of his balls in with my tongue while circulating my finger around his end. "Oh Izzy," he screamed out, "you are one dirty bitch!"

In any other situation I would have gone nuts right now. But strangely I liked him talking down to me, I liked the idea of being his, of him telling me what to do. "No, I'm *your* dirty bitch," my lips replied. He looked down at me with surprise and pulled me up to him. I wanted him to know I was his. Completely his. We smiled at each other for a brief second. His warm, deep brown eyes could tell me anything and I'd believe them.

This was very dangerous. I was getting into unchartered territory here. I had never been this expressive in sex. What disturbed me more though, was that I liked it. I craved it. I needed it. I had to have him inside me. Now. "Fuck me Edward – please just fuck me now," I pleaded.

"Patience…" he teased. Grabbing me by the hair, he pulled me up to his face. His fingers stroked the back of my neck; he looked into me contemplating his next move. I waited patiently for his command. I wanted to kiss him, to touch his skin, and feel his body press against mine. Slowly his hand reached for my zipper, unleashing my cleavage, massaging my breast as he pushed me against the wall. Then he kissed the length of my body as he found his way to his knees, hitching my skirt, and raising his hands to follow my thighs, I could sense he was about to lick my clit. Moving the crotch of my knickers to the side he gently parted my labia and started to stroke his tongue across my clit. I let out a moan at the intensity that had been allowed to ferment inside me. I wanted his cock inside me now. He felt so good, I didn't feel like I had the strength to stand up, I wanted to crumple to the floor to allow my body to fully relax and enjoy him, and with it feel the full force of his thrust deep inside me. He moved his tongue away and inserted two fingers up into my vagina. At last, some force where I wanted it! He pushed them right up into me and with the pads of his fingers he massaged a part of me I never knew I had. My feelings were so intense, I couldn't contain myself and I had to push him away – it was too much, my knees started to shake. Pulling me down to him, he kissed me, I could taste my sweet juice on his lips. I searched for his length, I had to have him inside me. "I want you in me," I whispered.

He lay down, and pulled me on top of him. "I want you where I can watch you." I slid up on top of him, taking my place riding his cock. My hair fell down over my face, I liked I had a shield. He tucked my hair back over my ears, he wanted to look into my eyes. He was so beautiful; how did I get here? My pussy sank down onto him and clenched around his girth, my buttocks pushed up and down, he held my waist. My hands lifted my hair up from behind my head, I was riding him free style with my hair around my face. As he pushed into me, I gasped with pleasure. I loved riding this handsome man, why did he want to be fucking me out of all the women he could choose from? I was the luckiest girl on earth.

He sat up to meet me. "I want to take you from behind Izzy, bend over," he said. I slid off him and bent over the sofa in front of him. I loved doggy style, it allowed deeper penetration, the deeper and harder the better as far as I was concerned. His hands slid up my outer thighs, slightly hitching my skirt up, revealing my naked arse. His penis gently kissed my opening before sliding gently into my wetness. He teased me at first, pushing in slightly and then pulling back, I pushed back into him, trying to pull him deeper into my sex. He smirked. He knew I just wanted him to power-fuck me. His hands steadied me, not allowing it, this was at his pace, he controlled my wanting, my passion, my desire for him to fuck me hard. As he quickened the pace, I couldn't contain myself, wailing out deep moans of excitement. I was so wet he slipped out of me, and as he pushed to go back in, it wasn't my pussy he was burrowing into.

'That's the wrong hole," I whispered.

"No it's not," he replied sternly. I didn't move, this was new to me, I was so turned on. It was wrong, we shouldn't be doing this, but I was powerless to stop it, I wanted him so much, he turned me on so much, I pushed my arse up to him, trying to show him I was enjoying the moment.

"I'm told it's better if you rub your clit," he said.

"I can't move, it's too erotic," I replied. Truth was I didn't dare move, this was the perfect position, if I removed one arm I might fall over, and that would ruin the glorious sensation happening in my arse right now. I never knew anal could be so pleasurable.

"You are such a dirty bitch; I love it Izzy." There it was again, the way he said my name, so erotic, I loved that he used my name whilst his dick was working its way inside me. He reached a palm round to gently start to massage my right breast, which was heaving for him to mould it. "I want to see you," he said as he pulled out of me. He kissed the back of my neck, and slid underneath me, looking up at me, so that I was straddling him. His fingers found their way to my clitoris. He kissed my neck, whilst slowly stroking me, I squirmed with delight as he made me come, playing me to his melody. "Where do you want me to come? Your mouth, your arse, over your tits, tell me, where do you want it?" (As turned on as I was, that thing had been in my arse, so as much as I would've liked to, there was no way I was swallowing it now!)

I rolled him over, so he was back on top of me, offering him my tits. I was surprised at how much of a turn on it was to watch him wanking himself over me. He looked right into my eyes, which I tried to close out of embarrassment.

"Open your eyes, look at me." His request was seductive and full of intent. How did I get to be here in this moment experiencing the sex of my life with this beautiful man? The way he looked at me made me melt. He could have asked me for anything and I'd have given it to him willingly.

I moved my hand to take control of his shaft and he pushed his fingers up inside me. As he came, he re-claimed his cock and shot his load into my cleavage. As the passion died, reality hit me. There I was. On the floor, cum all over me – if I stood up it would ruin the carpet. Thank goodness Ed noticed the box of tissues on the side and threw them at me playfully as he headed upstairs to take a shower.

I put the kettle on and made us a cuppa. When Ed came downstairs, he was wearing my robe. I laughed hysterically.

"I thought I'd stay over tonight."

"Yeah, sure," I said, smiling at him.

"Thanks honey." I could feel myself blushing. That was the first time he had addressed me with affection. And he was staying the night. Apart from anything, I really liked having him around. If I was honest with myself, I'd loved him awhile, I was just waking up to the fact.

"I'll cook us breakfast in the morning," he said swinging open the fridge door. "Eggs, bacon, mushrooms, toast – I can work with that."

"I'll look forward to that, I forgot you cook, Ed. You always used to cook such a delicious fry-up."

"Oh yeah – I cooked for you and Daniel, didn't I?"

"Well, you weren't employed!"

"Ha ha, you know what I meant."

"I used to like it when you stayed over. It was the only time we were allowed a fry-up. Dan is so health conscious. Plus, you always did what you wanted – I liked that about you."

"Yeah?"

"Yeah." He moved to stand in front me, his arms stroking my sides.

"Well, we're here together now," he said.

"We are, and I like it," I said, smiling at him as he leant in to kiss me on the lips. "Drink your tea, it'll get cold."

He picked it up and reached for my hand. "Come to bed."

I had a feeling I'd sleep well tonight next to him. He made me feel safe. How could I not feel that? He was so strong, muscular and oozed masculinity. It felt comforting knowing his scent would be all over my robe the next time I put it on, that he'd linger on me.

"That's my side," I said as Ed got into the right side of the bed.

"It's my side too."

"But I always sleep on that side – all my stuff is on that side."

He didn't move. He was taking my side of the bed.

On the up side, now I'd smell him on my pillow too. I got into bed next to him and he automatically opened his arm for me to snuggle up into his nook. I rested my right hand on his chest. My fingers started to massage his dark hair, caressing him. He kissed my head.

"It's time for sleeps, maybe I'll wake you up early," he said, holding me tight.

"You better woman – I'm expecting a full English!" I teased.

Was this really happening? Was Edward Coolidge actually in my bed? Was my life starting to align and was I getting everything I'd ever wanted? Was I getting my mate for life? I was too happy and excited about the future to sleep. I listened to the sound of his breath and studied the contours of his chest. I didn't want to miss a moment of him being here. My contentment turned to a dream world and I drifted off to sleep safe inside his embrace.

I awoke to the smell of bacon and ventured downstairs to find Ed again wearing my robe, bacon sizzling, mushrooms about to join them in the pan.

"Morning!" I said, smiling at him dancing around my kitchen. It looked like every pan had been used and every utensil had a part to play. But I didn't care. Ed was cooking me breakfast and that made me the happiest girl in Badersley.

"Morning honey!" he said, planting a kiss on my head. Hmm. Morning breath… I should have brushed my teeth first. But the smell of the bacon had drawn me downstairs.

"How do you like your eggs?"

"With no snot in them."

"Huh?"

"You know what I mean, when the egg white hasn't been cooked properly and it looks snotty – I hate that – I like my egg cooked properly."

"Right, no snot for Izzy it is!" He flipped it over in the pan and let it sizzle with the bacon. I sat at the table waiting expectantly. I couldn't wait to get stuck in. Ed put the breakfast in front of me and we started eating.

"This is so good, I forgot how good a cook you are."

"It's just a quick fry-up."

"What have you used on the mushrooms. They've got a zing to them."

"Lemon juice and some *herbes de Provence*." Christ, I didn't even know I had lemon juice and herbs in stock.

As I took in my fourth mouthful, Ed stopped eating. "There's something I need to tell you." He looked serious. Enough so that I could feel a bombshell about to go off.

"What's up?" I asked.

"I've been offered a contract working in Abu Dhabi. It's a lot of money – it means I can start my pilot's licence."

Abu Dhabi – that was like, halfway around the world! This was it then. Our last supper. I meant nothing. This was just… well, sex.

"Wow – congratulations, that's awesome." Somehow, I managed to fake my best smile and look happy for him.

"That's a relief – I wasn't sure how you'd react." *Please don't go* my heart cried.

"What right do I have to react, Ed? I'm not your wife. What did Ella say?"

He looked to the floor. "I haven't told her yet. I can talk to you Izzy. I like talking with you, you're cool, you listen to me. You don't go off on one. It's different with Ella."

"Well, she's your wife, it affects her, doesn't it? You going away means she's a single parent. You must do what you think is right Ed. I'm not gonna tell you what to do."

"Legally, yes, we're still married. But our relationship has been dead for years. I don't want to be with her."

"Is it easier for you to run off to Abu Dhabi and leave it all behind you – rather than face into it and get some resolution?"

"I don't want to hurt her."

"I think it's a bit late for that, mate."

He laughed. "Mate?"

"We're mates, aren't we?"

"Yeah of course, but… oh, I don't know."

"What?"

"Ner it's nothing." He picked up his glass of orange juice. "Here's to you Izzy."

"Why are we toasting me?"

"Because you're amazing." I wasn't sure why I was amazing, but I didn't feel like pushing the conversation either.

He was moving to Abu Dhabi. I wasn't going to see him. I'd been a fling. A re-bound following the break-up of his marriage. I'd been stupid to allow myself to think a guy like him would have been interested in me for anything else.

I wasn't hungry any more.

"I'm gonna go grab a shower," I said, taking my OJ from the table.

"Are you ok? You haven't finished your breakfast."

"It was too much for me, lovely but more than my stomach can handle."

"I'll have it then," he said instantly, scraping it onto his plate. I went upstairs. I could feel the barrier going up. I had to distance myself from him. No point in prolonging the agony. He was going. He wasn't meant for me. This wasn't going to be our time after all. I'd just been a bit of fun to him. He'd been so much more than that to me. I'd dared to dream about a future with him. I was such an idiot.

I went in my room and turned on the shower. I took a pee before getting into the warm water. I let the steam consume me as if to cleanse my mind of all my feelings. I cupped the water in my hands and allowed it to overflow.

He was leaving. Tears started to flow. The warm water carried them away, down the drain. We'd slept together twice. We'd been running, had dinner. It wasn't anything serious. It was just…fun… I guess. Although it sure didn't feel fun right now. You'll be ok, Izzy, I told myself. Just keep moving forwards. I turned the water off and stepped outside of the shower, wrapping myself in a towel.

Ed appeared. "Thought I'd jump in the shower myself before I go," he said, pulling me in for a cuddle and kissing my ear. "Although, now you're all clean, maybe I could get you dirty again?" I pulled the towel tighter to me, I didn't want him to see my body in the light of day – feeling my wobbly bits was one thing, but seeing them? Even I didn't want to do that.

Sensing my discomfort, he said, "Hey, I love you the way you are."

Loved me? He loved me? His face looked sincere; his words felt true. One flash of that smile and I was putty. It was pointless to resist. With one kiss my towel dropped to the floor and our lips set to doing all the talking our voices seemed incapable of. Why did he have to go to Abu Dhabi of all places? He said he loved me but if I meant even the snippet of something to him, surely, he wouldn't go. He kissed into my neck awakening my senses. His skin felt firm against mine. His touch, the way he held me in his embrace with such passion and intent.

I pushed him to the bed, straddling every thrust while I could.

"I like looking at you while you're riding me, Iz." Damn. He was so attractive, he made me feel sexy and alive. Like out of all the woman he could have, he only wanted me. No one has ever made me feel as desired as I felt I was by Edward Coolidge.

"This isn't the end Iz. I'll still call you; we'll still talk. I'm not losing you. I can tell you anything. You're my best friend."

He held me tightly as he came in me. Silent tears fell into his chest. He wouldn't have noticed from the sweat between us.

"I need another shower now," I said, lightening the mood.

"I mean it Iz. You are."

He got out of bed and got down on one knee, taking my hand in his.

"Izzy, will you take my hand in best friend-dom? Will you be my best friend for better or for worse? Will you promise to fuck me whenever I demand it, from this day forward until death do us part?"

I laughed, covering my blushing cheeks with both hands.

"I'm serious Izzy, I want an answer!" he said, his voice sounding a little hurt.

"I will Edward, yes," I said, sliding out of bed to take him in my arms. "I love you as you are too." I snuggled into his arms, and felt an honesty in our embrace.

The sad thing is, this was the best proposal I'd ever had. My ex-husband had asked me mid-row and to my shame my first response was to tell him to fuck off – even though the thing we'd been arguing about was getting married! Daniel asked in bed when I was six months pregnant. It wasn't romantic – it was more a conversation. *Do you want to get married then?* More matter of fact. Then Ed – out of sheer silliness, gets down on one knee and sweeps me off my feet by asking me to be his bestie. Priceless.

4

The rain hammered against the window. I sat in the lounge cuddled up under a blanket on the sofa. Maddy would be home soon. Any minute now a burst of energy would come running through the front door and I'd be Mum again. I watched the overcast sky wrap around the houses in the street. Each drop of rain seemed to be sharing my sorrow. Liv had told me to enjoy it whilst it lasted. "Take it while you can," she'd proclaimed. I guess she was right. I was never gonna keep a guy like Ed Coolidge. He made me feel so sexy just by the way he looked at me. I wondered when he was going. I hadn't even asked when the contract started.

A whistle - a text from Ed. *Hey honey, how's your day been?*

How had my day been? I have to confess I hadn't done much. The washing and household essentials. I didn't want to appear boring, so I replied: *Had a busy one thanks mate, how's yours?*

Dan's car pulled up outside, and then the sound of Maddy's feet running up the driveway. A tiny continuous knock followed; she always does this until I get to opening the door.

"Mummy!"

"Hello darling," I said scooping her up into my arms. Her little face looking up at me in wonder.

"Mummy's upset, what's the matter Mummy?" she asked. I'd put my best mummy smile on my face and everything, and my five-year-old saw straight through it.

"Mummy's probably just been asleep and we've woken her up," said Daniel. Clueless as ever. I didn't mind he was oblivious really – it was one less person to fool that I was ok.

Beep beep.

"Yeah, just tired, and I missed you Maddy Waddy!" I said, squeezing my baby girl.

Beep beep.

"Someone wants you," said Dan, glancing at my phone.

"I'll get it later." I knew it'd be Ed and I couldn't risk Dan seeing the text.

"See you next week Maddy, be a good girl for Mummy."

I put Maddy down so she could say goodbye to Daniel. We waited at the door as he drove off down the road.

"Right Maddy, what would you like for tea?"

"Nuggets!" she declared. I could do with an easy tea tonight, besides, one of us had the right to be happy. "Shall we put *Jake and the Neverland Pirates* on?"

"Yay!"

"Ok, let's get your jama's on Mads, and then we can sit down, cuddle up and eat tea."

"Oh!"

"You haven't got to go to bed yet love, let's just get you ready, ok?" I got the nuggets out the freezer and poured the baked beans into a pan. I didn't feel like eating. In fact, I didn't feel like doing much anymore.

Beep, beep. I checked my phone. Three messages from Ed.

Mate? I think I'm a bit more than that!

What you doing tonight? Thought I could come over.

Oi! Where'd you go?

He made me laugh. I called him mate to establish a boundary. To remind myself that was all we were. He wanted me to think of him as more than that but at the same time he didn't want me. And men think woman are complicated!

I texted back. *Sorry Maddy just got home and Dan came in and I couldn't reply straight away. I'm at home tonight, I have Maddy but she'll be in bed by 7.30 if you want to come over. We could get a take away.*

I didn't really know if I wanted a take away but it seemed an obvious thing to suggest. He was certainly keen having been here last night already. Maybe he didn't know what he wanted. All the same, even if we didn't have sex tonight, it'd be nice to see him. Actions speak louder than words after all. He could be in one of a million places, and he was choosing to be with me. A smile beamed over my face as I stirred the beans.

Beep, beep. *Oh, I see, yeah wouldn't have wanted him to know we were in text would we! Ok honey cool, I'll come over later – see you soon.*

I snuggled up with Maddy. She sat on my lap with her tray on her knee, eating her nuggets and beans. I loved my little girl, she was the light of my life. It could be difficult being a single parent. Dan always helped out financially, I couldn't fault him for that. It wasn't the life I planned though. Single, unmarried mother. We don't always get what we want though. The way I saw it, I was Queen of the remote, I took my own bins out and I was the mistress of spider watch. I didn't necessarily want those titles, but whilst waiting for my prince to come, certain things still needed doing.

I tucked Maddy into bed with Tigger and Doggy after reading *Ten Little Chicks* for the third time. She had little fairy lights around the end of her bed, every night I'd tuck her in, and every night as I reached the doorway, she'd kick her covers off.

"Night night baby, Mummy loves you."

"Maddy loves you too," she'd say as I hit the landing. If I made the mistake (which sometimes I did) of going back for another cuddle at that point there'd be fun and games trying to get her to stay in bed – and tonight Ed was coming, so I had to be firm. "Be a good girl darling and cuddle down and go to sleep," I said softly as I walked down the stairs, feeling like the biggest arsehole for not going back for that extra cuddle of the night. It was 7.15. Tonight, I wasn't bothering with my appearance. Ed knew Maddy was home and that to me meant no sex. Tonight would be about friendly conversation, catching up with his move to Abu Dhabi and rolling with the punches. I put the telly on and tried not to watch the clock. 7:30 – he wasn't here yet. Oh well, time for another episode of *Friends*. It was the one where Ross said to Rachel *but we were on a break!* I pondered on whether Ed would say that to Ella should she find out about us. 7.47 – still no sign of him. No text. I'd hold out the hour before calling him. What if he'd had an accident though? Ner, he was just delayed. But with what? Or with whom? I checked his text reply. He'd said *Ok honey cool, I'll come over later – see you soon.* Later? That meant tonight, right? Or did he just mean later, later? Had I misinterpreted what he said? Did he mean he was coming over *tonight?* Or was it like *later dude?* I could feel anxiety rising within me, suddenly he was all that mattered. 7.53. If he wasn't here by 8pm, I'd just call him.

7.55. *I'll make a cup of tea.* I got up and filled the kettle. He was always right on time. I must have got it wrong. Disappointment rushed through me. I wasn't going to see him tonight. Why was I bothered? I was playing it cool – *remember, Izzy? Yeah great job girl!*

Knock knock.

He was here! I ran and opened the door. There was Ed, holding a Sainsbury's bag and 12 red roses.

"Hi honey, I got you these," he said planting a kiss on my lips and handing me the flowers.

"They're beautiful – thank you!" I said pulling him back for another slower kiss.

"I also thought I'd cook us tea. How does steak and chips grab you?"

"Sounds great!" Wow – he'd brought me not just flowers, but a dozen red roses. Oh my God! And now he was cooking me dinner. I so should have bothered!

"How do you like it?" he said looking at the steak.

"Well done please." I sat on the stool and watched him work his way around the kitchen. I liked having him here, that was the problem. But he was only on loan, and I knew at some point he'd go and then the sadness would start to creep up on me.

A banging of cupboard doors lifted me from my thoughts. "Chopping board?" he inquired.

"Bottom right, near the oven… So, any more on Abu Dhabi?" I did, and didn't want to know more.

"I've got to go through reference checking yet, could be a few weeks."

"You're definitely going then?"

"I have to, I need the money."

"Have you told Ella yet?"

"Yeah, I told her this morning. She cried. Said she's going to move back to Hereford. The kids miss it there."

I had great empathy for Ella. She hadn't got what she was promised either. An unfaithful husband who was deserting her, leaving her with two kids while he went off to work miles away. A catch like Coolidge would be off after his next victim instantly too. He'd likely already be looking up Arabian women on plenty of fish. He was sent for fun, that's all, to liven me up and get me back out there. My heart sank a little deeper. My smile hung a little lower and my eyes fought back the trickle forming behind them. He was here now, his strong arms tending a spatula to the bearnaise sauce he was stirring. I liked how his t-shirt cut off around his biceps. His arms were so beefed up he had to stand with them slightly further away from his body than the average man. His legs fell slightly ajar as he stood in front of the hob orchestrating the vegetables and sauce. This was what I'd always wanted – someone to share ordinary life stuff with.

I had two weeks – I could enjoy what we had or mope around because it was temporary. I'd always believed in regretting what I had done not what I hadn't. My smile returned and my heart lifted as he opened the fridge and passed me a beer.

"Do you want a hand with anything?"

He paused, turning down the gas on the hob to its lowest flicker.

"There is one thing that goes well with steak Iz – especially on 14th March."

I was confused. "What's that then?" I really had no idea.

"It's steak and a blow job day," he said with a glint in his eye and moving his torso into me, taking back the beer from my hand and placing it gently on the table. "You've got five mins Iz."

I looked at the clock on the oven – 20:28. "I'll only need two," I said with confidence, dropping down to my knees and pushing him up against the door. He'd undone his jeans and they dropped to the floor around his ankles. I whipped his boxers down; his erect penis was waiting to greet me. I licked the end, taking his length in my mouth, my hands holding his firm buttocks as he pumped my mouth. Wrapping my lip over my teeth, I held him in my mouth, squeezing down on him tight as he thrust into my mouth. My tongue circled his end, I took my finger and poked it deep up into my vagina to make it moist, then as Ed was moving in my mouth, and I was licking his end and squeezing him as he thrust into me, I inserted my finger into his anus, and pushed down onto his gland making him scream out with an unexpected delight.

"Oh my God Izzy – that's amazing, I can't control myself."

I looked up into his eyes, which reflected my devilish glint, allowing him to watch me watch him as I sucked him off with confident enthusiasm. His juice released into my mouth as I swallowed it down and slowly removed my finger from his rectum while licking my lips. I looked at the clock on the oven – 20:30.

"Two mins!" I rejoiced.

He smiled at me breathless, I knew I'd done good. I could see in his eyes that he wanted to reward me. He dropped to his knees and inserted his fingers deep into my sex, making me want him inside me. I craved his touch, he released me like no other ever had. He was a sex God and I his faithful student.

He looked into my eyes. "Dinner's ready." There was something alluring about being on my knees in front of Edward Coolidge. I liked that he took control of me. Being submissive was sexy.

We took our food into the lounge and ate in front of the TV. Afterwards Ed laid out on the sofa, his head resting in my lap. I stroked his hair and caressed his back as he fell asleep to the sound of the TV. It was nice to not be alone, to have him here. I let him sleep and flicked the TV from *Plane Crash Investigation* over to *Friends*. An hour later Ed stirred.

"Did I fall asleep? I never do that. I must feel relaxed with you."

I could feel something start to glow inside me. "I'm glad you feel relaxed enough to doze off if you want to."

"They say if a man falls asleep with a woman after sex it means he loves her."

Random, I thought. "Well, they also say that if you've had a big feed it can make you drowsy!" I said smiling.

He cuddled into my chest and I continued to stroke his black wavy hair. "I don't want to go," he said.

"What do you mean?" I asked searching his eyes for truth.

"It's late, I don't want to go though, and I can't stay over because of Maddy."

He was holding back. I had the feeling he didn't mean the hour.

"As long as you're gone by 7am you can stay. She wakes at eight."

"I'm tired."

"Stay then. It's ok. I'll wake you up in the morning. Come on, let's go up to bed." I could get used to him sleeping next to me – if I allowed myself.

They say you meet someone for a season, a reason or a lifetime. I had to remind myself that Ed was only for a season.

Luckily, I could busy myself at work, which helped for at least some of the time to keep my mind off Ed Coolidge. He'd been in Abu-Dhabi for two weeks now. He was staying in a five-star hotel, all paid for by his employer.

He'd text me daily, often with pictures of his cock or with a picture of him sending me a kiss goodnight, his lips puckered up. I missed him.

Beep beep.

It was Ed. *So – got a question for you if you're game.*

I typed back. *Sounds mysterious – what's up?*

I want you to come and see me. Will you fly over?

He was inviting me to fly out to be with him!

We'd go out around Dubai, have some quality time.

Have sex.

Absence must make the heart grow fonder. Finally – maybe this would really be the start of something.

I typed back. *I'd love to!*

Amazing, when can you get here?

Let me check with work and ask Mum if she can look after Maddy and I'll let you know!

I can't wait. I miss you Izzy. Ooh you'll need to book a room.

Why can't I stay with you?

This is the United Arab Emirates Izzy. We have to be discreet.

Can't we pretend we're married?

LOL – no we can't, you need your own room.

Are you going to pay half then? For this room we'll never use!

I'll make it worth your while baby, my cock is hard for you.

Just reading him say that made me wet for him. One thing was for sure. I needed to get time off and my mum up to look after Maddy, and I needed to book me a flight.

5

The taxi arrived at 5am. I'd been up since 4. I didn't mind the eight-and-a-half-hour flight, the early morning pickup or even arriving at the airport three hours before I needed to fly out. I didn't mind waiting – because there was a purpose. In fourteen hours, I'd be with Edward and the waiting would stop.

Even that early in the morning Heathrow was alive with activity but thankfully there was only one person ahead of me at check in. I felt my phone vibrate.

Are you at the airport yet honey?

It was 10.30 in Abu Dhabi. A bashful smile crept over my face. I liked that he was excited to be seeing me. I typed back: *Just arrived, gonna check my bags in.*

You didn't pack your vibrator, did you?

No – won't need it!

I headed straight for the security gate. I wanted to jump through all the hoops straight away, then I could relax with a coffee, and I was bound to need the loo at least three times before I boarded. I hated using the loo in the air. All those people waiting outside the door, listening – it put me off going. My phone went again. Ed was on constant chat. I felt I could sense his excitement. He was wanting to share my whole journey with me. I didn't mind. I lived for his text messages.

Good, came the reply a few minutes later. *They frown on that sort of thing in the Arab States. I don't want to have to bail you out of jail.*

Crickey – glad I left it at home! I replied. *There's so many rules out there – basically don't do anything. No hand holding, kissing or touching.*

Plus, Ed replied, *if someone finds what you're doing an offence and reports you – then you're in trouble. Oh, and it's Ramadan – so no eating/drinking in public either.*

It's a good job I'm not coming for the food then isn't it! Maybe we should just behave as friends. I don't want to get arrested for touching you. Maybe I shouldn't even be coming. It was fine before, when we were just mates, but now feelings have got involved. We should have just kept it primal. Just sex. No kissing on the lips!

Are you freaking out Izzy? Come on, you know how I feel about you.

Not really. How do you feel about me?

Oh God, did I really write that? How long would I be waiting while

51

he searched his soul to answer? I distracted myself with a decision to make. Costa Coffee or McDonald's breakfast? I decided on both and got in line for the coffee first.

His reply came. *Look we don't have to say it — we can just know it.*

We can just know what?

How we feel about each other. Come on Izzy I'm mad for you, you know that.

That sounds like lust.

I feel lust, happy and all sorts for you, you know I do.

I shouldn't be coming.

No, coming is exactly what you should be doing — over my face!

Ed I'm serious, and then I stopped. Where was this conversation going? What was I really trying to say? What did I want him to say? And why now? The thrill of seeing him was suddenly tainted with apprehension, and with guilt about Ella. Was this all just horribly crazy? And Ed? He was having his cake and eating it, wasn't he?

My appetite had suddenly gone. I felt sick. I paid for my coffee and took it over to an empty table.

We shouldn't be doing this.

I pressed send.

Ed's reply came almost instantly, as if he'd been expecting this. *Izzy please come. I need you. You're what keeps me going. Imagine my lips on your lips. You know how I feel about you Izzy, deep down you know you do. We don't need to say it.*

52

We both know the feeling is there.

A weakness swept through me I couldn't escape. This was as close as Ed had got to telling me he loved me. *I'll come out if you tell me how you really feel. Am I just someone you like to hang out and have fun with, your best friend, or do you feel more for me?*

You're impossible. Alright I love you for fucks sake now get on the bloody plane and get over here!

Lol - ok.

What are you wearing?

Eh?

What have you got on? Tell me. I'm on the bed.

Black vest top and jeans.

The one where your cleavage shows when you bend over?

Yes, that one.

Have you got a hoody?

What? No.

Be careful honey, you need to cover up out here. Don't show anything.

Bollocks. I'd dressed for the heat! Could I wear my backpack on my front?

Stop worrying, I told myself. *Go and get that breakfast.*

Ed had told me he loved me. I'd had to wheedle it out of him. But still I should have been over the moon. And I was. I hustled my way into the McDonald's queue. After breakfast I'd go to one of those shops selling holiday clothing for people panicking at the last minute that they'd brought all the wrong things for a hot country and find something to cover me up.

In departures I was met by a sea of white-hooded heads, bodies covered in white robes. It was an Emirates flight, going to the United Arab Emirates. Of course, it would mostly be populated with Arabs. The women wore khimars, their heads and shoulders concealed. I looked like a typical Brit in apprehension of hot weather. I felt uneasy, and for one of the few times in my life, different. I was the minority. A single travelling white female. For now, I was still in my own country, so maybe the rules didn't quite apply to me here standing in a Heathrow departure lounge. But once I boarded that plane, and then in eleven hours when we touched down in Abu Dhabi, I'd stick out like a prostitute at a funeral. The floaty scarf I'd found wouldn't be enough. I texted Ed.

Please can you bring a T-shirt with you to the airport?
It'll be fine honey – just don't bend over and show off the ladies!

Once we landed, the only thing that stood between me and Ed was customs and luggage collection. I walked as fast as I could to passport control. *The more people behind me the fewer in front of me...* I turned my phone on as I waited in line. I texted Ed.

Landed!

I'm here – see you soon.

Through customs, my luggage retrieved and suddenly I was facing a wall of people waiting for their loved ones. This should be easy – Ed would stand out. He'd be the only clean-shaven white guy. I walked more slowly to allow myself time to survey the crowd. There he was! Black t-shirt, guns bulging, smile set to smolder. I wanted to throw my arms around him, instead I stopped a metre in front of him.

Ed greeted me, laughing his arse off.

"What's so funny?" I asked.

"You – blending in – in that ridiculous orange scarf!" I'd forgotten I was wearing that.

"Well, it was a panic buy before I left Heathrow – to keep the ladies hidden." I smiled – I'd missed his laugh.

"How am I allowed to greet you?" I asked, looking around to see what everyone else was doing.

"Come here," he said confidently, pulling me in for a hug. Oh, how I loved the safety of being back in his arms.

"Good flight?"

"Yeah, it was thanks, I can't believe I'm here."

"I can't either – I'm glad you are though. Let's get back to the hotel."

He took my case and we headed outside. The night air hit my lungs, drying them of every ounce of moisture. My nostrils started to feel intensely dry, as if I was walking into an oven.

"I can't breathe Ed – I can't breathe," I said panicking whilst doing an about turn back inside the terminal.

Ed followed laughing. "Oh yeah I meant to say, it's a bit humid here."

"I can't go out there Ed – it sucked the life from me and I couldn't breathe."

He laughed. "I forgot what a pain in the arse you are honey. Come on – you'll be fine; besides the sooner we get back to the hotel, the sooner I can welcome you properly."

My vagina hydrated itself instantaneously and before I knew it, my feet started following that smile. I concentrated on my breathing – in through the nose, out through the mouth – and followed Ed. I loved how he took control. When we reached the taxi, Ed sat in the front. Sensing my upset he turned and said, "It hurts my back in the back seat – I have to sit in the front." I wouldn't have been able to touch him anyway so it was probably just as well. He started pointing out things of interest – Abu Dhabi looked so beautiful at night. The air con made me forget the humidity that awaited outside. Ferrari World appeared, a mass spectacle of pastel-coloured lights. Palm trees lined the road as we pulled up to the Yas

Island Rotana Hotel. Ed took my luggage, and I paid the driver. Once I'd checked in, we went up to my room.

As we walked through the doorway of my hotel bedroom, one thing raced through my mind. *Is he going to fuck me?* He placed my suitcase at the end of the dresser.

"Wow – great room," I said. "Oh my God! There's a window in the bathroom? Who the hell needs a window from the bathroom into the bedroom?" I said laughing.

"So you can do this," he said, raising the blind. "Look, you can watch TV from the bath!"

I ran into the bathroom like an excited child, eager to see for myself. When I stood back up from peering through the window, Edward was in the doorway of the bathroom. He held out his arms and held me tightly to his chest. He wore a black T-shirt which showed off his guns. I wanted him. Why the hell did I have to go and get all moralistic and try to set boundaries before I flew out to meet him? In a stupid attempt to keep my feelings to myself, I had talked about not kissing on the lips, so that we could just keep it primal; keep it about sex and not emotions. Now he was in front of me, I realised how stupid a suggestion that had been. I didn't care anymore, I just completely wanted him.

"Ouch, you are going to cut off my circulation," I said laughing, pushing myself from his grasp so I could see his face. When I was in Ed's presence, I couldn't control myself, one flash of that smile and I was putty waiting to be sculpted into his desire. The way he looked at me, a flash of his lips, the slightest touch of his hand, his flesh on my flesh. I was an addict and he my drug of choice. I stood in the bathroom looking through that window at the fresh linen on the bed.

"I don't care," he said sternly, yet softly. "I don't care about the rules Izzy." Then he kissed me so deeply on the lips I thought I was going to melt into him. His fingers caressed my back. His lips pushed against my lips (I was reminded of his text message, *imagine this – my lips on your lips*) and I knew there was no turning back. I was falling deeper and deeper into this fucked-up situation that was turning into us. He held me tightly and reminded me of the thrill of the feeling of being with him – of being chosen to satisfy his needs. Never before had I been so desired. Sexy. Powerful in my femininity, while maintaining an unconscious state of vulnerability. His touch traced my soul like no other before him.

I moved towards him, forcing him to move out of the bathroom, we were still holding each other, kissing and walking in sync. He turned me around putting himself in control and walked me towards the bed, and bent me over the end of it. He slipped his hands underneath my vest top and peeled it from me, cupping my breasts and moulding them in his palms before relieving me of my bra. Turning me to face him, he moved his head towards mine and kissed me passionately. Each of our tongues found the other, connecting for the first time. He threw me onto the bed. His head moved towards my sex, planting gentle kisses along my inner thigh as he went, the light caress of his fingers and little rushes of chemistry followed throughout my body. My clitoris became wanting, I could feel it start to pulse in excitement and expectation of his touch. My breath became shallow as I waited for his tongue to lightly lick across my clit. I'd wanted him so much this last eight weeks, I orgasmed almost immediately. Edward wasn't forgiving, he knew he had me where he wanted me and he would make me come over and over again before he would allow me to suck him. He craved knowing that he had truly made me orgasm as much as I craved tasting his sweet juice in my mouth. I was nothing but a perfectionist, and thank the Lord so was he.

As he creamed me it made my body stiffen, I had become so sensitive – caught between the barrier of wanting and not.

"Give it to me Izzy," he said warmly, almost pleading. "I want it... gush for me baby." As he inserted two fingers deep into my vagina, my back arched, my body playing to his melody, I started to shake as he caressed the gland at the back of my vagina.

"Oh my God Ed," I screamed out.

"Sshh baby, you can't be loud here..." he whispered. I reached for a pillow and rammed it into my mouth. Every breath in my body wanted to express itself. His fingers were relentless. I could feel the excitement building deep inside me, and my junky sex-crazed cunt was out for all she could get. At first it felt like I was going to urinate, this was a new sensation and I didn't know what to do with it. It was as if he knew.

"Just go with it, don't hold back Iz." I loved it when he said my name during sex, it really turned me on, it was as if he was really conscious he was with me, and somehow it made me feel special, wanted, and for those few seconds when he said my name, it made me feel like I was the only one. His fingers continued to massage my inside, and then suddenly he got all vocal.

"That's it, you're doing it, oh my God, look at it all." He threw warm cups of my juice up onto my chest and stomach. Surely I hadn't generated all this? "Oh, Izzy I knew you could do it, there's more I know it. Come on." His persistent fingers carried on playing me, he pushed my legs above my head, and pushed deeper and deeper into me, penetrating me where I'd never experienced before. As he pushed into me with his fingers, I could feel the yearning build again. I began to push back against him, my hands holding onto the bed sheets, gripping them taut, I couldn't move, like my face would explode if I did. "Breathe baby," he said. I couldn't, it was like I had to hold my breath, to feel it, for it to last, for the wave to come. Only afterwards, could I breathe. As I sank into the bed exhausted from my climax, he mounted me, sinking his cock into me. He whispered in my left ear, "Did you miss me?" A little rush of goose pimples brushed across my body as he said it. My nipples hardened. He knew I did, but I couldn't speak, I was so full of elation and exhaustion from him. Then, the excitement of his cock digging into my vagina started to fill me, awakening my senses. He pumped me slowly at first, and then with each thrust he went in deeper and harder. As he moved inside me, I could feel the wetness pouring out from my dripping wet sex. He looked into my eyes, and I smiled up at him, I was so in love with him, he must have known how much I loved him by the way I looked at him, by the way my smile sparkled back in his eyes.

That was the twelfth time we'd had sex. Whatever it was between us was so fucked up there was no way it could last. Yet still in that Abu Dhabi hotel room, I found myself longing for the impossible. Him.

Afterwards we lay together, I felt safe in those arms. This was where I'd longed to be. We were quiet, content with each other. After half an hour Ed said, stroking my hair, "Come on, let's go and get something to eat and have a beer. There's a nice bar in the complex I'd like to take you to."

I was covered in bodily fluid – I needed a shower. "Ok, but I need a wash first," I said, lying in a soaked bed of our own making.

Ed smiled. "Yeah you do – so do I – come on, up you get Izzy squirty pants." He reached out his hand to help me out of bed.

"I seriously can't believe how wet the sheets are. I've soaked

61

through the duvet for goodness' sake."

"I love it Iz, I love I can make you squirt like that." He turned the shower on and pushed me in it with him. I didn't mind him seeing me fully naked. He made me feel like his goddess. His hands lathered up the soap and he set to cleansing me. His hand slid between my legs. No stone left unturned with Ed. His finger brushed past my clit; I gasped a little. I took some soap in my hands, turned and started to trace the contours of his body. I cupped my palm and softly glided under his penis, scooping his balls lightly in my fingers, massaging them with the soap. He looked at me with an expectant longing, his lips moved down to gently press against mine. "Room service?" he said.

"Room service," I agreed. I loved being in the clutches of this man. He pressed his lips against mine, and our tongues started to dance. He lifted me up against the wall, looking deep into my eyes. As he pushed his cock into me – we came alive, our animal instincts making us feel the thing we both knew but didn't speak of. The chemistry between us was so intense that it didn't last long for either of us. "At least we're in the right place to get clean," he said, pulling out of me and lowering my feet back to the floor. The water trickled over us – he lathered his hands with soap and ran them over my body before washing himself.

"Right – room service," he said turning off the water and stepping out of the shower. "Let's go to my room, I'm literally across the hallway and my sheets aren't wet!" He threw me a towel. We'd come a long way since the running track. Literally – we'd come a long way! And now here we were, in this magnificent hotel with all its splendour. I couldn't help but dare to dream a little about what it could be like to spend my life with him. *Isobel Coolidge.* It didn't sound ridiculous – I quite liked the ring it had to it. I'd feel proud to introduce him as my husband. He was so handsome, strong and manly. A true protector. Where would we get married? On a beach. Just us, at some remote island.

"Here – put this robe on." Ed pulled my towel away and held open a dressing gown to wrap around me. Slipping my room key into my pocket, he said, "Come with me."

We walked across the hall straight into his room. It looked identical to mine only his room was dressed to the left. Ed turned on the TV and started ordering our food while I slipped into bed. I could smell him on the sheets as I cuddled into his warmth and drifted off to sleep.

My nostrils awoke to burgers and chips. "Izzy – Iz – wake up. The food's here." It smelt good, although I didn't much feel like eating, my body clock was on UK time. I sat up as Ed threw a plate on my lap.

"There's a good movie I've been keeping for when you got here – you'll love it – it's called *Paul*." I dug into my chips. "It's about two dudes that go to America and tour the UFO heartland, so funny, made me think of us – we should do a trip like that – it'd be fun to do that with you."

"Two sci-fi geeks together eh! That does sound fun!" It was reassuring to see Ed running around the room excitedly. I liked he was thinking about a future together. The thought we might go on a road trip filled my hope glass. The last eight weeks without him had been so hard. Now I was here, with him, hanging out. Time could stop now.

"How's your burger?"

"Really good." A sudden question rose to my lips before I could stop it. "Ed."

"Yeah," he said devouring his plate.

"What are we doing?"

"What do you mean?"

"Well, what is this? What are we? It feels more than fuck buddies or friendship. But you're still married… and so I'm not sure what this is. What is this to you?"

He stopped eating, paused a while and announced, "We're having an affair."

An affair? So, I am the other woman. Every girl's dream…

"To have an affair, at least one of us would need to be in a relationship and I thought you weren't."

"I know. I don't know what I want Izzy. Ella's coming out to see me next week with the kids. All I know is I feel an obligation to her – but I really love spending time with you. And I don't want to lose my kids."

What the hell! So that's why we have to have two rooms. He can't have a pretend wife when the real one is coming out here next week. Why am I here at all? Why does he want me here if she is coming out? They must still be together! I understand about his kids. But all I've really just heard is he wants to have his cake and eat it.

I felt like I'd been kicked in the guts by some unseen force. Somehow, I put another chip into my mouth. I didn't want it, but it gave me something to do. It meant I didn't need to say anything. I hadn't known what would happen when I flew out here, but I'd hoped for more than this. A quickie in a hotel room and the stereotypical "I can't leave my wife". I could feel my dreams dying inside me. Four thousand miles to get my heart broken. What had I been thinking? And not so much as an apology or any recognition from Ed for how he may have thought this made me feel.

This had never been going to be any more than just sex. Why had I allowed myself to think otherwise?

You're so stupid, Izzy.

"You're quiet – you ok?" Ed asked finishing the last bite of his burger.

He eats like a pig.

He started laughing at the movie. I didn't feel like laughing. I'd come all this way to be with him and I meant nothing more to him than a quick fuck.

I put my plate on the side and did up my robe.

65

"You're not going? The movies only just started," he said, surprised.

"It's been a long day, I'm gonna go unpack."

"Like fuck you are – come here." He got up from his side of the bed and ushered me back into his nap trap. "Let's enjoy the time we have together, come and spoon with me." He pulled me down under the covers and cuddled into me to watch the movie.

This was what I had wanted – us – together – yet we weren't. Not really. It was no more than a stolen moment. Next week Ella would be lying here in my place.

But somehow I allowed myself the indulgence of nodding off in his embrace and pushed her out of my mind.

"Wake up sleepy head, the movie's over – you best get back to your room."

"We aren't sleeping together?"

"Best not – we are in the Arab States after all." He pulled me up and out from under his covers, tied my dressing gown around me, then steered me towards the door. "See you tomorrow," he said – pushing me away without so much as a kiss.

Still dazed from sleep, I stood in the corridor trying to understand what just happened and where I was. I put my hand in my robe pocket and found my key. As I pushed my door open, I wasn't sure if I felt confused, rejected, or like I should have collected money from the nightstand on my way out of his room.

My clothes were still on the floor where he'd shed them from me. The bed covers lay tumbled across the bed. The duvet had dried out.

Must be the heat… I need something to focus on. Some tunes… I reached for my phone. I put on the Stereophonics and started to potter around hanging up my clothes. I'd travelled all that way to be with the guy of my dreams only to be told he was back with his wife and I could sleep in my own darned room.

I really am a frigging idiot. Got what I deserve, though. Bottom line. He's married – they never leave their wives.

6

Ed knocked for me for breakfast and we headed down to eat. The waitress

checked me in, then turned to Ed to say, "Good morning, Mr Edward",

flashing him an extra curve in her smile of hospitality.

I turned to Ed as we walked to the table. "She's friendly."

"Yeah, everyone is so nice here." He said with a smile I didn't trust.

I could sense from the attention the maître d' gave him there could be more

to it. "There's a buffet and you just help yourself. If you want an omelette

the chef will cook that to order for you." Ed rushed off like he only had

five minutes to hunt and gather on a supermarket sweep.

I ordered a tea and sat pondering. Something wasn't right here, but

I had no evidence – only my guts hunch. I'd have to let it go for now. I

didn't feel much like breakfast, I fetched a yogurt. Ed returned with a full

English and two rounds of toast. "Is that all you're having? Breakfast is included, you should eat all you can."

"I don't really feel like breakfast. I'll eat later."

I was still chewing over his wife coming out next week, and now that woman on the way in. I didn't care for the way she smiled at him. Something about it was too familiar for my liking.

"What would you like to do today?" he asked.

"How about we chill by the pool?"

"Ok, you had a busy one yesterday, we can chill out. You've got to try the gym with me later – you'll love it."

Great, the gym – nothing like sweating your tits off when you're on holiday. I sipped my tea. Tomorrow I'd have orange juice. Tea abroad doesn't taste like proper English tea. I don't know why I bother – I always hope for that same morning taste I get at home – and every time it's never the same. I watched Ed devour his breakfast, then we headed upstairs to get changed. "See you by the pool in thirty minutes," he said. I was changed in five so I decided to head out to the pool and get a good spot in the shade. I plugged my headphones into iTunes and laid out on one of the huge comfy round throne beds. Shade overhead, sun keeping me warm. I could get used to this. I'd give it an hour before jumping in the pool and doing my workout. I closed my eyes and snuggled up under the Abu Dhabi sun.

Something hit me in the gut at speed. I opened my eyes to see Ed. "Are you coming in?"

"No, not yet," I said closing my eyes.

"Oh, come on!" He wanted to play. He scooped some water up out of the pool and threw it at me. I screamed as the cold water hit my hot skin.

"Come on then Ed, let's see how good a swimmer you are," I said, getting up from my comfy haven and walking towards him. The fool had decided to stand near the edge of the pool. I could see there was no one behind him and rushed forwards to push him in. He'd predicted my move though, and pulled me in with him. We emerged from the water laughing.

"You swine!" I said laughing.

"You were the one that pushed me in!"

"You didn't have to take me with you!"

"I knew you'd try to push me in… I couldn't resist it."

"You never can, Edward," I said, turning to swim the length of the pool.

He swam up alongside me. "I'm glad you're here."

"Am I the only one that would fly out? Your other women busy, are they?" I wanted nothing more than to feel close to Ed, but keeping a distance between us was the only protection I had for myself.

"Ella's bringing the kids out next week." A sadness crept into his tone of voice.

"That'll be nice for you." I swam faster to outpace him. Why was I such an idiot?

"I didn't want her to come. She said I owed her a holiday. She's the Mrs – what can I do?"

I hated myself for starting this thing with Ed. He seemed so sure his marriage was all over when we first started having sex. Four months on, and suddenly I'm the bit on the side.

"I'm gonna swim now," I shouted out. I needed to burn off this anger I had with myself. I churned up fifteen lengths. Not looking up once. It was me and the water.

A familiar touch grabbed hold of me as I started my sixteenth. "I'm glad you're here Iz. I want you here. I couldn't wait for you to get here so we could have fun together. I want to take you to the water park. I haven't done Ferrari World yet cos I've been waiting for you." He held me as much as he dared – in an Abu Dhabi swimming pool. "Let's enjoy what time we've got together, eh?" He flashed me that scoundrel smile of his and before I knew it, I was smiling at him in agreement of a truce. Already I wanted him.

"How long can you hold your breath under water? My brother and I used to play this game – he always won! Come on, I'll time you."

"That's unfair! You'll be way better than me!" he protested.

"Want me to go first?" I teased.

"Ner." He plummeted down under the water. I set the stopwatch

71

going on my watch.

He emerged less than half a minute later.

"Not bad – twenty-two seconds," I smirked.

"Your turn then," he said, holding his watch ready.

I was at home in the water, I slipped down taking a huge inhale with me. The vibrations from the pool echoed in my ears. The pings of the water. Muffled laughter from the poolside. A bubble left my mouth. I didn't want to completely annihilate Ed's attempt, but it felt good to be good at something that he wasn't. I let out a few more bubbles and came to the surface. "Well?"

"Fifty-eight seconds! Right, I'm going again."

Oops. I'd dented his manhood. Now he'd have to keep going until he matched me and then broke my attempt.

"How'd I do?"

Shit, I hadn't timed it. I improvised. "Forty seconds. Smashing it Ed!" I laughed.

We'd caught the life guard's attention. He shouted over to Ed. "You have a great friendship with your wife sir – you are very lucky." Wow, he thought we were married. I breathed it in and held the thought for a while.

"Oh no – she's not my wife – we're friends," shouted Ed.

Yeah, that's right, we're just friends that screw each other, I wanted to reply.

Then I thought about saying – *I'm just his bit on the side – his wife is over next week!* But then I remembered where I was. So, I said nothing.

The lifeguard looked at Ed in amazement. "No sir, she is your wife, you get on so well, you have much fun, I have been watching – she's your wife!" I wondered what he'd make of Ed's real wife when she rocked up next week. I wondered if he'd have as much fun with her. Ed looked at me and I smiled.

"The man can't help what he sees," I said as I flashed Ed a wink that meant *we should be together*. "Anyway, next week he'll meet your real wife – I wonder what he'll make of you two together…" He flicked water at me to silence me. I pulled my arm back and sent an almighty wave his way. He stood up.

"Alright – ok."

"Conceding, Mr Coolidge?" I was surprised to have won so easily. The lifeguard shouted back, "Yes, yes – you must be married – look at you two!" he said, beaming.

"See, we must be married. What's it like to have two wives Ed? Well, I guess you're in the right country – so next week when Ella turns up at the pool that guy won't be shocked!" I teased.

"Do you wanna go and fuck?"

"Spoken like a true friend, eh Ed!" I said, laughing.

"Well – do ya?"

"Not yet." It was good to know he wanted me. I liked having a little power over him. "How about we hit the gym? Burn off some energy?"

"Ok, but let's dry off first in the sun."

The thing with the Abu Dhabi heat was it didn't take long to dry out.

Ed leaned over from his sunbed. "Iz."

"What?"

"I like your tits in that bathing suit."

"Thanks." I blushed a little.

"Iz."

"Yes, Edward?"

"Do you wanna fuck yet?"

"What's the matter with you, contain yourself man."

"I've missed you."

"Well, your wife will be here next week – you can fuck her."

"She'll have the kids."

"That's the only reason you can't eh? You'll find a way Romeo, I'm sure. Right – gym – now – let's keep your mind focused on something, shall we."

"It already is." He raised an eyebrow and gave me that cheeky half-grin of his. I had to confess, if only to myself, I did want to fuck him. I was enjoying playing hard to get though. We walked into the leisure area and the air con hit me with the cold of a dark winter's night, making me rub my arms for warmth.

"Changing rooms are over there." Ed pointed.

"Ok – see you in there."

When I reached the gym, Ed was already killing himself on the running machine. Great, now I'd have to kill myself to show I could keep up. I put my headphones in and slipped into my own little world. I'd run it out to my tracks and this would be ok. I was doing my fitness routine – not his.

I've got this.

After ten minutes he slowed down from running and I could see him heading for the weights out the corner of my eye. I had another twenty minutes to run it out, whilst also completely not watching him pump iron through my peripheral vision. He looked so hot. Right, don't look at him Izzy – he's doing it on purpose because I said I didn't want to fuck him yet. Somehow, I made it through the run and managed to step off the runner looking like I belonged in a gym. I walked over to Ed.

"Can you hold my feet?" he said, taking to the floor to do sit ups.

"Is that all you want me to hold?" I said playfully.

"You didn't want it – you can bloody wait now," he said laughing.

"I meant your towel." I gestured to the towel in his hand. "I'm gonna hit the shower after this. Then shall we get some lunch?" I asked.

He finished his reps.

"Iz – you've got ten minutes to have a shower."

"Why – is lunch finishing soon?"

"Ten minutes, and then I want you in my room."

"Well, that doesn't give a girl long to get changed!"

"I said you had ten minutes to shower. I want you clean – not dressed."

"We'll see," I said, heading off to the changing rooms. Wow – someone wasn't waiting anymore!

I decided I'd shower in my room; I had all my comforts up there. I let the cool water trickle over me. It was refreshing. Here I was in this great hotel with the hottest guy alive, and I'd been ordered over for sex it would seem. Something started ringing. I pulled the curtain back to look. Crickey, there was a phone in the shower! *Of course there was in a swish hotel like this.* I turned the water off and picked up.

"Where are you?"

"In the shower, they have phones in the bathroom Ed!" I said laughing.

"I know, I'm calling you from the shower." He laughed too. "What you doing?"

"I'm washing Ed, I'm in the shower."

"I know that – tell me what you're doing."

"Well, at the moment I'm standing in the shower without the water running to speak to you on the phone!"

"Right forget it – you won't play the game," he said in his best stroppy little boy that didn't get what he wanted tone of voice.

"Oh – I see, you wanted me to tell you in every small detail exactly what I was washing and how I was doing it… Well, first I let the cool water run down over my head, finding the contours of my body. The freshness slightly causes my nipples to erect as I start to run the soapy sponge up and down my torso. I bend over to rub my legs and bring the soapy lather up to my inner thighs as I reach under to clean…"

"Izzy – my door's open – get over here right now – I want you."

I smiled to myself. I liked I had this effect on him, it felt sexy, hot, a little naughty even. I put my hair up in a towel and donned the hotel dressing gown and slippers. Just what you needed to slip over to the room opposite for lunchtime sex. It was so handy that the hotel provided this attire. I opened my door to check no one was in the corridor, then darted over to Ed's room, opened the door and locked it behind me.

Ed was lying on the bed naked. He had his cock in his hand and as I walked in the room his eyes met mine as he continued to stroke himself.

"Come here, lie with me." He had a soft tone to his voice – I liked how it sounded on him.

I kicked my slippers off, and lay next to him. He kissed my lips and held my side. My right hand made its way to his hard cock, taking over from him. Our kiss became more intense. He undid my robe and kissed my neck. Our bodies began to rock together. I was aware of music in the background. It was Stereophonics, 'It Means Nothing'. He was gentle. He took his time with kissing me, his fingers tracing my breasts as he looked at me with such adoration. He might never tell me he loved me, but actions speak louder than words, and this sure felt like love. He pushed into me to the same rhythm, slow and meaningful. The tenderness in his every move made me gasp. Not from longing or wanton hard, raw sex. But from the truth of his actions. This man loved me. I could feel it. There was an honesty in the way he moved inside me. His eyes looking straight into mine. He'd never say it – but this was as good as I was going to get. I don't know why but it made me want to cry. Somehow it was too much truth to bear. This man that I adored, being so honest with me, yet not. Having him within my reach whilst also accepting his wife would be in my place next week. I pulled myself up into his shoulder so he wouldn't see the tears escaping. I couldn't do this.

"Roll over," I demanded. "I want to sit on you."

I had to fuck him properly – I couldn't deal with all this honesty. It felt like goodbye sex. I'd get up on him and ride him to the point of exhaustion. That would snap him back to reality. He held my hips and stopped me from fucking him, slowing my movement to match his pace.

"No," he said. "I want you like this, I want to feel you, you're so sexy Iz, I love having sex with you." I guess that was as close as he was going to get to saying it.

"Do you love having sex with your wife too?"

"That's different. That's just sex. With you, it's exciting." There was a compliment in there somewhere. He wrapped his arms around me and brought me back under him, kissing my face and holding me tightly.

He gently squeezed my hand and said, "I'm gonna come inside you Izzy."

"Fill me up," I gasped as I allowed my climax to release.

He stayed above me for a while. Staring into my eyes. Still not daring to say the words.

"Don't say it," he said.

"Don't say what?"

"We can both think it, we can know it – but don't say it." His eyes smiled honestly into mine for a few seconds, then he kissed my forehead and rolled to my side - scooping me in his arms and holding me close to his chest. I could lose time here forever. There was nowhere else I wanted to be ever than under the safety of his embrace. Whether I told him or not didn't change the fact that my heart was his.

"Right Miss Izzy – we need another shower," he said, rising from the bed and heading to the bathroom. I followed him and he took my hand leading me into the shower. I took some soap and rubbed it into his chest. That manly chest that I adored. He returned the favour, massaging my breasts and then cupping my face in his hands and stealing a kiss from me. The water ran over us, shielding us from the outside world for a few minutes. The looming thought that I only had three days left with him began to fall over me. Next week she'd be here. It made me shrink into myself and withdraw.

"What's wrong?" he asked.

"Nothing," I said, shaking my head.

"Come here then, I want to hold you while I can." At least being in the shower he couldn't see or feel my tears, I thought, as I buried my face into his chest.

7

Ed sprang up from the bed. "Let's go out to dinner, I want to take you to the Red Lobster."

"Ooh, that sounds good, I've always wanted to try lobster – but never have."

"Right, that's where we're going then, I'll book a table and order us a taxi."

I stood up. "I'll just go change."

"You've got twenty minutes and we're leaving."

"I only need ten," I said, sticking my tongue out as I opened his bedroom door to head back over to my room. I knew what I was going to wear. I had a navy summer dress with a sweetheart neckline that fell just above my knees. It was conservative – but if I leaned in and wrapped my arms under my chest, he'd see more than anyone else. I dressed and lightly applied some make up – the heat made it run from my face so just a touch was enough. A knock at the door. I opened it to reveal Ed.

"That was barely eight minutes!" I laughed.

"I know but I'm ready, let's go."

"Well as long as you're ready, I've just got to put my shoes on."

"You look nice, I like your legs in that." He sat on the bed to wait for me.

I bent down in front of him to tie my shoes. I knew he was watching me, so I took my time.

"I like you in that dress – can't wait to get you out of it later."

"Now now Mr Ed – we'll be late – we best get a move on – taxi's waiting." I walked towards the door and he rose from the bed and held my back as I walked out. I liked it – made me feel protected, that I was his woman, and somehow it made me feel wanted by him.

When we got in the taxi, to my surprise he sat in the back with me and held my hand. Tonight, was going to be a good night. I flashed him a smile, he smiled back.

"Don't get used to it," he laughed. "It's just for tonight," he said, squeezing my hand and pulling it over to rest on his lap.

The pretty lights lined the way to the mall. Abu Dhabi sure was more beautiful than I'd imagined. The green of the palm trees, the summer haze across the sandy landscape. Men wore white clothing. It was a bright whiter than white – I wondered what detergent their wives used. I was glad of the air conditioning in the car. You couldn't walk far in the heat – especially during Ramadan with the no drinking in public policy during daylight hours. But people were polite, everyone kept to themselves. I just had to make sure I didn't indirectly cause offence to anyone. That's what can land a girl in jail out here. I decided my strategy was to let Ed do the talking with the locals and I'd stand quietly next to him unless spoken to. I'm not normally so submissive but the customs here scared the life out of me. Worst case scenario – I didn't want to be that woman that was on the nine o'clock news back home *detained* because a local took offence to the way she smiled at the man she was with, or something I wouldn't give a thought to doing in England. If I was conscious of anything here it was that men ruled.

As the taxi pulled up to the mall, I had by now got myself into a frenzied state of panic. "Are you ok hunny – you've been quiet," Ed said, pulling my hand to get out of the taxi.

"I'm scared."

"What of?"

"I don't understand all the customs here, I don't want to end up in jail."

Ed laughed at me and smiled. "Come on, it'll be fun, I won't let anything happen to my woman."

My panic evaporated with those words. *His woman.* I'd never been with anyone that made me feel so safe and protected. It was the feeling I'd been looking for my whole life.

The mall was elegant, with wide marble steps leading up to the entrance. As we walked in, we were hit with the usual escalators, and name brand shops of a large mall.   Next, H&M, Victoria's Secret – it was like being in West Quay back home. We stepped on the escalator and I saw two Arabs sat in Costa having a meeting. One of their phones went off and I burst into hysterics. Ed turned to look at me.

"What are you laughing at?"

"That guy's ring tone – it was different."

"What was it?"

"Arab music I think."

"Not the usual opening ringtone then!" Ed laughed.

I couldn't help but notice that the women followed their husband, like ducklings. I walked next to Ed. They followed in a row. I actually saw a man with seven women walking in a row behind him.

"Look, he's out with his seven wives," said Ed.

"I wonder why they are allowed seven."

"One for every day of the week I expect."

"That'd suit you wouldn't it, Mr Ed," I said playfully with sass in my voice.

"Nerr, I wouldn't want seven fucking women moaning at me."

"Out here, I'm sure they'd treat you like a god!"

"Well. If I ever did have seven wives – I'd fuck you the most," he said with a wink, guiding me into the restaurant. I knew I didn't need to put on any blusher – being with Ed was enough to make me glow.

We were seated and Ed said, "What do you think of it here?"

"It's beautiful." The mahogany bench style booths had little blue lit lanterns hanging above, the pictures on the walls displayed sail boats and the warning beacon from light houses. Then I noticed the lobsters in the tank. Stacked on top of each other, cornered into the glass – with only one way out.

The waiter came over and Ed took over ordering the food. I didn't mind, he always made good choices.

"To start we'll have the Mozzarella cheese sticks - with tangy marinara sauce, crispy calamari and vegetables and some roasted garlic mussels please. Then for main – Izzy will have a half lobster tail – wood grilled, and I'll have wood grilled lobster, shrimp & scallops with a side of asparagus and saffron rice please."

Ed looked at me "What do you want to drink?"

"Lemonade please."

"And a raspberry lemonade." Ed looked over the menu at me.

"Trust me – you'll love it – and a Pepsi please."

The waiter took our order.

"You're going to love the mozzarella sticks; the sauce is a little spicy but not too much – I think you'll like it," he said excitedly.

I loved his smile. I'd do anything for that smile.

"What are you smiling about?" Ed asked.

"You – you look happy – I like it – it suits you."

"Suits you too Izzy. I like being here with you."

The waiter arrived with our drinks and discreetly went off.

"I like being here with you too Ed. And next week you can bring Ella here." I picked up my glass and rose it to toast his.

"I wouldn't bring her here – she wouldn't appreciate it." He looked sad. I couldn't help but wonder if Ed felt trapped by her, obligated to do the right thing because of the children.

"Cheer up – you're out with me – you can have a face like a smacked arse next week!" I said laughing. Ed laughed and we were back.

He was right about the mozzarella sticks; they were delicious. But when the lobster arrived in the shell I was horrified. I mean when you order a steak it doesn't arrive on your plate in the form of a cow, does it? Ed noticed my horror.

"They just do that for presentation – here…" He lifted the shell off the top and underneath was the lobster meat. I started to feel bad about the little lobster that would have come from the tank to my plate. I also couldn't help thinking if all meat arrived on your plate inside the body it came from there'd be more vegetarians – me for one.

"Why have you got a sad on?"

"The lobster was alive before you ordered it."

"If it wasn't sat on your plate, it'd be on someone else's – get it down you woman."

I picked the white meat up to my lips and took my first bite of lobster.

"Well?"

"Oh my God it's delicious!" I'd never tasted anything like it.

"Try it with the sauce," said Ed.

I liked how he knew his way around a menu and chose things he thought I'd like. It took me out of my comfort zone and made me try new dishes. I found his confidence attractive; he wasn't afraid to have fun and laugh at himself either. I wondered if he could ever be a one-woman man.

"Tomorrow, I was thinking we get a taxi into Dubai, have a look around – see the sail hotel, go to the Palm Islands, hit the mall?"

"Yeah, that sounds good, be good to get out and see some landmarks – plus I wouldn't mind picking up a Bose docking station."

"You should – way cheaper out here and they've got a Bose in the Dubai mall."

It felt nice, planning our day and thinking about what we were going to do together. I felt an ease inside of me. Like we were meant to be.

"That was delicious," I said finishing my plate.

"We won't need dessert after that."

"Really? No dessert?" I teased, leaning slightly inwards towards him.

"Ok – we won't be needing dessert until we get back to the hotel then." His eyes widened as he glanced at my cleavage.

"I can wait until we get back," I said sitting back into my seat.

"Good – cos you'll have to – we'd get arrested if I so much as held your hand out here!"

We arrived back at the hotel and got the lift to our floor.

"Your place or mine Mr Ed?"

"Mine – we can watch a movie through my laptop."

"Are you going to kick me out again afterwards?"

"Probably, yeah."

"In that case you can come to mine and bring your laptop with you – then you can do the two am walk of shame!" I laughed. I was playing it cool. But I hated that he sent me back to my room. I was all right to have sex with, but not sleep with – what gives?

As we got near our rooms, he pulled me into his room. "I want you stay in my bed, I like the smell of you on my sheets."

"Oh, I see, you like the smell of me but not so much my actual presence through the night!"

"Look, I didn't want you to stay all night while you were here, and then when you were gone, you know…"

"No, I don't know – what?"

"I didn't want to miss you."

Aw. Who'd have thought he had a soft side.

"So, if I don't sleep in your bed throughout the night – will that mean you won't miss me then?"

"No."

"We may as well then – since you'll miss me either way."

"Shut up and kiss me." He held me, wrapping both arms around my shoulders and pulling me into his long, deep kiss.

"You do something to me Izzy. You're different. I feel alive with you. You're funny, kind and you enjoy sex as much as I do."

"You do something to me too. I love being with you Ed, you make me smile," I said looking up into his deep brown eyes. "So, am I staying the night?"

"All right," he said, looking at me like he was a little defeated but didn't really mind.

I slipped into bed and had the most restful night's sleep I'd had in forever.

In the morning I awoke snuggled into his chest, his arms wrapped around me. I'd dreamed of this moment. Ed stirred.

"Morning," I said, sinking further into his embrace.

"Morning honey," he said. *Honey. I could get used to this.* "Right, we need to get up and get breakfast! Busy day today, I'm taking you to Dubai – we'll see the sights and there's something special I need to pick up."

Something special? I wonder what he's up to – maybe he's going to get me a present. He knows I really want that Pandora heart-shaped charm with "Best Friends" engraved on it. Maybe he's going to finally seal the deal!

I decided I'd wear my bracelet today – just in case.

After breakfast we got a taxi into Dubai. Today was going to be another great day. I didn't care what we did – I was with Ed and that was what mattered. We went to have our photo taken outside the sail hotel. We took our shoes off to stand on the sand and it was so hot it burned the soles of our feel and we flapped about like a couple of ignorant tourists and fell into the car laughing at ourselves.

"Whose idea was it to take our shoes off then, you muppet?" laughed Ed.

I think, it was your idea, but I go along with his script.

"You seemed happy enough to do it at the time!"

"My feet are burning, man," moaned Ed from the front seat.

Ali our driver smiled at me into the rear-view mirror.

"The sand is hot, ma'am," he jested.

"It's hotter than the sun Ali – I'm sure of it!" I laughed.

"Where would you like to go next, sir?" he asked Ed.

"Can you take us to Palm Jumeirah please?"

"You have an address or just a drive around?"

"Just a drive around please."

The air con cooled my skin, my body absorbed the warmth from the Dubai sun. I looked out of the window in wonder at what lay outside. The dust from the sand skipped at the wheels like dolphins off the bow of a ship. As we entered the man-made island, palm trees waved gently. The sky was the brightest blue I'd ever seen, and completely cloudless. The water sparkled as if reciprocating my smile. The Atlantis Hotel looked like a palace.

"Next time you come out we'll stay there," said Ed.

"Only if you're paying!" I laughed.

"I'll take you there, honey, you deserve to be in a palace." He turned round to flash that smile at me. He had a way of making me feel special, like I was the one person that made him happy.

"Would you like to stop for a photo?" Ali asked.

"Ner, I think we'll save our feet this time," said Ed. "Can you drop us off at the mall – I have something I need to collect." He looked at me mischievously. Much as I'd have liked the photo opportunity, I was also curious about his mission.

As we entered the mall I took to walking by Ed's side.

"What are you up to then, Mr Ed – what's this special something that you need to get?"

"You'll see, it's over the other side of the mall. We'll go to the Bose shop for you first."

As we walked in the shop, I saw the speaker I wanted instantly. "That's it!" I was happy to just buy it, but Ed started chatting with the sales person and trying to barter the price. The sales guy invited me to play my own iPhone on the speaker and choose a song. I knew exactly which song I was going to play. Ed looked around the shop. I selected a song called 'Slowly Raining Over Orange Manchester.' As the music started to play out it only took Ed three seconds to clock the song.

"That's my song, that's my band! How did you get that?"

"Well, there's this place called iTunes, and you can get most music from it – it's great. You should check it out!" I winked. "Besides – anything that can make you sound awesome must be worth the money!" I wanted to stick my tongue out, but I wasn't sure if it'd cause offence so I resisted.

"You're lucky we're out," he said with that devilish smile.

I paid for my purchase, pleased with myself to have surprised him by knowing his old band and listening to his album.

Walking through the mall, I don't know why it surprised me, but I noticed the children's dolls in the toy shop were dressed as Arabs. Things in the mall were the same yet different. The little ducklings followed their men here too. I wondered if the wives got on. If they had their own jobs or if they switched things up. Did their husband sleep alone? With all of them (it'd have to be a huge bed!), or did he pick who he fancied that night? Maybe one was good at massages, one might be a better talker, or the best at keeping house. Maybe it was one's turn to produce an offspring. Did they all pitch in with the baby? Would it be easier to be married with all that potential emotional support from other women? True sisters that would understand each other's ups and downs with the same man? I was curious. The more I thought about it, the more I thought that to have such support must be priceless, a real community. I'd struggle with the whole idea he'd have six other women to fuck mind…

"Here it is, come with me honey." Ed led me into the Swarovski shop. The pretty sparkles came with quite the price tag – I'd only dared hope for the charm I'd mentioned to him.

"Right, what do you think of these – I was thinking either the sapphire or rose. Which do you like?" He pointed to two very pretty pendants with matching earrings. Not to sound ungrateful but I didn't really want either – my heart was set on the heart-shaped best friends charm – it was more meaningful to me. He was making the effort though, and I didn't want to sound like a brat.

"The sapphire, it's my favourite jewel," I said, my smile glowing because it meant so much that Ed wanted to do this for me.

"Yeah, I think she would too. That's what I'll get for her then."

It isn't for me. He's buying the set I said I liked for someone else.

"Um… so who is this for?"

"Ella's coming out next week. She's my wife – I have to get her something, you didn't think I was buying it for you did you, ya loon!"

He laughed and went to find an assistant. My stomach lurched and I felt suddenly cold. I decided to wait outside while he paid.

He'd not mentioned buying her anything once. Not out of duty or love or anything. He'd talked like it was a surprise – like it was for me – at least that's what I was led to believe. Well. It sure was one hell of a surprise, I'll give him that. I wasn't the sort of girl that needed money spending on. I didn't need gifts. But to be asked to choose what I liked, only for him to buy it for someone else – how could he do that? I was reminded of my place in the pecking order of things. It was simple. I had no place. I was just the other woman to him.

Ed appeared from the shop triumphant with his purchase for Ella. "She's gonna love this. Thanks for your help, honey." He gave me a prolonged and exaggerated smile. My heavy eyes flicked up at him.

Back home I'd be calling you a cunt and telling you to fuck off.

94

Instead, I started walking at pace ahead of him.

"It's ok. We have five minutes before the dancing fountains start," he shouted. "We don't have to run, babe."

Don't babe me you arse!

I followed the crowds of people apparently heading outside for the 5pm performance. I figured they knew where they were going. We found a spot on the bridge and Whitney Houston's 'I Will Always Love You' started to play, accompanying the elegant movements of the dancing water. It was a real moment… it could have been a real moment. My heart started to break and the floodgates of my eyes failed. Whitney sang softly "*and I… will always love you*". I looked over at Ed. He was oblivious to my feelings. It was as if he didn't realise, I had any at all. Instead, he looked back at me, not noticing my wet face, and said, "I'll have to bring Ella and the kids here, they'll love this."

I clung on to the handrail.

The music built up to a dramatic climax, the fountains spiralled and swayed, rose and fell for the last time. I'd never seen such graceful heartbreak.

Non-reciprocated is definitely the worst kind of love, Whitney.

"Right, that's that over, let's get a cab back to the hotel." Ed's voice was unemotional.

The fountains had been beautiful. Yet it was like he hadn't even seen what he was looking at. Not really. It was like he had no emotion

sometimes. I didn't understand him. It was as if there was a side to him, I

didn't know.

8

When we arrived back at the hotel, we decided to have a drink in the hotel bar. It was in the basement, it was dark, and I could feel a veil of distrust wrap around me.

I was numb with disbelief… Ed had got me to choose jewellery for his wife. I didn't want to be the other woman. When we met, he'd said it was over with her. And now here I was being the very thing I despised. I needed clarity. Now. Once and for all. I downed my shot and held the glass firm on the table.

"How do you feel about me, Edward?"

He looked down at his glass, I could sense he didn't like I'd asked him this. "I don't know. I'd be upset if anything happened to you. But I thought we locked all that stuff up in a box – I thought we weren't doing emotions. I thought we weren't going to say it. I just wanted a bit of fun."

He said taking a swig of his beer.

I swallowed hard and blinked back my tears.

"Ok. In that case, I'll leave you to your life with Ella and I'll stop being in the way."

I got up from the table, out of the bar, and headed for the lift. Some old guy had to get in too, didn't he. So as the lift slowly ascended, stopping at each floor, I had to restrain myself and keep the tears inside. When I got to my floor, I ran to my room and slammed the door shut. I threw myself onto the bed, held the pillow tight to my face and allowed myself to cry it out. I tried to silence my pain. Have I mentioned I'm an ugly crier? Well I am. And the noises that came out of my mouth and nostrils then, the faces I could feel myself pulling from the anguish that escaped from inside me – any pig would have been proud. The feeling hurt like no other. The realisation that I wasn't enough. I was pitiful.

Exhausted from crying, I blew my nose and wiped the snot from my face. My mind was in turmoil. *What am I doing? I've got a four-year-old at home. I shouldn't be here. He doesn't want me – he's using me for entertainment – to fill the void until his wife gets here. I'm such a fucking idiot!*

I sat up on the bed at the realisation. Flight mode set in.

Right. I'm going home. What do I need to do?

I googled Expedia and got the number.

I texted Ed. *I'm moving my flight.*

But you don't know what I've got to say. You're being irrational. How can you leave when you don't even know what I'm feeling?

He had a point there, no denying it. I needed him to confirm what I already knew. Then I couldn't look back filled with what ifs. I stopped packing my case and made my way to his room. Breathing in deeply first, I knocked on his door. He pulled it slowly open and I searched his face. He looked solemn, the way people do when they want to console you, but at the same time have nothing they can tell you to take the pain away. He didn't love me. His eyes now, and all the things he hadn't previously said confirmed that. I was such a fool to even retain a glimmer of hope that he would take me in his arms and confess his undying love for me. This is no fairy tale after all, it's my life, and happy endings don't feature. I braved up and asked the question anyway.

"So tell me, so that I can't be construed to have been irrational for leaving without you having told me how you feel, tell me Ed." The very fact I had to ask – that I had to go to his room to ask – and that he looked so uncomfortable said it all.

After the silence, he said in a murmur, "I can't say I'm madly in love with you, Izzy."

His words burned me as they fell from his lips. Scalding me like hail as they caught my skin. Each word carrying its own silent blade that cut through me.

He tried to explain. "There's a difference between sending each other sexy photos and actually being together. I just wanted some fun."

What?

Inside I felt weak, filled with disappointment and grief at losing him. Mind you, to lose him I would have had to have had him in the first place, and that I never did. I was not a weak woman. I would not cry in front of him when he was the object of my tears.

Although I had seen it coming, he may as well have stabbed me through the heart. But instead of crumbling in front of him, I looked him straight in the eyes and said softly, "I know that." He looked surprised. I was unemotional. Matter of fact. *Never let them see you bleed.* One of the few things my dad had told me that I carry with me. Then I smiled at him and turned towards the door. "Right, I'll carry on packing then, as it would appear there is still no reason for me to stay."

As I opened the door, he was the one that looked lost, he looked weak, like his world was crumbling and he was powerless to stop it. He looked pathetic. "At least let me know when you are going," he said.

I turned away and walked across the hall. Once I was safely inside my room, I threw myself on the bed and once again allowed my tears to sink into the pillow. I hated being right, especially where Edward Coolidge was concerned. I should have known better at my age. How could I have allowed myself to get sucked into his devilment? I deserved what I got, after all, *they never leave their wives.* Why would they? Being married is protection for them against spending a lifetime with each of the many women they choose to fuck along the way. (*If things were different... It's just bad timing... If I could leave her I would, but she's too unstable...*) Just a few of the many excuses that I had lapped up from him whilst still daring to dream that I was somehow different for him, that I could be the one that saved him. Whom he could be himself with, whom he could tell anything to. What a pathetic woman I was. No one could win a man like Edward Coolidge; he wasn't for the winning. I sat up sharply, wiped away my tears, and started about re-scheduling my flight. I would be leaving in twenty-four hours. Three days ahead of schedule. It was the earliest they could get me out.

Something inside me made me text him to tell him I was on a flight home tomorrow. He sent back, *I can't believe you are going.* I wanted to reply, *I can't believe you don't love me!* But I didn't, I kept it together and held my head up.

I didn't sleep much. I still couldn't believe it had ended like this. It had to end some time, I knew that, but I'd only been here three days. What happened to all that great sex we were supposed to have? All the texts he had sent me that, I wanted to believe, said how he had fallen in love with me, how he wished he could be with me? All those dirty things he said he wanted to do to me, and the promise of *we are so going to do everything we have discussed.* Disappointment filled my veins, and I was aware of a needle-like pain in my heart as that old question haunted my mind – *why aren't I good*

Suddenly I found myself comparing this to every break up I had been through. I summarised. Out of four relationships, I had ended two of them. I was reminded again of what it felt like to be on the receiving end. Karma I guess, it would seem it was my turn. It sure does suck when the person you love doesn't love you back. We humans should be made so that we can't love someone who doesn't love us, we need a protection system. Although technically, I hadn't been in a relationship with Ed. Ours ended before it had begun. Things must end, so that new things can begin. This wasn't my happy ending, but it wasn't the end either, I knew that. Ed Coolidge wasn't out of my life. *You're like a library book Edward, loyal to no one - available to everyone.* I fell asleep, exhausted thinking about him.

I awoke to the sheer brightness of the Abu Dhabi sun. I laid amongst the softness of the pure white sheets and rolled over to cuddle my pillow as it started to come back to me that I was leaving today. I thought I'd spend the day by the pool. I glanced at my phone and a text was waiting from Ed.

Have you had brekkie yet?

Followed by another... *I can't believe you are leaving me.*

I'd calmed down from my upset from last night, from rallying round to get the heck out of here. Not seeing him before I went wouldn't stop the tsunami of pain I'd experience on the plane. I texted back.

Not yet, just getting dressed, late night from re-scheduling my flight. Do you want to eat breakfast together?

I got up and went about getting washed. I looked like shit – I didn't much care – after all it was a true reflection of how I felt. I pulled on a top and some shorts. No reply from Ed – so I texted him. *I'm going down to eat.*

On my way into the dining room, I passed the 'Mr Ed maître d'; she didn't really greet me, but she noted, 'No Mr Ed this morning?' I smiled and went through. *Bitch.* I circled the buffet, but I wasn't really hungry. I felt sick. I took a banana for later, and poured myself a cup of tea. At least tomorrow morning I'd be back at home and I could make a decent cuppa! I checked my phone – still no reply from Ed. I figured he didn't want to see me. I stirred my tea and tried to look comfortable with my loneliness.

A familiar figure appeared in my peripheral vision. I looked up from under my fringe. It was Ed. He looked me in the eye, and I started to get all fidgety expecting him to sit with me. He didn't. He sat alone. My gut twisted at his absence. I finished my tea and left.

When I got to my room, I decided to finish my packing so that I could relax the rest of the day. Twenty minutes in – a knock at the door. Ed. He'd brought me a banana. He looked sad – I hated to see him so sad. I half-wanted to slam the door on him, but I couldn't. He stepped inside looking humble.

"What right have you to have a sad on – you're the one that broke my heart Edward – remember?" He walked over to me and held me in his arms.

I knew it meant nothing to him, yet, somehow, it's what I needed.

"Why didn't you sit with me at breakfast?"

"I didn't see you, I thought you'd eaten."

"Ed, you looked right at me with a face like a smacked arse and then sat somewhere else – you completely blanked me. May I remind you it was you that asked about breakfast, and I replied to ask if you wanted to eat together, and you ignored me. Then you come to my room, acting all upset about something of your own making. Why?"

"I didn't see you at breakfast – I've brought you a banana."

I laughed. "That's as good as baby saying, 'I carried a water melon!'"

We both laughed. The ice had been broken.

"Come and lie with me," he said. "I want to hold you." Those sad eyes pulled me in and I lay down next to him, cuddling in under his arm, wrapping my arm around him. This would be the last time we'd hold each other. I didn't want to let go but I knew I had to. All this on–off; it was messing with my mind and starting to make me feel ill.

I wish I didn't love him so much.

"I want to say something and it's really inappropriate," said Ed.

"Go on – out with it…"

"Do you fancy a sympathy shag?"

"No Ed – I don't."

"What time are you leaving?" he asked.

"At two," I replied.

He checked his watch – it was ten-thirty – then pulled me in closer to his chest.

"Two am," I confirmed.

"So, we've got today?" he said, smiling.

"Yes – we have today." I smiled back.

"In that case I'm taking you to Yas Island Beach – you'll love it there; I want you to see it before you go."

The secluded beach was only a ten-minute walk, but the intensity of the sun beat down on us with all its might. Sweat poured from my brow – I watched it hit the pavement like a trail of vanishing breadcrumbs.

"It's too damned hot," I complained.

"Man up!" Ed said laughing.

"It's just so unbearable!" I moaned.

I'd never been so pleased to see the sea when we finally reached it. The sand looked inviting – but it was deadly to touch – like hot coals it would easily rob you of the soles of your feet. The sun beds looked like four-posters, with veil-like sheets that wrapped around each post to offer shade. We threw our towels down but kept our shoes on and headed straight for the water. It was warm. I just went for it and started swimming. As I breathed out through my nostrils under the water, the salt was so dense it burned my nose. I swam out to the platform where Ed had raced off to, and as I climbed on board, he could see I was having difficulty.

"My eyes, my nose, it hurts, it stings…"

"Yeah, I had that the first time."

"Thanks for the heads up!" I said, pissed off at his selfishness.

I couldn't bear it, I had to go and wash myself off, so I swam back to shore with my eyes shut. As I exited the water, I grabbed my drinking flask and poured it into my eyes. A few minutes later Ed appeared. He grabbed me by the hand, ordered me to put my shoes on and took me to the showers.

"Better?" he asked.

"Yes, thank you. You're still a cunt for not warning me though," I said smiling.

We headed back to the sun beds and lay down and talked for a bit. He had that look in his eye as he scanned my body up and down.

"What?" I asked.

"Do you wanna go back to the hotel and fuck?" he asked casually.

I so did. Instead of saying so, I looked all put out.

"What, just so you can announce after ten minutes that it's not going to happen cos you can't keep it hard enough in this heat?" It just came out before I had a chance to stop it.

"Right, that's it, fuck you, you ain't getting it now." He looked dejected by my words. *Ha! Good.* Only the truth was, I did so want to have one last go on him before I left.

"I'm sorry, I didn't mean it, sorry, I'm just a little frustrated, please don't take it off the menu."

He smiled at me and winked. "Come on," he said, getting up and putting his flip flops on.

"Where to?"

"Back to the hotel – it's too hot here, I need a drink."

"Yeah, me too."

When we got back to the hotel, we collected some drinks from the bar and took them up to Ed's room. The air con gave it a welcome freshness after the Abu Dhabi heat outside. I sat in a chair and sipped my lime and soda.

"Shall we watch a movie?" I asked.

"Yeah sure, I know just the thing!" he said, springing to his laptop.

Two women appeared on screen kissing each other.

"Er, what's this?"

"My fantasy. It's what I want to do with you and another woman."

"Ed, I'm leaving today – because you don't love me and I don't want to be your plaything."

"You're mine Izzy. You promised to fuck me whenever I wanted it."

"I love you Ed, and you can't say the same."

"Because we put our emotions in a box, remember, it's too complicated. I didn't want to fall in love with you."

"What do you mean, you didn't want to?"

"Exactly that."

So, he's saying he does love me now?

Ed stood in front of me, stroking my hair. His hands had a softer touch. His voice was quieter.

"I don't want you to go without a proper goodbye, Iz." His hands cupped my face.

Maybe I'd been too quick to jump to conclusions. Maybe he'd needed time and I'd pushed him too quick. But I didn't want to be just his plaything while he carried on with his wife.

"But Ella?"

"I don't love her. I just don't want to lose my kids. Come and lie with me. Please."

I followed him to the bed and we spooned for a while. He continued to stroke my hair and made no advances on me, although I could feel his cock pushing into me through the covers. Would I feel less upset if

I did or if I didn't have sex with him one last time? I turned and kissed him, holding his head in my hands, pulling him into me.

"Take me, I'm yours."

"I know," he replied.

We rolled away the hours. He was gentle and it felt more of a loving sex than the usual lust. My mind wandered.

Why have I been so hasty to leave? We could have had another three days. But that wouldn't have stopped the fact that his wife is coming out next week.

It hung over me like a widow's veil.

Ten pm. I looked at Ed. "I need to go to the airport."

"Did you have any UAE money you wanted me to have? You won't be able to use it."

"I want money for the airport, and I'll exchange what I don't spend when I get home."

"Are you sure?"

"Am I sure I want to keep my money? Lol – yes thank you!"

"I'll come to your room with you, help you with your bag."

"Ed, my room is right across the hall, I'm literally going to grab my bag and go."

"I did say I'd ring Ella." He picked up his mobile and started to dial out. "Have a good flight."

"Thanks." His lack of attention re-installed the reason I was leaving. I turned towards the door. I'd already had our goodbye sex. It was right that I just left. I flashed him one last smile. He didn't catch it. He'd already moved on – or back. Ella had picked up.

"Hey honey, sorry it's late, how are you?" He looked so happy, cuddled up in bed talking to his wife. The woman he'd promised me four months ago he'd left, or I wouldn't have started this shit. *What a cunt.* I closed the door quietly and went to my room. I took one last look around. This was it – I was leaving early. It was my choice. It was breaking my heart. But he didn't love me. Those were his words. *I can't say I'm madly in love with you.* Judging by his last action, I believed him. The trouble was, I was madly in love with him. But when it's not reciprocated, you have to keep your pride, right? Take the higher ground, wish them happiness and move on in peace. As I left my room I looked over at his door, closed my eyes tight, took a deep breath, then headed for the lift down to reception to get a taxi.

When I arrived at Abu Dhabi International, auto pilot took me straight to the nearest Costa. Wherever I find myself, it's just the place I head to, especially if I'm at an airport after the rigmarole of getting through security. My round-the-corner home from home. Costa is like McDonalds – reassuringly the same wherever you go. I investigated the cabinet – banana bread! I liked banana bread. It reminded me of when Dan and I went to Australia and the life ahead of me was full of hope. I needed some warm familiarity – so I ordered a slice with a skinny latte.

In the history of air travel there has to my knowledge always been a size limit for carry-on luggage. It never ceases to amaze me just what people will try and take onto the aircraft with them. There was guy in a suit, a businessman – he'd come over for a few days to clinch a multi-million deal. He was flying first class – so the rules didn't apply to him – that's what he thought anyway… He had a toy camel that was five feet tall. For his kid – to make up for missing something, maybe their birthday, a big football match or just their kid growing up… He was ahead of me at security and this thing went in under the scanner. He walked through passport control with it. He'd got so far. Then at the gate before we boarded, the lady on the desk broke it to him – he had to check it in. He'd lugged this thing all around the airport. And now the thing he'd been trying to avoid doing, he had to do anyway.

I guess at times we all try to escape the inevitable. I'd known in my heart this thing wasn't going to work out between Ed and me. I'd hoped I wouldn't get hurt, but I did it anyway, knowing that I would.

I tried to be positive. But here I was still – stuck, checking my baggage in.

As I walked onto the British Airways Boeing 747, it was nice to be met by someone with a British accent. More familiarity. I took my scarf off. Home. Nearly.

It wasn't the flight home I'd imagined on the way out. I wasn't full of the excitement I'd hoped I would have been. I didn't get what I went to Abu Dhabi to get. But I did get a kind of resolution.

It was 2am as we took off the pan toward home. The flashbacks started coming at me. Ed meeting me at the airport. The way he kissed me in the bathroom. Going out to dinner. Feeling the warmth of his presence. His glance across the table, making me wet. The dancing fountains and Whitney singing her heart out – 'I Will Always Love You'. The look on Ed's face as I watched him watching the dancing fountains, my hope lost in reality. The way he emerged from the sea – James Bond style. shades on, blue shorts, guns on show, his confidence, his swagger, his style. His total lack of anything for me.

The Stereophonics played me out with 'It Means Nothing' as the tears rolled quietly down my face. I leant my head against the seat, pulling the blanket up around me. Thankfully sleep took me, allowing me to escape my own distorted hell.

9

It's been five long, cold months since I've seen him or had any communication from him. I've somehow learned to move on with my life. I feel free. I've grown in my job, I'm earning a good wage, and my little girl is growing up so fast. I love my life. I'm happy. My little Maddy and I, we make the most of the weekends, we laugh, we run, we play. Finally, I feel like a parent.

Last weekend, we took a kite to the seaside, we ran along a pebble beach, we laughed, we got wet from the rain, we fell, we got back up again – and we learned to fly the kite! The sound of Maddy's laughter as we clung onto the string will stay warm in my memories forever.

I was focused on my training for the Blenheim Triathlon. I was doing a 750m swim, 19.8km bike ride and a 5.4km run. I'd been training four times a week and this evening I was back in the pool. Swimming was by far my best leg. It also allowed me the indulgence of not thinking about anything. It was just me, the water and breathing.

Out of nowhere it came. From far-left field. Just as I was starting to re-build myself. As I walked out of work for the day, I reached into my pocket to retrieve my mobile. A text from Domino's, it was Two for Tuesday. (*No thank you, not with my training schedule.*) A text saying my Barclaycard statement was available. (*I'll put that off until I'm sat down later with a cuppa.*) And a WhatsApp message from Ed. I carried on crossing the road towards the leisure centre, but my insides stood still. My whole body missed more than a beat.

A WhatsApp message from Ed.

What to do? My feet dragged, a weight pulled me from within. I don't think I was ever really not going to read it, but I thought about it as I made my way down the road to the pool.

Greetings from Abu Dhabi. Hope you're well.

To reply or not to reply?

He was bad for me. I knew I couldn't take him seriously. He'd never leave his wife. I'd always be left alone, crying on the floor, as he drove off up the road having taken what he needed from me. Yet still my fingers typed back to him.

I'm good thanks, how are you?

And with that, I'd hit re-set and the carousel had started again…

When I got to the changing rooms, I got into my swimsuit and decided not to check my phone before my swim. I needed my head to be in the zone. I was aiming for 64 lengths inside fifteen minutes today. My day wasn't changing just because Edward Coolidge had decided to sniff me out again. I needed a wee before I got in the pool. I pondered. Why was he contacting me after all this time? Had it not worked out with his wife? Had he changed his mind about us? Or was it the same old Edward? Curiosity got the better of me. I decided I'd just look at my phone before getting in the pool. I fumbled with the locker, pulling my clothes out of my backpack to reach inside it for my phone.

No reply yet.

He was already inside my head.

I took each length up and down the pool.

Right, come on Izzy – focus, swim – clear your mind. It's just you, the water and your breath. Come on.

I was getting quicker – not because of achieving my goals, but because other swimmers (the ones that had no right being in the fast lane in the first place and would be best off in the coffee shop) got out of my way, and, reaching the end of the lane, offered for me to go first. I'd turned into one of those swimmers! Today though, my thoughts weren't blank. Had he replied? Would he be coming home soon? Would I see him? What was going on with Ella? After five months, why had he contacted me now? I'd been cast aside, hadn't I? Ok, it was me who returned from Abu Dhabi early, but it looked like he was wanting to make it work with his wife. I thought I was doing the right thing. It hurt like hell, so I must have been doing the right thing. And then, *Greetings from Abu Dhabi. Hope you're well*, and I'm thrown into anguish. Filled with hope, and the knowledge that I love him now as much as I ever did. Longing for him to say he'll be mine.

Breathe Izzy. Just keep swimming.

I finished my lengths: 14:48. I did it! Got the swim leg in the bag! I felt victorious as I exited the pool and made my way to the showers. Now just to work on my cycling and the run – which was my worst leg. Running to me felt like dying – slowly.

The warm water in the shower was revitalising. I pulled my swimsuit away from my skin to allow the water to wash the chlorine off. I made my way to my locker and without thinking had reached for my phone. A text was waiting from Ed.

I miss you.

I stared at the screen. I took my things slowly out of my locker and went to a cubicle and locked the door.

I miss you too. How's Ella?

It didn't work out. She just doesn't trust me. I think about you all the time. That last time you were here, how I moved inside you. I wish you were here now.

I thought you didn't want me. What are you saying?

I can't stop thinking about you Izzy. I miss you. I wish you were here. I

116

want you.

That's easy to say when you are miles away. Different when I'm in front of you... that's what you said isn't it?

I was scared. I didn't want to fall in love with you. I didn't want to lose my kids. Ella makes life so difficult. I don't love her, I've tried but she's not you.

He didn't want to fall in love with me? So, he did love me? He just couldn't say it before? He loved me?

And she left you because she didn't trust you. So it's not exactly like you chose me Ed.

The reply came straightaway.

It had to be that way around for her to let me go. She had to not want me.

Will she ever not want you Ed? Sure, she doesn't want you now, but if I'm back on the scene she'll soon change her mind and it'll be the same old pattern and you'll be oblivious to it.

You're right. She does do that and I'll look out for it. I won't let her ruin us this time.

Us? There's an us?

Yes if you want there to be. I love you Izzy. I want to be with you.

I stared at the screen. *Bloody hell. Here he is, saying everything I wanted to hear. And yet... still there's something that doesn't feel right. Am I sabotaging myself? Denying my own happiness? Do I trust him? Will he break my heart again? I've fought so hard this last five months to rebuild my life. But the truth is – nothing*

117

compares to Ed. I need him.

A volcano of happiness erupted inside me.

Does this mean you're my boyfriend then?

Yes and you're my woman.

I couldn't stop smiling at the fact that he wanted me. I was so made up.

I'm holding my cock. What are you going to do to me?

I'm going to take your end in my mouth.'

Then what? Tell me.

I'm going to lick your length like a lollipop and tighten my grip around your ball sack as I suck you between my lips.

Yes and?

Then I'm going to lick up around your starfish and circle your rim with my tongue, while playing you with my left hand.'

More.

And taking the middle of finger of my right hand, I'll suck it and moisten it, before sliding it into your arse.

Yes?

Moving it in and out of your tight arse while gripping your cock and moving my left hand in rhythm with my right until you explode.

Oh baby that was good! You still turn me on. I'm all wet now.

Glad I still do it for you! Lol. Later, boyfriend. I have to collect Maddy from

Dan's.

Always you do it for me Iz. You're amazing. I'll facetime you later tonight.
Can't wait!

I was still sitting on the seat in the changing room. *It's true what they say. What a difference a day make. This morning, I was single. And now at 18:22 the man of my dreams is my boyfriend. It doesn't seem real. Yet still I feel elated. At last, we're together, a proper couple.*

A picture message came in from Ed.

Can't wait for my lips to meet yours again. It was a picture of his lips, puckered up to kiss me.

I sent a picture back of my lips reaching to kiss his. *Me too.*

10

My iPod sang out across the kitchen as I merrily moved around tending to the vegetables and preparing the table. Ed was coming back for a visit today. I stopped to peruse the kitchen while opening a bottle of Bud. Pausing for thought before swigging a little of the cold beer. The meat was in the oven, the table was set – complete with R2D2 droid salt and pepper shakers. The veg was simmering and the trifle had been topped. 16:40 – all that remained was to make the Yorkshire puddings. I still had twenty minutes before he'd arrive and I was pretty much ready.

Knock knock.

I swung the door open. "You're early!" I said happily.

"Come here, I want to kiss my girlfriend." He planted a nice one on my lips.

"Welcome home!" I said, smiling into his eyes.

Ed's eyes scoured my apron. "What you wearing under that?" he asked.

"I've got clothes on," I said. "What would you like to drink?"

"Something cold."

I handed him a bottle of Bud and confessed, "I'm a little tipsy. I'm not sure why I told you that. I'm such a lightweight! I feel a bit wobbly." I sat up on the kitchen worktop, opening my arms out for a hug. He came over to me and held me tight and we started rocking each other gently for a few seconds.

"Right, come on, let's save this dinner." His announcement put him in control. I stayed on the kitchen worktop watching him. He was good at cooking and I loved to watch him work.

"Have you got any seasoning in the veg?"

I shook my head and took another swig of beer.

Ed took some from the kitchen table and flicked it across the pans.

"I'm not sure how to cook slightly pink meat," I said.

"How long has it been in there?"

"About an hour." I jumped down and took the meat out of the oven to show him. "I'm no good at gravy either."

"Have you got any wine?"

I took the wine from the table and passed it to him.

He poured wine around the meat, added some water, salt and pepper, covered it in foil and then returned it to the oven.

I sat happily swinging my feet on the side looking at him. I liked him being here. I liked that he got stuck in and helped his little tipsy Izzy. I sat and smiled, content at just being with him and doing an everyday activity, cooking dinner together. This was what I missed about being in a relationship the most. The normal everyday stuff that other people take for granted. I quite envy people at work who say, "Ow – what am I gonna cook for tea?" I envy them because they have someone to cook for, someone to cook with. I have a romantic notion of cooking in the kitchen and the man of my dreams coming home and wrapping his arms around me as I stir the custard in the pan, cuddling into my back. Only Ed has ever done that. Once. It felt so natural, like it was the way it was meant to be. It was a sneak peek at the future and what I imagined could be, which made me lust after it all the more.

We ate dinner in the kitchen then retired to sit in front of the TV. I sat on the couch next to Ed and laid my feet across his lap.

"All right boyfriend?" I winked at him. He rubbed my feet slowly. Feeling his touch made me start to get excited. He looked a little tense. I wanted him to feel relaxed. "Would you like me to run you a bath?"

"Yeah, I should, I stink!"

"I didn't mean that, I thought it might be relaxing for you after the long drive you've had."

"That'd be nice, yeah."

"I'll go run it for you."

Ed stood up to follow me up the stairs. "It'll take a while; I'll call you when it's ready." He followed me up anyway.

"I want to look at your bum," he said playfully, which made me run up the stairs with him chasing me. I went into the bathroom and pushed the door behind me. Kneeling over the bath, I put the plug in and ran the water. "Sleep Easy or Muscle Soak?"

"Muscle soak sounds good."

I poured the bubbles in the bath and he started kissing me. His lips were magnetic to mine. Once I'd started kissing him, I just wanted to devour him all the more. He clasped my hair and pulled me down, the bath still running, pulling my body up into his, he swung me round and pushed me down into the sink. My arms fell in, cushioning my head. He slapped my arse, then pulled my panties down and inserted his penis into me. I let out a moan of joy. My leggings were half way down my legs, his penis slipped out and I turned to face him. His fingers rubbed my clit, I moved his hand to insert his fingers up into my cunt, he knew what that meant. I wanted him to gush me as only he could. Ed took no time to working his fingers deep up inside me, my leggings caught the river that flowed out of me, the wetness that fell to my feet.

"Get in the other room," he said. Stopping only to turn off the taps, I ran to the bedroom and he followed me. His fingers rose deep inside me and I screamed out in ecstasy. I loved the way this man played me and knew my body so well. I wanted to feel him inside me so much.

"Right, no arguments, I'm taking your arse."

It sounded so erotic to me when he took control like that and made me submit to him. I liked submitting to him. I also liked surprising him.

"I'm taking your arse first – no arguments Manchester."

I took the KY jelly from the bedside drawer and ran it over the anal beads, then I inserted them up in his arse, and watched his face explode in delight. Gently I pushed each bead up inside him, until he had taken the lot, then I gently moved the beads in and out of him, fucking him with them. His attention turned to my arse as he took some jelly and pushed it up inside my hole.

"Be gentle," I said. "If it hurts, stop, won't you?"

"Of course," he whispered, breathless.

I was worried it was going to hurt. Sometimes it did, sometimes it didn't. Alcohol sure helped though, and I was still feeling the effects of the king of beers. I concentrated on rubbing myself, my fingers brushed over my clit, my wetness starting to flow. When Ed pushed into me, my inhibitions cried out within me it was wrong, naughty like we shouldn't be doing it and the anal police would bust through the door at any minute. But it felt wrong in a really good way. He moved slowly and gently to start with.

"That feels so good," I said. "Tell me what you are going to do to me, tell me what you are going to do when I'm naughty."

"I'm gonna spank you, Izzy."

"Tell me how you're going to do that."

Coolidge was more a show-me kinda guy. He raised his hand and spanked my arse cheeks four times as he penetrated me, as I rubbed my clitoris. I'd never felt so hot for his cock.

"Are you gonna bend me over your knee?" I said, taking a breath. "Pull my pants down and spank my sorry arse?" I liked talking dirty to him. I liked how I knew it drove him wild.

"Yes, that's exactly what you're gonna get, Iz," he said as he spanked me again, followed by another four erotic blows to my cheeks. I thought about what colour they would be, if he'd made my cheeks shine – Christian Grey style. I pushed my arse up into him, willing him to fuck me harder and faster. I never thought I'd enjoy anal as much as I was right now. He's taken my anal virginity and I like it, I liked it a whole awful lot. I could feel the wetness run through my fingers, trickling down my wrist. I'd never been so turned on.

"It's not so bad is it?"

"It's fucking awesome! I love you fucking my arse, please don't stop, it feels so good."

"This is so wrong," he said in a pleasing whisper.

"But it's so fucking good!" I said. "Do you prefer fucking my vagina or my arse more?"

"Your tight little arse, Izzy."

"Me too," I sighed. "Talk dirty to me."

"You are such a dirty little slut, Izzy."

"No! I'm *your* dirty little slut – get it right!" I yelled at him.

He pulled his penis out of my arse; I was still bent over the bed.

Oops, maybe I've gone too far with the seductive yelling – could be a penalty for that – if I'm lucky...

I could feel him positioning himself. He flipped me over to face him. Then to my surprise he started lightly striking my vagina across my clit. *I loved it.* Each tap made me wet to his mercy. Then he spun me over his knee and administered six of his best to my arse cheeks and still I wanted more.

"You dare to correct me Iz? Me? I'm in control – never forget that."

Still I wanted more, I loved this dynamic we had going on. He took the anal beads and inserted them deep inside my arse, awakening my senses in places I didn't know I had. "Oh my God, Ed that's amazing. I want to feel you inside me. Put your cock in me and come in my arse."

"You are such a dirty slut," he said, pulling the beads out of me.

"I'm your dirty slut and you fucking love it!"

He lay on top of me kissing my face and feeling my boobs. He passed me the beads and lay next to me. "Suck my balls," he said.

"Tell me how you like it, and I'll do everything you ask." I whispered.

I kissed his sac, taking each ball lightly in my mouth. "Suck this one," he said, pointing to his right nut. "Gently" he added. I licked him and kept his right ball in my mouth and slid the beads up into his arse as I sucked him. With my other hand I tightened the grip around the back of his sack, sucking his ball and moving the beads slowly in and out of his arse, then with one swift movement moving my mouth to the tip of his penis and sucking him in whilst withdrawing the beads from his hole.

"Oh, bloody hell, Iz," he screamed out as his juice poured down my throat. My reward for a job well done. I licked my lips and looked up at him.

"You lucky boy." I said teasing as I got up to return to the bathroom and clean myself up. Ed followed me, cuddling into my back and causing me to stop walking he whispered. "I need you Izzy. I can't be without you. I love being close to you." I started moving and we shuffled along back to the sink in the bathroom. I could see his reflection in the mirror. He buried his face into my neck and pulled me close – his arms fully wrapped around my waist. I melted into his arms and held him close. We stood there, in the silence. My hands started to rub along his arms – showing comfort that I was there. He held me tighter. When he released me from his embrace, I turned to face him.

"I'm so glad you waited for me. I need you Iz."

"I need you too." I said smiling into his eyes. He smiled back at me and kissed me with an intensity that convinced me he must love me. No one kisses like that unless they truly love you.

"I'll finish running that bath now then," I said, looking up at him.

"Yeah – we both need it now," he winked. I leaned over the bath, swirling the water with my hand to get an even mix of temperature. Ed sat on the loo. He rubbed my back lightly with his fingers. "I'm so relaxed when I'm with you. There's no stress, no drama. Somehow, I just feel like I'm home." He looked so happy.

My hands paused from stirring the water.

He stopped caressing my back and pulled me into him.

"I love you Izzy."

Our lips met and his kiss took me back to heaven.

"I love you too Ed."

11

I was never late. Every month as regular as clockwork. Somehow this
month's period had escaped me and I hadn't noticed its absence. I went to
the calendar in the kitchen. I was four weeks overdue.

Ok Izzy calm – it could be stress.

I went to ASDA and picked up a pregnancy test amongst a load of
groceries I didn't really need. I was going through self-check-out but
somehow it still felt shameful to be buying a pregnancy test when it was one
that wasn't planned for. I remembered my mother telling me that when
you needed to do a sample for the doctor always do it in the morning. I
was freaking out now. I had two tests. I could do one now and another in
the morning. I didn't hesitate, as soon as I got home, I dumped the
shopping on the kitchen floor and ran upstairs to the loo to take the test.
One line – not pregnant; two lines pregnant. I peed on the stick and put
the cap back over the top of it. I stayed sat on the toilet, knickers around

my ankles, contemplating how allowing my knickers to fall around my ankles had got me in this position in the first place. What would I do? What would Ed say? Don't let yourself get carried away, another thirty seconds and then I'd either have something to worry about or I wouldn't. My right hand started to rub my tummy, reassuring myself that everything would be ok. Time was up. I turned the stick over.

Two lines. I flipped it back over and then turned it and looked at it again. Still two lines.

Our baby was inside me. I smiled. A seed was growing. I stopped. I was already a single working mother. Life was hard enough. Could I cope with two? Did I want another child?

Fuck.

I pulled my pants up and got off the toilet. If I was four weeks late that meant I could be eight weeks pregnant. On another note, this did explain my sudden craving for sausage rolls. I reached for my phone and called Ed. He didn't answer. I didn't leave a voicemail – he'd call me back after seeing I called.

A text came in. *Hey, can't talk right now – what's up?*

I didn't want to tell him over text, but also, I wanted him to know I wasn't ok. I wanted to talk to him – I needed to talk to him.

Something's happened; I need to talk to you. I thought that might encourage him to call me.

Another text came in. *What's wrong, tell me – I'm worried.*

Then just like that I blurted it out in a text.

I'm pregnant.

I wasn't expecting him to be elated about it. But I wasn't prepared for the trail of abuse that followed either.

You're fucking what?! What is the matter with you? Why haven't you been on contraception you bloody idiot?

As I finished digesting that, in came: *Do not expect any money out of me if you keep it. You're on your own. I haven't got money for that.*

Wow. Money was far from my mind.

I don't know what to do.

GET RID OF IT! It's only cells. Go to the doctor, you'll get a couple of pills, take them. End of. Simple. WE DON'T WANT A FUCKING BABY! GET RID OF IT AND TELL ME WHEN YOU'VE DONE IT!

Capital letters – he was angry with me.

I didn't expect him to be pleased, but I'd hoped he might have been supportive. It was so easy for him: *get rid of it.* My hand touched my tummy. I couldn't help but feel the love I had for Ed inside me. Sure, he was being an arsehole now, but he was probably scared and lashing out…

But having another baby terrifies me too. Maddy's birth was complicated. I've always vowed I'd never have another one. But can I consciously kill what's inside me? I don't think I could live with that. I've got time to think, I don't need to rush into

131

anything. I can mull this over for a week. I'll give myself that time to make an informed choice and then I'll know what I want to do. I won't be bullied into a termination when I don't know if that's what I want to do. Even thinking about it feels wrong. I'm a firm believer that everything happens for a reason, and if it's meant for you, it won't pass you by. Maybe this baby is meant to be. Who am I to say it isn't? Who is Ed to demand I get rid of it? It's here now, living inside of me. A piece of us. My own mini-Ed that will need me and stay with me. It'll give him a reason to come and see me. Maybe I should follow suit. Maddy's four now. I've made it through the hard years…

But God, can I really go back to that? I don't know how I'll ever afford the childcare. Dan was always reliable with money. Anything Maddy needed, he'd always go halves, I'd never have to ask him twice. His mum's been brilliant with helping me out with childcare too. She's never let me down. With this baby though. There'll be no 'other side' of the family around. There'll be no help. I'll be just like Ella. Alone and tied to responsibility… My poor friend Liv had to make the difficult decision to have a termination. It's never an easy decision. The universe can be so unfair – all those women desperate to get pregnant that can't – and then those like me – one mishap and instantly pregnant without trying.

After romancing the idea, I was still none the wiser about what to do. This was really tough. My hand naturally started rubbing my tummy again and the tears of what should've been fell down my face. The fact he hadn't called me back. The fact he'd been 'busy'. It said it all. This right here, right now, would be my reality.

Beep beep. *Have you called the Dr's yet?*

I wasn't going to be bullied. I'd make my decision and then I'd let him know. If he wanted to see how I was coping with this news, he could have called and sped up the process. But I can see he doesn't care for me and cares still less for our child. *Our child.* It felt right trying that one. I needed to know what I thought about things before I called my friends and canvassed opinion. I started to feel peckish. I reached in the fridge for a sausage roll with HP sauce. With Maddy it was banana milkshake. With baby number two it was clearly sausage rolls.

Maybe it's a boy this time. I'd like a son.

My hand started involuntarily rubbing circles on my belly. I found myself saying, "It's all right little one, it'll all be all right."

Maddy burst in through the door like a whirlwind when Dan dropped her home.

"Mummy, Mummy, guess what?" she gasped in excitement.

"Maddy, Maddy – I don't know! What?" I teased back.

"Daddy's taking me to Disneyland Paris!"

I'd always wanted to be the one that took Mads to Disney. It's been a childhood dream of mine to go there myself. My parents never took us. But she was so excited; I couldn't put a dampener on it, even though it broke me inside. I scooped her up.

133

"That's so exciting Maddy, I bet you can't wait!" I hugged her tightly so she couldn't see my tears.

"I'm going to see Mickey!" she squealed in delight.

"Yes, and Minnie," said Daniel.

He looked at me like I was an afterthought. "Oh – is that all right?"

I silenced my voice. "Yes of course, how exciting! When are you going?"

"We got one of those coupons from the newspaper. We were gonna go in April."

I nodded. "How long for?"

"Just a weekend, Friday to Monday."

Maddy hadn't started school yet. I'd still have to pay for the childcare though.

"Maddy will love it, how exciting Mads – Disney!"

Maddy came in under my wing and stood gazing up at me.

"Come on Maddy Waddy – time to get tea on for you." Dan scuttled off and I shut the door behind him. My heart started to hurt again. He was taking my little girl away without me. When would this ever get easier?

After I'd fed Maddy and read her a story, I tucked her in and headed downstairs to contemplate what life would be like with two fathers in the mix. I dozed off in front of the TV and was awoken by my phone. It was Ed calling.

"Did you call the doctor then, have you got rid of it?"

"What? No, I haven't. I don't know what I'm doing yet."

"Well, you can't have it, it has to go, we don't need a baby. You don't need a baby. You'll get no money from me. Seriously what's wrong with you? Get bloody rid!"

"I can't just kill it Ed. It's part of us. Part of our love."

"I'm back with Ella. I have to look after the kids I already have. I don't have time or money for new ones. You're on your own."

He was back with Ella? Again? Same old pattern.

I really did mean nothing to him. I sank into a thick numbness. He was back with Ella. I'd thought things would be different this time. I'd hoped he'd choose me. I'd hoped he wanted to be with me as much as I wanted to be with him. I'd put so much belief and hope into the hope of a life with him

Why did I want to be with someone who treated me so badly? Who ran back to his wife at every opportunity? Why didn't I value myself? And what the heck was I going to do about being up the duff? It was all too much to bear. I crawled under my duvet in the hope sleep would lead me to escape.

As I awoke, I tried to outwit my consciousness by waking up ahead of myself. I wanted to embrace that two-second window before my brain reminded me of the life I was living. The two seconds before I'd remembered that Ed was 'back with his wife'.

I felt sticky between my legs, but my dreams weren't wet ones. Not last night anyway. I remembered feeling in pain, and rolling around holding myself. It's true what they say. Love does hurt. I put my finger down beneath the sheets and felt myself. I was sticky and there was gloop. It felt clotty, like blood. I pulled back the duvet and there was a liver like substance on the sheets. I sat up and looked down at it. I'd been bleeding. And there was a jelly like substance looking up at me. It was about the size of a raspberry. I don't know why but I instinctively picked it up and placed it gently in my palm. As I did bits of it came away with the rub of my finger. A tiny embryo cushioned in my hand.

It's only cells – get rid of it echoed in my mind.

It was our baby and it was far from only cells. I thought I could see its eyes, the shape of its face. Tiny little fingers. I'd lost it. I'd lost our baby and no one would care, or even know about it. I sat in bed, my legs bent, my hands cupped, holding this tiny little human. It was real. It was so tiny. Like a baby bird fallen from the nest. Helpless. Lifeless. Dead. I just sat there staring at it. Was it a boy or a girl?

What would I have named you? What am I going to do with you?

I didn't want to let go, but I knew I couldn't keep it. It didn't feel right to just scoop it away like the aftermath of a period and flush it down the loo or put it in the bin. I laid it carefully on my bed. Then went to the loo to clean myself up before venturing downstairs to look for something I could put our child in. I found a matchbox in the kitchen. I went back upstairs, took the scissors from the bathroom and cut up my favourite fluffy socks to make a tiny blanket, so I could tuck our baby up in its matchbox bed. I still didn't know what to do with it. I had an hour before Maddy would be awake. To bury it in the garden didn't seem right. All I could think of was the cats digging it up again. I didn't have cats myself but other people's cats seemed to dwell in my garden. As with any situation where I don't know what to do, I Googled it.

How do I bury my miscarried child at 8 weeks?

Back came the answer. *When a **baby** dies before 24 weeks of pregnancy, there is no legal requirement to have a **burial** or cremation. Even so, most hospitals have sensitive disposal policies and your **baby** may be cremated or buried, perhaps along with the remains of other **miscarried babies**.*

There. Google had spoken. I'd contact the hospital.

I went to the hospital chapel and saw the vicar. I didn't tell him much. Just that I was holding my miscarried child in this match box. It didn't feel right to just hand the baby over without some kind of acknowledgement of its brief existence. I opened the box, and the vicar blessed my unborn. He asked the child's name. I said 'Hope', for I'd felt hope die within me last night.

There are times when all we want is for that special someone to just reach out and save us. When all we want is to hear from them. We know we can do things on our own and we'll get by, but it sure would be a lot easier with the person we long for the most by our side with us. No amount of longing, pining, or wishing has ever got me what I wanted. There's the hope (*I really hope he calls, or turns up on my doorstep like they do in the movies*), and there's the reality (*I'm gonna have to do this myself – alone – like I always do. No one's coming to help or save me. I just need to crack on and get through this*) Hope versus reality. Hope is all your dreams come true. Reality is the bump that jolts you back to where you are at in the real world. Yesterday, I found out I was pregnant. I didn't know how I really felt about that until I held my eight-week-old foetus in my palm, felt the love I had for it in my heart and wrapped it up in a sock blanket in a matchbox. That doesn't sound like hope or reality. It's wrong. I'm not sure what the universe wanted to teach me with this lesson.

12

I am no stranger to loss. I understand only too well what it means to lose someone – and not just to death. It's possible to lose people you love to life too. My brother is one such person. As children we hated each other. As teenagers we understood each other. My bro always had my back. He went down to school and 'sorted' out the bully situation. I'm not sure what he said, but those bullies didn't dare even look at me in the classroom from there on in. I was blessed with having a six foot one, built-like-a-brick-shit-house older brother. He could do intelligent arguing too. Which meant if you took him on in a row you'd look a twit and he'd look glorious.

Unlike me though, he wasn't forgiving. If you upset him, you'd have to do your time. I went six months once before he'd speak to me again. Previously I'd served a month or a three-month ban. Currently it's been five years. I think about him every day. I've tried to reach out over the years. He never replies. He's got two boys now; I've never met them.

Liv reckons the reason I like Ed is he reminds me of Brian. That sounds sick to me. I'd be lying though if I said there weren't similarities. Ed and I banter like me and my brother used to. We shout out random film quotes to each other and the other one completes them. Ed is stocky and protective like my brother was. He makes me feel safe. I could ring my brother at any time of the day or night and no matter what he'd answer the phone and help me. I don't feel like that with Ed. But it was nice to have one person in my life I knew I could call when I needed to. Everyone should have that in life, I think. Brian would have this way of looking at me when he knew something was wrong and I needed his help but was trying to deal with it alone. He'd look at me and say, "Iz – come on – I'm your brother." That meant – just tell me so I can deal with it. It meant everything to me when he'd say that and just take away all the upset going on in my life. The bullies when I was fifteen. The wicked stepfather through my teenage years. Brian was the only person in my life that fought for me.

It got too close to home though and I lost his protection.

When we were kids, I would always sneak into my brother's room after our mother had put us to bed. We used to talk. I'd tell him my woes and he'd make me feel better about them. My dad wasn't home much. We liked it that way. He'd drink and get verbally abusive and violent. I remember one

Christmas he got pissed on Scotch and fell asleep on the couch and us kids thought it'd be a good idea to put holly stems in his mouth. My mother was worried, although at the time we all found it hilarious. He slept like that for a good hour, before waking up splattering and swearing at us at the top of his voice. We were saved many times by the lock on the bathroom door. My mum wasn't so lucky. I made him a cup of coffee once and as soon as I gave it to him he threw it at my mum. She said nothing and just walked out the room. It took me decades to realise that wasn't normal behaviour. Men terrified me.

My dad would do things that as I became an adult I realised weren't normal. It made me feel uncomfortable. I remember I was about five or six and we'd go to this pizza place we loved going to in Poole. Some of the seats were benches, furnished with a deep maroon velvet. I'd walk along a bench, behind my dad. He'd put his arm up behind me, and put his hand down my pants and hold my bum. I hated it. But I didn't know any better and never dared to challenge my dad. As I grew older and developed breasts, he took me round to his friend's house and announced, "Look, she's got things," to his mate, and then said to me, "Go on Izzy, show him." I was horrified. This friend also had a daughter and thankfully he was equally horrified. It was the first time I'd seen anyone challenge my dad about the way he treated me. One night, while swapping secrets with my brother, I told him that my dad used to slide his hand down my inner thigh and leave it there – up close to my personals (which was the term me and Brian used to describe such things). I told him I really didn't like it and I didn't want to see my dad; I wished my mum would divorce him. Stu told me that my father did that to try and intimidate me and I shouldn't let him see it bothered me. He said he did it to him too and I wasn't to let him win by allowing him to make me feel vulnerable. We were just children trying to make sense of behaviour we didn't understand.

Flash forward to thirty years later, and I became pregnant with Maddy. I felt this absolute rage at what my father had done to me, and complete 'mumma bear' protectiveness over my unborn child. That man would never touch my baby. Never make my child feel like he made me feel. And I did the thing I'd wanted to do all my life. I cut my dad off and I've never looked back. During the fallout, I lost my brother. I don't know if he felt guilt over not being able to protect me from such a predator. Or if it was because I'd reminded him of a past he'd forgotten. He's never coming back to me – I know that. Yet in my heart I hope he will. One day, I'll open up Facebook and there'll be a message or something. Hope. Whilst in the real world I live my life one day at a time, and I try to be a good mother to Maddy, I also live on hopes. Hope versus reality. Today's reality is I took my unborn foetus to hospital wrapped in a sock blanket to be incinerated in a matchbox coffin. Tomorrow's hope is for a day when my brother puts his arms around me and tells me he's here and everything will all be all right again.

A week went by before I received word from Ed.

Have you got rid of it yet?

He really didn't want our child. Cold and to the point. I decided I'd make him squirm and replied *No*. Technically that was the truth. I didn't get rid of it; I had a miscarriage. My phone sprang into life like it was the bat phone. He was worried – he was calling me for round two.

"Hi," I said.

"Izzy, are you insane? We don't want a child. Why haven't you gone to get rid of it yet?"

"I don't need to get rid of it, Ed."

"I know it's your decision, but you'll get nothing from me. I want nothing to do with it, do you understand?"

I hated like this side of him. Cold, distant, no consideration of my feelings – it was all about him. He'd had his fun with me and now it was back to his wife. I fell silent. There were no words,

"Izzy!" he yelled at me from across the miles.

"Ed. I don't need to go to the doctor because there is no baby any more. I miscarried."

"Thank God for that – that's the best outcome we could have hoped for."

I didn't expect it, but there was no *are you ok?* There was no concern at all. Only for himself.

"Why you had to tell me in the first place I'll never know, I didn't need to know about any of this! I've been worried sick about what this would have done to Ella."

About what it would have done to Ella? What about what it has done to me?

"I don't see why I should have had to go through it alone – although as it happens, I did. It was half yours – you had a right to know."

"Next time just deal with it; I don't want to know about it."

Next time? As if.

"You don't want to know about the consequences of your actions Ed? I've always been clear I wasn't on any contraception. Anyway, you're the one that chose to come inside me."

"You wanted me to. Look, I can't talk to you anymore."

"That's right, you're back with Ella. Again! Let's see how long it lasts this time shall we. I give you three months."

He laughed.

"Well, it'll be at least nine months."

My heart froze.

"Why nine?" I already knew but I had to hear him say it.

"Ella's pregnant."

"How many weeks?" I murmured.

144

"She thinks she's about eight weeks."

So that's why he'd been so frantic. We were both pregnant at the same time. *Bastard.* He'd been doing us both. I *was* the other woman. It made sense the universe would take my baby and allow hers. She was his wife. I was nothing. The pain kept rolling through me, torturing me from the inside. Playing on repeat in my mind.

"Eight weeks?" My lips started to tremble.

"Yeah thereabouts, I think that's what she said."

He had no idea, did he? Of the pain he was causing.

"So, we were both pregnant at the same time Ed. You had sex with both of us in the same week."

"I didn't want to, she's, my missus. I couldn't say no, could I?"

"But you kept telling me you were split up from her."

"It's complicated."

"There's nothing complicated about it, Ed – you were screwing us both over – literally." With that I hung up. He's not worth it. And I should never have gotten involved with a married man. This was my penance. She got to keep her baby and her husband.

I wasn't going to get in the way of that.

13

For nine weeks he blanked me. Every morning started the same. I'd wake

up thinking of him. Every night ended the same. I went to bed thinking of

him. I didn't know if I obsessed over Ed more when I was or wasn't

speaking to him. Either way it did my head in. After everything we had

done together. Whenever I thought about contacting him, I was faced with

the answer – *he doesn't care about you Izzy* – and then I deleted my text and

put my phone back down, and the wave of pain rolled through me again. I

agonised on what I could say that wouldn't come across as needy, how I

could be funny, say something that would make him miss me somehow.

And all that pain, the knots in my tummy, the excitement, the

disappointment, it all sits there in the base of my stomach – reminding me

of my loss.

    I finally raised the nerve to contact him.

    Hi, how's things? Keep it simple, I thought.

It was tempting to just sit and wait for a response. But I had to keep my mind active. I fully accepted I might not get a reply at all. I took my camera and went for a walk in the nearby forest. It was in-between seasons. Winter was disappearing but spring hadn't arrived yet. The leaves looked beaten and torn. The colours faded and dying. The trees were waiting for new growth, for life to start again. Looking through the camera lens, it was easy to be so judgemental in my surroundings. A squirrel darted down a tree and ran across my path. I stood still. Watching. It sniffed the air and scampered up an opposite tree. Oh, to be free like a squirrel.

Beep beep.

Hey, things are good thanks. Ella and I are really happy. You?

Not quite what I was hoping for, but I guess I was prepared for it in a way.

I'm happy for you. Glad it's all worked out for you.

I wasn't happy for him. I wasn't glad it had all worked out for him. But what else could I say? We're supposed to be happy for others, aren't we? It's what you say – even if they are the person that's broken your heart.

Well, I still work abroad so we're happy across the miles! I promised I'd return for the birth. I'm sorry things worked out like this between us. I had to push you away.

Why?

I got too close to you and it scared me how much you loved me. Plus, the wife

147

got pregnant – I had to do the right thing.

The right thing? That was just a point of view.

You're happy now, though, right?

I prayed: *please don't let him be, please let him be miserable and long to be back in my arms.*

Yes I am. I speak to Ella every night and we have plenty of text sex while I'm away.

Did he even realise how much his words were cutting me right now?

Well like I said I'm happy for you Ed.

I wasn't. *Fucker.* I hated him with a passion. Why should he get to keep his wife after all he'd done. Why did he get to play with who he wanted, and then not be alone for how he'd treated me? Why did the universe reward him? Why wasn't he punished for what he'd done?

What about you – are you with anyone?

As if, you twat! *No not yet.*

At the end of the day Iz, you have nothing to offer me that I don't already have. If I didn't want to be with Ella I wouldn't keep going back to her, would I?

What? I had nothing to offer him?

You also keep coming back to me.

Well, I do like your cooking, especially those after sex bacon sandwiches!

It wasn't much to be left with really. There was no sugar coating it.

No choosing the words carefully. Out they fell onto his text screen, to be sent casually to mine.

Look, I miss talking to you. I can talk to you. We can be friends but nothing more.

As if that was ever going to work out!

I miss talking to my best friend too.

Right that's settled then – we're friends.

We could never just be friends. There was too much chemistry between us.

Does this mean I'm released from the promise to fuck you whenever you desire until death us do part?

One step at a time Iz. I didn't say that now did I?

Knew it!

Same old Edward. Same old games. I didn't sleep that night. It haunted me. We'd done all that stuff together, shared all that intimacy, how was it that he had the ability to make me feel alive and irrelevant all at once? Whatever way I looked at it, however I diced it, it hurt. How I wished he hadn't got that power over me, power to destroy me.

I awoke early and decided to take the bike out over the New Forest. The terrain was perfect to train for Blenheim. Plenty of hills and turns and flat-out straights. I'd burn away this impossible feeling inside of me – use it for good. The air was crisp and full of promise. Rabbits came out of their warrens and played amongst the hedgerows. My legs pedalled hard, trying to outrun the thoughts in my head.

You offer me nothing I don't already have...

I looked ahead and concentrated on the next bend, leaning into it.

I speak to Ella every night and we have plenty of text sex...

I wiped the tears from my eyes and felt the breeze on my face as I powered down the hill to take the next up.

I miss talking to you...

This hurt. Inside and out. My legs pedalled hard up the incline, my heart lost the will and my soul had given up. My shins hurt, I couldn't breathe, I tried to keep going, but I couldn't reach the top – jumping off, I panted, holding onto my bike, making myself stand up. I walked slowly onward. As long as I was moving, it didn't matter how slowly I moved – I had to keep going. Had to reach the top. I moved off the road and fell to the grass. My body aching, my heart racing, my breath unable to keep up. I sat up, and drank some water. Taking in the green grass, the trees, the peace – deafened only by my own inner turmoil.

After feeling like I'd abused myself enough for one day, I packed the bike up in the car and drove home.

I decided to recuperate on the couch with a big bag of Maltesers and a movie. It was comforting to snuggle up under the blanket – especially as

Mads was with her dad so I could do as I pleased. I decided to text Liv.

Hey, how's your weekend going?

Fucking nightmare! Bloody kids are being bastards today! And Mike is being a complete dick! What's going on with you? Any more from the cunt?

Liv – my down to earth, tell it as it is, please or offend type friend. I loved her for it. There was no mucking about with Liv – straight to the point.

Went for a cycle over the Forest, nearly killed myself, came home! LOL. Currently sat with Maltesers watching Bridget Jones. Radio silence from Ed.

He'll be back! They always are! It'll never work with his wife. He's only with her because she's pregnant. It won't last.

I hope you're right Liv. God, I feel awful thinking that.

We'll see I suppose. Why have the kids been bastards?

The usual, not listening to me, doing as they please. Mike doesn't help, giving into them, taking them out for ice cream when I'd said they couldn't have any!

Oh dear.

Quite! I wish I was at yours eating Maltesers and watching Bridget!

You're welcome over if you want to leave the kids with Mike – his penance for going against you! LOL.

I fucking should do that mate! But I can't today. Catch up soon though!

I stuffed a handful of small geezers in my mouth and savoured the short-lived pleasure. Poor old Bridget. The bad boys always break our hearts.

Beep beep. It was Ed's tone.

I'm taking some holiday, coming home next week.

That'll be nice for you – get to see your kids.

I was hoping we could catch up? Well actually I wondered if you'd be able to collect me from the airport.

Won't Ella and the kids be collecting you?

Ner – she wouldn't do that! She's not kind like you are.

I'm surprised you want me to. Lack of options I suppose.

No, I want to see you, I miss you, I thought it'd be nice.

When are you back?

Next Saturday, around 7am.

I wanted to say no. But the truth was I really wanted to see him too.

Yeah sure, no worries mate.

There you are again with mate!

Well, that's what we are isn't it – your rule not mine. Anyway – where am I driving you to?

I need to get to Cambridge – left my car there.

Ok.

I'm staying at a Travelodge though. I'll be knackered. So I'll have a night there before travelling back to Hereford. You could stay over with me.

We'll see Ed. I didn't think friends slept together.

We'll always be way more than friends Iz. Thank you — you're amazing!

No worries, I'd collect any of my friends from the airport Ed.

I'm not just any old friend though, am I?

No, you're not — you're way more complicated than that! Lol.

Can't wait to see you.

I've missed your face too. Be nice to hang out for a while.

I was still lying on the couch, the Maltesers beside me. I stared at the phone screen for a long time. I felt sick. It was partly anxiety and partly excitement.

Here I am — again, changing my life to run around England after him. I can't bear the thought of a missed opportunity to see him though. I've always got that one shred of hope for things to be different. I'm so pathetic. Someone once said that the definition of insanity was doing the same thing over and over again and expecting a different result. If that's the case — I should be committed.

14

Ed Coolidge will never choose me, I know this. Am I happy to be his bit on the side?

No, I am not. Can I allow him to have a double life, with me as the other woman? No,

I can't do that. Can I be friends with him, and be the person he confides in, but doesn't

go home to? No, I can't do that to myself. As long as I see him, I'll want him, I'll stay

in love with him. He'll get everything he wants and I'll get nothing. Can I walk away

completely, and have no more to do with him? No, I can't do that either. So what choices

am I left with? The way I see it, these are my options.

Option one: Do nothing, carry on as we are, and continue being used. Err, no!

Option two: Allow him to have us both by being a willing player in this circus.
No, I don't want to share him.

Option three: Be his friend, and no more, observe how he treats other women
and accept he'll not love me like I want him to. No, I can't do that to myself. I'll keep re-
opening the wound every time my heart sees him. I'll always love him; I can't go back.

Option four: Walk away completely. This would be the hardest thing to do, which means it's the right thing to do and what I must do to save myself. Sucks to be me.

I hate all of these choices so far! What I want to happen is for Edward to realise it's me he's in love with and wants to be with, and shake off all these other women, and have the balls to say he wants me. But that's never gonna happen. So, I guess I'm left with option four. Although option five has just come to me: I walk away for a period of six months. If within that time he finds that things don't work out with Ella, and if I was in his mind, and he wanted to explore a relationship with me, he can contact me and we can see how things go. It's goodbye, it's walking away, but it's not forever. There's an option in there if he wants it.

Or, option six: I could tell Ella the truth. Let her see what he's like? No, I couldn't hurt her like that. It's not her fault.

This sucks. I can't be his friend, can't put my life on hold for him in the hope he'll change his mind and be available. And I can't cut him off completely.

I won't touch him again in a sexual way, won't kiss him, while he is with Ella, unless he asks me to (and is no longer with her.) Right. I now know the boundary I need to keep in place. This is a test and I have to pass it for my own sanity.

I awoke at 4am to get up and make the two-hour drive to the airport. Even though I knew he wasn't coming home to me, I couldn't help but smile to myself – I was going to see Ed today. I had to keep reminding myself that Edward was not coming home to me, he was coming home to his wife and re-kindle their marriage. Edward had chosen Ella; after everything we had been through together, in the end he stayed with his wife. How very predictable.

I chanted to myself: *It's not you he's coming back to be with, all you are is a lift to get him to where he needs to go. He's not coming to be with you. He doesn't want you. Don't get excited. Be cool.*

I didn't know what I'd say to him, or how I'd greet him when I finally saw him. If I'd smile, if I'd hold out my arms and hug him. I had no idea. My face beamed as I drove into the car park and found a space. I was an excited child. Bitter sweet. Here I was, ready to welcome back to England the love of my life, and I wasn't the love of his. *I must constantly remind myself of that, I can't allow myself to fly off the ground. He doesn't want me, he wants her. I'm just the mug that agreed to collect him from the airport because no one else was available.*

When I walked into terminal three, I saw the arrival gate, the sliding doors that he would walk through. People were waiting in anticipation of their loved ones coming home. Some would give a casual wave as they saw them walking out the gate, some would walk quicker towards them to greet them, some a casual kiss on the cheek like they'd just arrived back from being next door.

I sit down. The arrivals board flashes – his flight is delayed by ten minutes. I keep watching the screen arrival time adjust: 7:03; 7:02; 7:02;

7:05; 7:09. The closer it gets the further out time moves. Story of my life. The closer I feel like I'm getting to Edward, the more he pushes me away, like it's getting too real, like he's sobered up with a bump and the drunkenness has evaporated.

I start to feel calmer. I wonder if I'll stay that way when I first see him. *Remember he isn't here for you Iz. He doesn't love you. Chant it to yourself. Say it. "He isn't here for me, he doesn't love me, I'm just a lift to where he needs to go, no one else was available."* Sad really. He has a huge family. Not one of them would collect him from the airport. I wonder why? Not one of his friends would be there either. Odd. Three months away, and he won't have the person that he loves meeting him from the airport. That's sad. I feel for him. If I was Ella, and he was coming home to me, I'd be here, with our kids, and a huge banner to welcome him home to us. But I'm not. I'm me. And all I have is an A4 piece of paper, his flight details on one side and 'Mr Ed' written on the other. Maybe he needs a big hug. After all he's been through. Yeah, I'll hug him. Hugs don't lie.

The screen says the bags are arriving now. Won't be long. I reckon by 07:45 he'll be in front of me. My heart is starting to pound, I wish it wasn't.

He's not here for me, I'm just the ride home, he chose her. Come on Izzy keep chanting to yourself. Do not allow yourself to fold when you see him. Stay strong.

I'm focused on the gate now. A bomb could go off and I swear my eyes would remain fixed.

A sea of heads bounces up and down from out of arrivals. Then there he is, with that confident, cocky, stocky, swagger. I don't think he's seen me yet, but the way he's walking, he's in no doubt I'll be here.

It was my heart that first saw him walk through the arrival gate, and without hesitation my body rose, bringing me to my feet. My soul following him from the side lines. He walked out into the open space. I walked up beside him. I didn't need to look at his face to know his eyes were searching for me.

"All right mate," I said in my coolest tone of voice. He looked down to see me, dropped his bags and scooped me up in his arms. My body started to involuntarily shake in his embrace. He held me for a while. My legs weak, I was grateful he held me up. We looked at each other and smiled knowingly. *He still loves me! You don't give a welcome like that to just anyone!*

"How was your flight?"

"It was good, I managed to sleep – I got changed and put some spray on so I didn't stink for you."

Making the effort eh Ed?

"Hey, I don't judge – it's a long flight and we're mates, it's all good." With that he looked into my eyes and pulled me to him, kissing me deeply on the lips. Edward didn't play fair.

158

"Yeah, mates that do that, let's get out of here." He picked his bag up and swung it over his shoulder, grabbing my hand.

I could feel myself shaking, I didn't know why my body was behaving like this.

"Are you cold honey?" he asked.

"No."

"You're trembling – come on – I'm here now – it'll be all right." He smiled at me.

I'd failed again. So much for boundaries. As I held out the ticket to the ticket machine, my whole hand was shaking, I couldn't get the ticket in the slot. I tried to concentrate really hard. I held out my hand again and again – I kept missing. It wasn't excitement, it was fear. I was terrified he'd not choose me this time, that I was doomed to never have him be mine. All I wanted was him. That first time I met him, when he opened his front door in Bristol, I saw his face and I felt something inside me that was new. There was an instant attraction. He was so beautiful. So handsome. A real man's man. Tall, stocky, well-built and firm. His smile swept through me, my every cell feeling his intent. His eyes got me. A lot was said between us in that first meeting that wasn't to be discussed for another seven years. Three years after that, here I was at an airport, trying to get a ticket to fit in the slot of a pay machine. That first feeling I had when I met him ten years ago never went away. Every time I saw him, I felt the same. There was a

159

comfort, a familiarity and a strong hope that we would be together. I'd never lost hope, yet with each strand of it, I lost a little more of myself.

"What are you doing woman, give it here." Ed took the ticket and slid it straight in the slot.

I'd never been so grateful; my nerves wouldn't allow me to do it.

"Right, what floor are we parked on?"

"Two," I replied. He was doing what he did best. Taking control.

I caught him eyeing me up as we walked to the car.

We got in, he looked at me and just stared. He was wearing the black t-shirt which he knows I love. "I noticed you straight away you know, when I walked out the arrival gate. I saw you spring to your feet and circle round." There were hundreds of people there, and he picked me out of the crowd in an instant and I him. I started to get that warm feeling inside me and my nerves started to fade away. He was here.

"Then you saw I noticed you straight away too," I said, turning on the ignition and reaching to set the sat nav to our destination.

"What's this?" he said, looking at the small black picnic bag at his feet.

"That's your welcome home, beer chilled with ice packs, scotch eggs – proper ones, and Walkers salt and vinegar crisps as requested. All part of the Izzy cabs door-to-door service."

His face looked like I'd just given him the crown jewels. "Come here," he said, leaning over and pulling me into his kiss. "You're amazing!! Mazing!! I don't deserve you." He excitedly started tucking into his food.

I turned to give him a seductive look. "You don't have me, Edward. I'm here to drive you to your wife, remember?" I stuck my tongue out at him and pulled a silly face as I started the car and drove out of the car park.

The traffic was hell. It was a Friday morning. I should have listened to Michael Macintyre. You should never drive anywhere on a Friday. I stopped at the roundabout, looking right, waiting to make my move to venture out. Ed's right hand appeared at my crotch.

"I've missed you," he said, gently stroking my inner thigh with his soft caress.

"Ed, don't, I'm driving."

"I know, that's the fun in it." He rubbed across my clit, his fingers slowly lifting my skirt. I started to feel breathless.

"Ed, please, don't." His fingers were playing my melody. Making me weak. I couldn't do this. I couldn't be in this car with him like this. There was a break in the traffic so I pulled out to join the chaos. Nothing but motorway and long roads. His fingers slid inside my panties, touching my naked flesh.

"You're so wet and ready for me, aren't you Iz?"

I was lost again. All that being strong, staying in control. It meant nothing compared to Edward's touch. He had me. I couldn't focus on the road. If there was only somewhere I could pull over. This was torture.

"Ed, please, I'm trying to drive."

"You don't want me to stop. Come on Izzy, concentrate – you can do both, you're an intelligent woman. You can multi-task. Show me you can do both."

There's no way in hell I can do both!

"Edward, stop it. You don't play fair. You aren't back for me. You don't want me. Stop torturing me like this. I need to drive. Just stop. Please." My eyes glanced over at him, to show him just how much I meant what I was saying. He held his penis in his left hand. That smooth, hard penis that he knew I loved so much. He was killing me here. The traffic was at a standstill. My palm moved over to take it, to hold it, to re-claim what was mine. As I touched his end, he let out a little moan. A turning approached; I pulled off.

"Where are we going?" he said.

"No idea but I can't sit in that traffic with you like this, it's killing me." I found somewhere to stop and turned off the ignition. The busy traffic rushed by. I grabbed his shirt and pulled him in to kiss me. My hand wrapping tighter around his cock. His fingers stroking my clit, making me moan out loud. "I want you inside me," I said. He pushed his fingers up into me, reaching for the back and finding my sweet spot, I could feel the warm release flow from me. "Imagine the warmth of my gush washing itself around your cock Ed, I want you in me – now."

He pulled me over to sit on him, lifting my skirt, moving my knickers to the side as he slid me down on him. His lips warm and caring, he moved me slowly, this didn't feel like fucking. His hands held my face. Looking deep into my eyes he said, "I do have you; you are mine, and you will always fuck me when I want you." Then he pushed me off him. "We can't do this here, drive on."

What the fuck? What was that about? It's like he's two different people sometimes.

"Why would you do that? Turn me on then deny me?"

"What are you talking about? Have you seen where we are? We have to go before we get stopped by the cops for having sex in public. What, are you insane ya lune?"

Am I insane? Who touched who first here?

"Do you wanna fuck or what?" I didn't understand. "What was happening there? I thought we were having sex."

"Bloody hell, woman, you're a nympho! You need to learn to control yourself. Come on let's go, I'm still hungry, let's find a McDonalds."

I didn't know what was going on here, but I didn't appreciate being turned on and then instantly denied. It made me want to drive angry.

163

I flicked the stereo over to a bit of Linkin Park. If he wasn't gonna give me a ride I'd bloody well give him one he wouldn't forget. I joined the traffic and erratically switched lanes to dart through.

"In a hurry?" he asked.

"I am actually, I need to drop you off quick so I can get home."

Fucking cunt.

"Oh, aren't you going to stay a bit?"

"Why would I do that? What possible good could come from me doing that?"

"Well, who says any good has to come of it, but I'm sure we could have fun."

"We could have had fun back there; you had your window Coolidge."

He started laughing. "You're funny when you don't get sex. I've never been with anyone who gets this pissed over not getting their leg over."

What a twat!

"Was Izzy feeling horny?" he said in a silly tone. "Aw come on baby, I'll sort you out at the hotel. We couldn't have done it on the side of the road. we'd have got arrested, you nutter!" He moved his hand over to touch my leg, I picked it up and shoved it back it at him.

"Oh dear, someone is having a stroppy moment aren't they." He was having far too much fun laughing at me.

He'd come on to me, then when I'd finally responded he'd pushed me off. I mean WTF? And here he was laughing his arse off at me about it. He was hard, I was wet – what was the problem? *Twat.*

"Come on baby, don't drive angry," he said, pulling a sad on over his face.

"You're a twat Ed," I said, my anger starting to melt.

"Honey, I'm not the one that pulled over to the side of the road and expected my passenger to have sex with me."

Oh my gosh, does he actually think he has a leg to stand on here?

"Excuse me?" I could feel myself hitting outrage mode.

"I only gave you a little rub, I thought you deserved it for doing all you have for me."

He actually believes the shit he is shovelling! "For your information cuntus, I don't just randomly pull my car over and fuck the passenger. To be clear – you had your fingers up my twat first." The road was clear, I put my foot to the metal.

"I like this feisty side of you Iz, it's making me horny." I shook my head and turned the music up. The golden M appeared on the horizon. I pulled over and turned off. "Right, you wanted food – here you are, go and get it," I said, parking up.

"Aren't you coming?"

"It would appear not, wouldn't it?" I snapped back. He laughed. "You're funny."

Funny? I was fucking fuming!

"I was just having a laugh Iz, I wasn't expecting you to pull over and want to jump me on the side of the motorway. I'll make it up to you honey, come on." He was almost pleading.

"With what? A double sausage and egg McMuffin meal?" I said with half a smile. I only had a few hours left of his company – we didn't have time to fall out.

"Come here," he said, kissing me with those sweet lips that make me forget everything. "We're arguing over fuck all. Let's get something else to eat. I've missed you – I don't want to row."

"I've missed you too. Come on." As we walked through the entrance, he tapped me on the bum seductively. "More of that later if you're lucky." He winked at me.

We ordered and sat down. He looked so happy to be back.

"Ask me anything!" he said, his face beaming. I pondered, pausing in front of my sausage and egg McMuffin.

"Do you love me?" I said taking a bite and looking straight into his eyes.

"Yes. But it's complicated. I miss my kids. If I don't keep Ella on side, she won't let me see them. I miss my babies Izzy."

I was a mum, I got that. But I still didn't know what to believe.

"Does Ella make you happy?"

"She's the mother of my babies."

"That's not what I asked. Does she make you happy?"

"She's negative, bitter. She's not fun like you. I don't laugh with her like I do with you. We don't have fun. She argues about everything. I haven't been the best husband. Ella deserves better. I need to be better."

"What do you want?"

"I want to spend time with my kids."

"I get that. I bet you can't wait to scoop them up and hold them." What I heard him say, was he loved me but he couldn't be with me. The only way he could have a relationship with his children was if he stayed with Ella.

I had to give up on the chase for him. He'd never be mine.

"It's too complicated for us Iz. You're Dan's ex. We shouldn't have got so involved. I didn't want to fall in love with you."

I took a sip of my orange juice. This was an impossible situation. I was so in love with him. He wouldn't be with me because of his kids and Dan. I couldn't change any of that. I had to do the right thing. I had to walk away.

"I didn't want to fall in love with you either – but some things are out of our control," I said, looking into his eyes.

He smiled back at me with an honest warmth. "I want you Iz."
He held his glance.

"I want you too."

"Wait for me."

"What do you mean?"

"I need to see how it goes with Ella; I have to for the kids. But wait for me. Promise me you'll wait for me. I need you."

Roughly translated that meant, I want to have my cake and eat it and I want to keep my options open.

Yet still I replied, "I'll always be yours Ed, you're all I want." He looked relieved.

Who knew eh? That I'd get trapped in a proper love story. One where they are doomed to never be together.

"Come on, let's see if we can get an early check in on that hotel."

My clit throbbed at the thought of it.

When we got to his hotel, we walked into his hotel room, it looked just like the Hereford Travelodge we once stayed at.

"This looks familiar," he said. He threw his backpack on the floor in the corner of the room. The curtains were already drawn. I pulled out the desk chair and sat down. He looked at me disapprovingly, miffed almost. He walked towards me and pulled me to my feet.

"It's not a good idea Ed."

"When has anything we've done been a good idea?"

Then he kissed me on the lips and I fell into his arms. He pulled me into him. I loved how he held me.

"I didn't think you wanted me, I didn't think we were having sex, we're just friends now," I said amongst the kissing, and pulling him into me. "I haven't shaved, it looks like a beaver down there. I don't even have matching underwear or a nice bra on."

"I don't care, I want you."

I reached to undo his belt, and at the same time we started undressing ourselves, it was quicker. I held his cock in my hand and instantly went down on him, he moaned out, three months was a long time for him not to feel the moistness of a woman's mouth around his rim. He grabbed my hair and pushed my head down, he wanted me to gag from him as I deep throated him. He pulled me to my feet by my hair, and kissed me, his tongue finding mine as he flung me to the bed and inserted his throbbing cock into my frothing vagina. I let out a gasp of ecstasy as he entered me.

"I want to come in you," he said.

"You can't. I'm not on the pill."

"I can." He said raising my legs above my head.

"I'm going to fuck you in the arse, just like you told me you wanted me too. I'm gonna come in your arse Izzy."

He started to push his cock in my arse, but it slid up and went in my vagina instead. I didn't tell him, he seemed intent that it was my arse, and felt so good, so tight. He told me he was going to come in me, I was stroking myself, I could feel myself gushing.

"I'm gonna come, there's loads, I can feel it, I'm gonna fill you up." As he came, I knew I shouldn't have let him, but I wanted him inside me. I wanted to feel his spunk squirt inside me, I wanted to feel that closeness, I needed him. He stayed in me briefly, before rolling off and lying next to me breathless.

"Do you want me to run you a bath?" I asked.

"That'd be lovely baby." I went into the bathroom and let the water mix with the bubbles. As I knelt down to stir the water, I had to reach for some loo roll to plug myself – what goes up must come down · after all. Ed stood behind me running his fingers though my hair – I liked feeling his touch. He stepped over me to enter the bath, I moved in, taking the sponge to rub over his chest. I like washing him and getting him clean after we've fucked. It feels intimate. Like that's where we are close.

"I've got a confession."

"You've got Aids?" he said joking.

"No!"

"That wasn't my arse you came in. It was my fanny."

"Was it? It felt like your arse. Why didn't you tell me?"

"Because I was loving what you were doing, and I wanted you. I'm sorry. I'll get the morning after pill."

He smiled at me, and didn't seem concerned as I moved my soapy hands over his body.

"Why don't you get the snip?"

"Never in the country long enough."

"Well, be careful, the wife will be after another baby now you are back together."

"No way, I've got enough kids. Anyway, be careful – says the woman who just let me come in her cunt with no protection! Between us we have enough kids, I don't want anymore."

"I don't either, I'll get the morning after pill, I promise."

We lay on the bed after, I fell asleep a little, I was tired from the driving. We talked, I could see he was tired, so I said, "I'm gonna make a move, let you sleep." I got dressed, and came to kiss him goodbye.

"Don't go getting all emotional later will you, sending me sad texts," he said. I put my hands over his mouth to silence him, then bent down to kiss him on the lips.

"I'm not going to message you Edward. That's it. I'm going to leave you to get on with your life now, with your wife."

He looked sad. "I don't want you to go," he said. He kissed me. "I'm hard again."

I looked at him, licking my lips. "Do you want me to get down there and sort you out before I go?" Without waiting for a response, I got down there, and wrapped my tongue around his penis. I sucked him, my tongue twisting around his end, I looked up at him, he looked back at me, his eyes turning me to putty. He pulled me off him, and threw me face down over the bed.

"I'm going to fuck you in your arse like you wanted."

"Be gentle, I haven't had alcohol."

"Shush," he said, pulling my arse cheeks apart and spitting into my hole, then watching as he inserted his cock into my arse. My hands gripped the sheets, my mouth bit down into the duvet, I loved his cock in me.

"Spank me!" I demanded. He slapped my left butt cheek playfully. "Harder! That was a pussy slap, Coolidge." He brought his other hand down hard on my right cheek. "Oh yeah, I love that!" I screamed out. "Spank me harder, punish me for tricking you into coming inside my wet cunt." He held my back down with his left hand, and with his right palm he smacked my right cheek.

"You're a bad girl Izzy, I must punish you."

"Yes, I understand." The blows kept coming, he hadn't spanked me this hard before, I was so turned on, I'd craved this kind of attention from him. His palm came down across my butt cheeks eight times. I loved it, but it was starting to sting, I could feel my eyes well up.

"What do you say to me?" he demanded.

"I'm sorry."

"When you are naughty that's what you will get and next time, I might take my belt off to you," he said as he pushed his cock deep into my arse. I pushed back into him, my bum rising up to meet his thrust. "Fuck me," he said. I raised up and pushed my arse into his cock as he stood still behind me. "You are a dirty bitch aren't you Izzy, you will always fuck me, won't you?" I was quiet, he pushed harder into me, he knew I loved it.

"Yes, I will."

"Say it, you will always what?"

"I'll always fuck you."

"None of this you aren't going to see me anymore, do you hear me?"

"Yes."

"Promise me, I need you Izzy."

"I'm yours, always, I promise." I liked this vulnerable side, it showed me maybe he cared.

"Gush on my face." He pulled out of me and lay on the floor, near the window, I straddled his face, and held onto the windowsill, he pushed his fingers deep into me, making me pour out. He held his mouth open to catch my juice and swallow it down. I leaned down to kiss him on the lips, tasting myself.

"That was amazing," he said.

"Yeah, it was," I said as I kissed those gorgeous lips.

"How's your arse?"

"Sore."

"Sorry, was I too hard?"

"No, it was just the way I like it, I've never been so wet." I licked my lips and headed to the bathroom.

I cried a little on the drive home. I so wished he was coming home to me, that he'd wanted me. As I drove, I started to think.

He didn't even ask me if he could have us both. He didn't even want that option with me. I really am just all right to fuck, but not to be with. Why does he think so little of me? It's not fair that I feel so much love for him, and he holds me in so little regard. I mean completely nothing to him. Why? He doesn't want me as his first, or his second or even his third. I finally get it; he doesn't want me at all.

15

Does it matter how many times your heart breaks in a lifetime? Does it hurt any less the more we feel the pain? Do we become immune? Does it make us stronger?

I knew what Edward was. I knew he could never be faithful. I knew he had a wife. But when he said he wanted me, I wanted to believe it so much. I wanted to dare to believe that we could be together, that I could have the guy of my dreams. The fucked up, twisted, sick guy of my dreams. Three years ago almost to the day we started seeing each other. A guy like Ed will never belong to anyone. He'll not be faithful to anyone but his own yearnings. I'm so hurt by him. Again. He never promises me anything. He never made me feel loved even. He just took, from the moment we first met. He took the light from my eyes, the sparkle from my smile, and turned them into tears. I thought he was going to be the love of my life, but how could he be? He doesn't know how to love. He only knows how to use women. To take what he wants and leave. He'll never settle. A long line of broken hearts awaits. And he'll not flinch as they queue up to be destroyed, each one in turn.

My insides stopped working. They were numb. I just wanted to cry. Seeing the man you love in the arms of another woman is unbearable. I couldn't go on like this. Texting him sweet nothings – for that's what it means to him – nothing. I was just his text sex bitch, I didn't even bleep once on his radar.

Beep beep.

Hey – are you sitting down? I have some news.

Oh God, what now?

What's going on?

Meet Robert. 8lb 6oz, born at 11.05 last night. It was a picture of his new-born son. Ed was all gowned up. Must have been a caesarean.

I couldn't help but wonder what our child would have looked like. We'd have been due around the same time. That could've been a picture of Ed holding our son.

Well, hello Robert, welcome to the world little man.

He's gorgeous isn't he, my son!

Your own mini you Ed.

I didn't want to ask but I had to. *How's Ella, is she ok after the birth?*

Yeah she's ok. She told me she doesn't want me hanging around.

She's likely just tired Ed, let her rest.

No, I mean she doesn't want me to stay. She prefers not being in a relationship. I can still see my kids though.

Oh, I wasn't expecting that. Are you ok?

Yeah I'm fine. I tried. It didn't work out.

What you gonna do now then?

Well, I was thinking me and you could give it a go – if you still wanted to?

What? I re-read his text several times to check he had said what I thought he'd said. He wanted to give it a go – a proper go. No Ella in the mix – she didn't want him.

Are you serious?

Yes, I'm serious. The only person that's got in the way of us is Ella and she doesn't want me. Do you?

Yes of course I do silly! Can you speak?

I'm at the hospital so not really. Are you excited?

What that you are finally coming home to me? What do you think? Of course, I am – I can't wait to see you!

On my evening run I was propelled along, like I was running on an escalator. I felt as if I was gliding around the neighbourhood. *Ed wants to be in a proper relationship with me, finally! Is this really happening? I can't quite believe it. That he will finally be mine.*

I thought about Ed's advice to create targets, to think only about the next goal ahead. I'd manged to steady my breathing over the last few months, which meant I no longer looked like I was dying as I ran down the road. I thought about the end of the road, the next bend and the home straight which was slightly uphill. I felt proud of my progress. How far I'd come, from spluttering down the road to arriving home with enough control to breathe. Training for the triathlon was a rollercoaster, but I was committed to get through the pain.

I was doing this to raise money for Macmillan Cancer Care. They'd looked after my grandad in his final weeks. They'd provided discreet information for us – to let us know it was ok to let go, that the body had to wind down, that food and fluid would ultimately stop in order for him to be released from his pain.

My grandad had meant the world to me – he was one of the few people I knew who knew what honour meant. I'd looked up to him. I'd call him, and I remember he used to say, "Hello little old Izzy – what have you got to tell me?" And then I'd tell him and he'd listen, and if I was worried, I'd always feel better for talking to Grandad. He's been dead five years, and my grandma has been gone ten. I still talk to him and he still makes me feel better. When I see white feathers, I know both of them are with me. It gives me the strength to keep pushing, to go on: *I can do this! I can complete the triathlon. I'll do it – because they can't, I'll do it for them.* Maddy was still too young to come and watch me do the triathlon by herself, and there wasn't anyone who'd come with her to see me: my mum didn't like crowds; my friends had busy lives of their own. I didn't expect Ed to come – he was so often working abroad. I'd do what I always do – I'd get myself through it. Besides I wouldn't be alone – my grandparents would be with me every bit of the way.

When I arrived home, I grabbed a quick shower and decided to clear some space from my wardrobe for Ed. It warmed my heart to know that his clothes would soon be hanging next to mine. I didn't mind giving up my side of the bed for him either. I couldn't wait to be falling asleep every night inside his arms. This time we were going to work, I just knew it.

Beep beep. It was Ed.

What are you doing?

I've made space for you in my wardrobe.

For me?

Well, for your clothes!

Oh I see. Thanks honey! Ella really doesn't want me here, so I'm going to move in tomorrow. I can't wait to see you.

Tomorrow? I hadn't told Maddy yet, and how was I going to explain this to Dan? I wanted to be with Ed, but this seemed to be happening so quickly.

Have you told Dan? I wanted to know if Ed was ready to tell Dan about us.

No not yet, I'll just tell him that you're helping me out at the moment as you have a spare room.

Not exactly the response I was hoping for.

I thought we were going to be together properly.

We are, but Dan doesn't even know we've been seeing each other, I need to let him know over time. First, I'll say I'm living in your spare room, then I'll ask him if he's ok if we see each other, then we can tell him we're a couple.

That made sense I suppose. Break him in gently.

So, are you looking forward to seeing me, roomy?

Of course I am — can't wait to welcome you home!

Good. It's going to be different this time Iz, we're going to be together properly.

I can't wait!

See you at midday honey.

Wow. That escalated quickly. I was excited, but also scared as hell. I'd have to tell Maddy that Ed was going to be living with us. She'd have to meet him. She hasn't seen me with a man. Ever. She is used to having me all to herself. I wasn't sure how she'd react. I could feel myself starting to panic. I picked up my phone and called Liv.

"Al right hun?" she said. Followed quickly by, "What's the cunt done now?"

I laughed. "Hi mate. I don't know where to start. It's all happened so quick."

"Has he asked you to marry him?"

"No, no nothing like that."

"Good – cos you're too good for him."

"He's moving in."

"What? When?"

"Tomorrow! I'm freaking out Liv, I'm frisking out!"

"How did that come about?"

"Ella said she doesn't want him, and he said he's ready to give it a go with me."

"Oh, so in other words he has nowhere else to fucking go!"

Ouch.

"Well he did ask me to wait for him before, to see how it went with Ella. He only went back for the kids. I think he knew it wouldn't work out."

"Just be careful Iz. You haven't even dated properly, it's all been about sex and him having this power over you to do what he wants. Do you want him to move in?"

"I do, I just didn't think it would happen so quick. As you say we haven't even dated properly. We're progressing straight into a relationship. I'm dreading talking to Maddy about it. And God only knows what Dan is going to think – he's not stupid!"

"Does Dan know yet?"

"No, Ed said he was going to break him in gently, tell him he is staying in my spare room for a bit, then progress to asking if he'd be ok if we saw each other."

"What if Dan say's he would mind?"

"I don't know. The shit will hit the fan I suppose!"

"Well – at least you will know once and for all Iz. You've wanted to be with him for so long, wouldn't look elsewhere or date anyone else. Maybe this is the right time for you both."

"I hope so Liv, it's been so long since I lived with anyone – a partner I mean. I don't want to fuck it up."

"You won't. Just be the cool girl, remember. And enjoy having him around. Think of all the sex!"

"I can't wait for all the sex – he's so bloody good."

"How good? Out of all your sexual partners how does he rate?"

"First definitely! Let's just say he really knows what to do with it and everything else! I love how he makes me gush."

"I don't know if I've ever gushed."

"Trust me Liv, if you'd gushed – you'd know. Everything would be wet. There isn't a wet patch as such – more half the bed is soaked!"

"Bloody hell – I haven't then!" she said laughing. "Must be a pain, all that washing!"

"I use those sheets that you use for kids for bed wetting."

"What, that you put under the sheet?"

"Yeah, when I know Ed's coming over, I lay them under the top sheet. Then it's just the top sheet I have to wash. Although saying that – there has been the occasion where I've made him wait whilst I lay out the mat or fetch a towel."

"Passion killer," Liv shouted away from the phone. *"Get to bed – now!"*

"Husband giving you trouble, Liv?" I said joking.

"Bloody kids! I'm going to have to go and sort them out. Let me know how it goes tomorrow mate."

"Ok, will do. Take care mate."

I decided I'd put the hoover round and tidy up before bed. I wanted Ed to arrive to a clean, tidy home tomorrow, with space to move his stuff in. I'd never sleep tonight. Too excited, scared and exhausted all at once. Although he was moving in, his next tour would start again soon. He'd not be here long, I needed to enjoy having him with me while I could. He'd soon be back in Abu Dhabi.

I watched the morning arrive from my bed, the sunlight streaming through the gap in the curtains. My stomach flipped and I could feel a sickness coming. I jumped out of bed and dashed to the loo. Would this happen? Would Ella have a last-minute change of heart? Was he really moving in today? My phone started ringing from the bedroom. Who'd be ringing at eight in the morning? I wiped myself and made a dash to look at my phone. It was Ed.

"Morning sweetheart! I managed to leave early; I'll be with you in 30 minutes."

"Oh my God!"

"Aw bless you – you're so excited aren't you! Can't wait to see you Iz!"

"Can't wait to see you either, drive safe."

"I always do honey, see you soon!"

At least he called to tell me I suppose. I hurried to get dressed and make the bed.

I heard Ed pull up and ran to open the front door. He got out the car and approached with a box, slinging it to me to take in the house. "Here you go – take that in for me, will you honey?"

I'd been expecting a kiss, an embrace or something. Not to have a box thrown at me.

"Er, excuse me mister."

"What? Come on, get these boxes in."

"Where's my kiss and cuddle? I've been excited to see you."

"You're a grown ass woman – it's my kids who wait for me at the doorstep! What's wrong with you?"

What's wrong with me? People greet the one they love, don't they?

"I haven't seen you for ages, where's my kiss?" I protested.

"Later – help me get this lot in first."

Well, that kinda pissed on my fire. What was up with him? He said
he was excited to see me; it doesn't look that way.

"The garage is open," I said, gesturing for him to unload his own
boxes.

"Thanks honey."

I took the box that he'd chucked at me inside and left it in the
lounge, and waited. Something didn't feel right. He didn't seem happy to
be here. It was like it was all run of the mill for him. Another moving day.
Another town, another female to come home to. To break my emotional
vortex, I decided to go out and help him unpack the car. I smiled as I
watched him going back and forth from the car to the garage. He didn't
smile back.

"Are you ok, Ed? Do you actually want to be here?" I asked him.

"I'm tired, I was on the road early. I just want to get this in and
then we can relax."

He must have been on the road by 5am to have got here now.

"I'll get you a coffee," I said.

"That'd be lovely."

This was happening. He was here. It must have been hard for him moving out from his family. But here he was. Moving in with me. Finally.

16

"I don't want a woman that looks like a stick insect, I like meat on my woman, I want something to hold." Ed had a way of making me feel sexy, that I could show him my true self without fear of being too fat, too ugly, not enough. He liked me for me. I could tell by his expression I aroused him and he found me a turn on. That made me feel sexy, daring, adventurous. He made me feel confident to push my limits. Spurring me on to dare to walk his path.

I'm not a slim girl. I don't consider myself pretty. I wouldn't say I had curves – more layers – like a good cake. There's not much I like about myself – but I do like my tits. My cleavage can dish out one hell of a viewing platform – if I so wish it. Only it's an exclusive club and the girls are rarely out on show. But for the right guy, one who makes me feel comfortable in my own skin, who encourages me to express myself – they're out a lot! I'd never sent pictures of myself to anyone before I was

with Ed. He was always texting *send a picture of the ladies* or *I want to see you —*
now — show me. Sometimes I thought I looked quite pretty. It made me feel

sexy, to rush upstairs, put on my lacy lingerie and then lie on the bed getting

my cleavage in the right position to send him a photo. His usual response

was to send me a picture of his erect penis in return. So hard and ready for

me. I'd then move my fingers down to my clit and start to lightly caress it

with my middle finger. My vibrator waiting in my other hand for me to

push it deep inside while I imagined Ed's penis rocking inside me. I'd push

it in as deep as it would go, so it was right up there, pushing on that magic

spot that made me gush, whilst my fingers massaged my clit causing me to

squirt. With the exception of physically fucking him, nothing made me feel

more alive than touching myself over Edward Coolidge. Even when he

wasn't here I still had to change the sheets. When I remembered, I put a

towel underneath me to catch the spillage. It was always satisfying when I

was able to make myself squirt as much as he did. When I looked in the

mirror, I saw my lumpy bits, my layers (what Liv calls 'the gunt' – this is a

merging of where your gut meets your cunt – hence 'gunt'). I hated looking

in the mirror. But when Ed looked at me – he made me feel like I was

some kind of super model, and he wasn't faking – I'd have known if he

was. He looked at me like he dug every one of my ripples. He didn't see fat

– he saw a woman of substance, he liked I dressed up for him, that I went

to the effort of wearing sexy undies, lace topped stockings and high heels.

He said he liked my confidence. That I'd tell him what I wanted to do to him, and how I'd do it, and then do everything I said I would. He'd devour me in seconds, but to be unwrapped by him in the first place and considered for his devourment tasted absolutely delicious.

Ed looked troubled as we sat and ate the curry he'd prepared.

"What's up?" I asked, with hesitancy in my voice. God only knew what bomb was about to go off.

"I'm fed up with working abroad, but there's nothing near home. I could get a job in Milton Keynes, there's one going up there."

I stopped eating. We were back here again. He'd agreed if our relationship was going to work that he'd come home, that we'd live together properly and he'd get a job in the local area. Now it was getting close to him having to uphold his end of the bargain and April was approaching, here he was, backing out.

"If you're going to work in Milton Keynes, you may as well be working abroad – at least it pays better." I sighed heavily.

"But at least I'll be in the same country."

"It makes no difference to me Ed – I still won't see you. Do what you want – you will anyway." I stood up and left the table, pushing my plate away from me. My stomach was too tight to eat. I was fed up with this carrot he dangled in front of me. Every time I had a solution, he'd find another problem. I was kidding myself. We'd never be in a proper relationship; I could feel the rage against hope forming within me. All I'd wanted was for him to get a job near home. To come home to me at night. To take joy in the everyday stuff – cooking together, doing the food shop, seeing his clothes in the wash basket. The trouble with Ed was he was so used to living away that when his relationships started to get close he ran for the hills. I wanted someone that wanted to be with me, and I wanted more than anything for him to want to be with me.

"I just don't see how else I'll ever afford to pay for my flight instructor training. Time's running out – if I don't do it before I'm forty, I'll be too old. I can't get a bank loan because of my credit rating."

"I know it's important to you and that's what you want to do. But you've been working abroad for years. You always say you earn thousands, 90k on your last tour. Where is it? If flying is that important to you why can you never actually save the money for it?"

"She has it, doesn't she? Or someone always needs something."

"*You* needed something. Money for flying lessons – that's why you're working abroad. If you keep giving your money away you'll never meet your objective. So how is anything going to change if you continue to work away? You'll just stay in the same situation. I think you like it that way."

"I don't, I want to be here with you – I do, really I do. There's nothing around here that pays anywhere near as much as I'd need."

"What would you need?"

"Well, I'd have to pay you rent, bills, food."

"You have to pay that anyway, wherever and whoever you're with."

"I pay her £200 per month for the kids."

"Is that all? Flipping heck, how does she survive?"

"Well one of them isn't mine so I don't pay for him."

"What about debts, other bills?"

"I don't know, it kinda comes in and goes out."

"Why don't we do a full review of what you pay out versus what you need and what you can save on? Then we can look at options."

"What options?"

"Options that provide the income you need versus the training you want to complete, in this area."

"I don't see how we'd achieve that."

"No, that's the trouble Ed, you don't see. Where there's a will..."

"There's a relative!" he said. Making a joke of it.

"I was going to say where there's a will there's a way." Looking over my glasses at him like a disappointed parent.

I opened up my laptop and started a spreadsheet. I took down all his outgoings and income. Then we looked at what the outgoings were for and if he still needed these. He had a phone insurance he was still paying for on a phone he no longer had. His breakdown cover was way more than

I was paying out – plus he was hardly in the country so why have it? If he stripped it all back, his outgoings per month could be kept to a minimum of £1,150.

"How much do you need to train to be a flying instructor?" I asked.

"£50k – maximum. I should be able to earn that in a year."

"And a bank loan is definitely out?"

"I've tried, I'm good for the money but my credit rating is bad because I had to go bankrupt years ago."

Another year of us not being together. Of barely hearing from him let alone seeing him. I couldn't take much more of this. The burden on my soul was too great. Seeing him once a month if I was lucky. Hearing from him every other week when he could be bothered to call. This wasn't the relationship I signed up for. I wanted him home – with me. Here to hold me in the night, getting in my way in the kitchen, coming through the front door at the end of the day and telling me all about his day and asking about mine.

I wanted my slice of normality. I was always waiting for something. For life to start. I had always been on my own. I did everything alone. I was sick of it. I wanted my man with me, no matter the cost. I wasn't waiting any longer. Three years was long enough to have been fucking about with this. He'd never save the money to then go on and do the course. The only way we'd both get what we wanted was if I stumped up the cash.

"What if I lent you £50k?"

"You've got £50k?" he said, amazed.

"I own this house outright. I could re-mortgage."

"I couldn't ask you to do that."

"You haven't, I've offered. But you'd need to train at an airfield near here and live here. I want us to be together."

The smile on his face said it all.

"Really, you'd do that for me?" he said, starting to believe.

"It'd be a loan and when you've got a job after your training, you'd need to repay it."

"I could have that paid off in a few years easy. You'd really do that?"

"Yes. It's your dream, it's what you've always wanted. I don't want you working away, I want you to be here with me, so we can have a life together. I support your dreams Ed; I want us to be happy."

"Wow. I don't know what to say. I won't let you down."

"I know you won't. Now, you best do your research and see where offers flight instructor training in Hampshire."

"No one's ever helped me like this before. No one."

"I believe in you Ed. I believe in us."

"I fucking love you Izzy." He pulled me close and gave me one of those 'cut off your circulation' hugs of his.

"I know," I said. It was our Hahn & Leia quote that we had going between us.

"I'll finish this tour, it's only another month. Do you think you can get the re-mortgage sorted out by then?"

"I'll get on it first thing Monday."

"How about you get on me right now?" His eyes were gleaming. "I've never wanted anyone more than I want you right now Iz." His eyes burned into mine as he moved towards me, to claim me. As he kissed me, my arms wrapped around his neck, pulling him closer to me. He lifted my thigh up towards his crotch. Positioning my crotch at his, we moved together, rubbing each other. He stooped and lowered my leg, pulling down my trousers and turning me around to push me over the kitchen table. His penis appeared inside of me, he pumped me deeply from behind.

"Oh Ed… Ed," I screamed out as the intensity grew inside of me.

"What Izzy? What do you want?" he said, continuing to thrust inside me.

"I want you to make me gush and I want you to fill me up," I said, breathless from the hard thrusting. He pulled out of me and spun me around. Looking into my eyes, he inserted his fingers up into me, and instantly made me gush. I could feel the warmth of my orgasm spray up

194

around my feet as it bounced off of the hard kitchen floor.

"I love how I make you do that," he said. He twisted my hips round and pushed me over the kitchen stool. His penis hard and ready. I clenched my vagina, gripping his dick tighter as he fell into me.

"Fill me up," I said. I could feel his orgasm rising within him.

"You're such a dirty bitch," he said.

"I'm your dirty bitch," I said squeezing his dick again extra tight. "Come on Ed – fill me up baby – you know you want to…" I teased.

"I'm gonna come," he said, releasing himself deep inside me.

I could feel his come dripping from between my legs, intermingling with my own. As I stood, it crept down my inner thigh, racing to meet my feet. I started to move toward the kitchen roll. Looking at the floor I noticed come-prints.

"Come on honey," said Ed "bath time."

I couldn't wait for him to be properly home. I'd call and make an appointment with the mortgage adviser Monday. I couldn't foresee there'd be a problem. I owned my house. I could hear Ed upstairs running the bath as I scampered around the kitchen, with kitchen roll held between my legs, trying to mop up our spilt juice.

"Bath's ready – come on honey," he called.

I ran upstairs and Ed was waiting for me. "You get in first – I want to bathe you." I lifted my arms up and he removed my vest top. He

195

slid my bra straps from my shoulders and reached round to undo my strap. He kissed me on the head and led me to the bath. I stepped in; the temperature of the water was hot – just like I like it. Ed lathered up a sponge and started to rub it across my back, lifting up the warm water to soothe me as he did. I laid into the suds and he moved to wash my legs – reaching up to my inner thigh he washed across my pussy, smiling at me as he set about teasing me. I lifted my leg up to stop him.

"I know your game, Manchester," I said beaming back at him. "Your turn." I stood up to get out the bath. He held out a towel and wrapped it around me, pulling me in for a kiss. I stepped out and sat on the toilet beside him. He started to clean himself. I took the sponge from him and kneeled by the bath. I wanted to wash that manly chest of his. To run the lather over his body, wash his back and show him I'd treat him like a god. I picked up the jug to wash through his hair and massaged the shampoo across his head, making sure to make my fingertips extra light, whilst rubbing his scalp gently. He closed his eyes and appeared hypnotised by my touch. "I still can't believe you're going to do that for me Iz," he said softly.

"I want us to be happy Ed. I believe in us – we have a future together."

"Once I've done my instructor training, we can work anywhere. How would you feel about America?"

"I've always wanted to go to America, I wouldn't mind working abroad with you for a while. Maddy would love it. What have you seen out there?"

"There's a helicopter company that do flights over the Grand Canyon for tourists. I'd like to do something like that. Or Florida, they have plenty of companies offering flights for tourists over the Keys. What about Daniel?"

"I'd have to speak to him about it – maybe if we could fly him out to see her it'd be ok? How long were you thinking of going out there for?"

"A couple of years? What about you, what would you do?"

"I could write anywhere – besides, it'd be your turn to work so I can achieve *my* dreams then!" I laughed.

"Deal!"

Was this really happening? Were we making plans together?

"Right, just one more month out here, then, if you can get the mortgage sorted, I'll be home."

"I'll get the money honey – don't worry."

"I need to take you flying. When I'm back next, I'll take you to meet Alan and we'll take the helicopter out."

I'd flown with Ed before, in a Cessna when Dan and I were together. That was seven years ago. I'll never forget it because Ed hadn't long passed his test and whilst we were up there, he got into slight trouble.

No one wants to hear their pilot say *oh shit* out loud.

"I'll look forward to that, I've not flown in a helicopter with you before."

"Have you been in one then?" He seemed surprised.

"Yeah, a few times. My dad was a photographer, he did aerial photography, I've been up with him." I paused. "I've never sat in the front though!"

Ed smiled. "I'll enjoy having you sat next to me. I know exactly where I'm taking you. You're gonna love it, honey."

I couldn't wait. It wasn't the fancy helicopter date – it was making plans to spend time together. It started to feel different. This wasn't stolen time any more. This was proper us time. We were planning our life together. There was nothing I'd wanted more for the last 3 years and now here it was, it was happening. I couldn't stop the smile on my face.

Am I finally getting my happily ever after?

Ed must have sensed my thoughts. He said, "It's all going to be ok Iz, this is our time."

Our time. I liked the sound of that.

"Yes, it is." I leaned in to kiss his wet soapy face.

"Right, I'm getting out."

"I'll go and get dressed."

"Do you fancy watching a movie before bed?"

"Sure, that'd be good. As long as we can cuddle up together."

"Let's watch it in bed." Ed smiled.

"Perfect."

I couldn't believe this was happening. We were going to have a proper life. As I pulled on my nightie, I started to think of him arriving through the door in his instructor's uniform. He'd look so hot! And he'd be coming home to me like that – every day!

"What are you smiling about?" Ed was wrapping his dressing gown around him.

"You – in your instructor's uniform…"

"Oh – are you now? I'll be hot and sweaty after a long day of it though."

"Well, you better be – I like the idea of you coming home dirty," I said, tilting my head and blushing at him.

"You're bad. I love it!"

"I know."

"Come on let's watch this movie before sleeps."

"What time do we need to leave in the morning?" I asked.

"I need to be there for 8am, so we'll need to leave by 6am."

"Ok, so up at 5am?"

"5.30 will do it honey."

I set the alarm on my phone – I was already dreading it going off.

Not because of the early hour but because the early hour would be taking him away from me.

The morning came all too quickly. "Only another month honey, then I'll be back for good." He leaned over to cuddle me, kissed me quickly on the lips before getting out of the car. He paused before shutting the door. Looking at me he said, "I love you, Isobel Burnell."

Instantly I replied, "I love you too, Edward Coolidge."

He flashed his cocky smile at me as if to say *I know*, shut the door and turned to head into the terminal. I watched him walk away in the rear-view mirror as I indicated to move out and join the traffic towards home.

17

Right, first up – I had to get that money. I searched online and looked through how much re-payments would cost. He needed £50k; I'd get £70k so we had a buffer in case he needed more. I made an appointment with the mortgage adviser at the bank. Since I already owned my house outright, getting a re-mortgage was easy. I'd have to wait three weeks for the paperwork to process and the money to come through, but after my hour appointment with the mortgage guy at the bank, that was it – done deal. This was going to happen – Ed was going to come home. I couldn't wait to tell him; he'd be made up.

I decided I'd use my excited energy to go out on a bike ride before I had to collect Maddy from school. I needed to get my distance up. I was averaging 10km per ride, at Blenheim I'd need to ride 19.8km. Today I was going to add another 2km to my training. I was confident that today's buzz was going to help me push that little bit further. As I cycled down the road my head went into daydream mode. With the sun shining and a gentle breeze in my face, the green of the trees spreading new hope warmed me. Just one more month and we'd be living a normal life. I laughed to myself – *I'll have to clear some space for a man drawer!*

I didn't notice the kilometres tick by as I cycled around Baddesley and on to Emer Bog. I sucked in the wildlife, the colours of the leaves on the trees, it was as if I had woken up to the world, that I was now a player in this thing called life. It sure felt good to feel happy. It was a feeling I hoped to become a friend to me. I spotted a rabbit's tail dart of the road into the bushes ahead of me. Maddy would like it here. She loves animals. By the time I reached home, I looked down at my Fitbit and I'd managed to clock up 15.3km, 3km over my target! And I didn't feel any the worse for wear. Just goes to show how your attitude really does influence what you can achieve. I've had some days where I've been out on the bike and literally felt like I was dying from the pain in my legs. They'd usually been days where I'd told myself I had to train even though I didn't want to. Then comes today, things are going well, the sun is shining and I smashed it.

As I got in from the school run my home phone was ringing – or as I call it the bat phone to my mum. Only Mum called me on the home phone. Well Mum and spam calls.

"All right Mum?"

"Yes, just calling to see how you are."

"Good thanks, managed to do 15.3k on the bike earlier!"

"What's that?"

"What do you mean?"

"15.3k in our language?"

"It's about nine and a half miles."

"How many have you got to do on the day?"

"What, ks in miles you mean?"

"Yes."

"Roughly it's just over twelve miles."

"You're getting there then, well done my love. How's the rest of it going?"

"The swim I can do, I'm not worried about that, the run is my worst leg – not a lover of running, and then I've just got to be able to do them all together one after the other."

"How far have you got to run?"

"Just under 3.5 miles."

"What's that in those k things?"

I smiled to myself – only my mother.

"That'd be 5.4 of the k things Mum."

"Well, it's a lot all that, however you measure it. Grandad will be proud."

"Thanks Mum."

"How's things with Ed? Has he gone back abroad again?"

"He's got one more month and then he'll be back, he's going to complete his helicopter instructor training."

"How can he afford that then?"

"He's been saving, that's why he works abroad."

"Hm."

"What do you mean hm? Be happy for me Mum, I love him."

"There's something about him I don't like."

"You haven't met him!"

"No, but you've told me things and I don't like it."

"There's two sides to every story, Mum. He makes me happy that's all you need to know."

"Well, for now. Until he's off again."

"The past is the past Mum. He's coming home in a month and we'll be together, he's what I've always wanted – be happy for me?"

"We'll see."

She was starting to bring me down, so I did the only thing I could.

"Maddy, come and talk to Grandma, tell her about your day."

Mother was always suspicious. She didn't like any man really, least of all one that was dating her daughter. I shouldn't have told her so much when we were going through those rough patches. It's tainted her view and I'll never get her to like him now. One thing's for sure, I couldn't tell her where he'd really got the money from. She'd be fuming. Especially as she paid off my mortgage when Grandad died.

I went about making tea, Maddy came in and announced: "Grandma said bye and she'd speak to you later." It was what it was but it sounded like a threat — like Mum hadn't given up the chase on this one.

"Ok, thank you Mads, get your hands washed for tea and you can watch some TV while I get it ready."

"What have we got?"

"Spaghetti."

"Yay!"

"With garlic bread."

"Double yay!"

I'd never be able to tell my mum about lending Ed the money, she was already hoovering up my happiness. I knew exactly what she'd say and I didn't want to hear it. I pushed her from my mind as we sat down to eat tea.

After Maddy had gone to bed and I'd done the customary three stories and four times back and forth saying goodnight and tucking her in… I opened up my laptop to wait for Ed's Skype call. I couldn't wait to see his face when I told him I'd be getting the money. I got myself a glass of water, I could feel something in my throat, and grabbed a biscuit too while I was at it.

The familiar Skype tune called out and I raced back to take my seat to see Ed's face.

"Hello!" he said all bright and breezy.

"Hello you!" I said beaming back at him. "How has your day been?"

"Busy, I've been in a confined space fitting cable."

"Sounds hot and dirty."

"And very sweaty!"

"I have some good news."

"What?"

"I saw the bank, the paperwork has to go through, but they'll re-mortgage my house, I'll have the money in three weeks."

He looked in shock, but it was a good shock. I could see he couldn't believe it.

"Really?"

"Really really!"

"Oh my God. Ok – so I'm going to do this?"

"Yes, you are Edward!"

"No one has ever done anything like this for me before, I'll pay you back, every penny, it's a loan."

"I know you will. And now you can start living your best life – we both can."

Ed's face was one huge grin. Like all his Christmas presents that he'd ever wanted had just been handed to him.

"Right – so I'll be home the end of the month then."

"I can't wait, and no more assignments abroad – you'll be coming home to me." I smiled at him. "All you need to do is find a flight instructor course near Baddesley, so that's your homework. I'm happy to get this loan for you, but my one ask is that you train near home – our home – here. You can take trips up to see your kids but if this relationship is going to work, we need to be living under the same roof."

"There's nothing I want more Izzy. I can't wait to be coming home to you. You are amazing! Mazing!" He said squinting his eyes like he does each time he calls me that.

"When are you going to tell Dan?"

"I'll talk to him when I'm back, face to face. I'll tell him Iz, I promise."

"It feels so good to hear you say that – I don't wanna be your dirty little secret."

"You're not – you're my little Izzy squirty pants and I'm proud to be with you honey."

"Will you tell Ella too?"

"Yes – I'll let her know we're together and she ain't coming between us."

"She'll come on strong for you as soon as she thinks you're with someone else. You know that, right? So, remember that, and when she does, remember we had that conversation and she's just trying to confuse you. She never really wants you Ed – she just doesn't want anyone else to have you."

"You're right. I'll remember. Now let's start planning our future, I can't wait to be home. I just want to get started now." Excitement oozed from his voice. It warmed me to know I'd been able to help him and support him with his life's dream. Sure, it would cost me financially, but I trusted him to pay me back once he'd graduated and was working in the job he craved. I could tighten my belt, cut down on the takeaways. Days out with Maddy we could do to the beach or park where it was free. I'd manage.

"Right, when I get back, I'm taking you flying, I want you to see what you're investing in."

"I'd love to fly with you, I'll look forward to it."

"I'll take you somewhere special – you won't regret this Izzy – this is the making of us."

"I know."

"Right, I have to go and get dinner before they stop serving. Speak to you soon – I love you Izzy Burnell."

"I love you too Edward – take care babe."

"I always do – speak to you later honey, bye." He said blowing me a kiss.

"Bye," I said blowing one back.

The next few weeks flew by. We'd both done a lot of research into finding a flight school near home, the prices down here were way more expensive – practically double. I wanted more than anything for Ed to be living with me, so we could do this together and I could support him when the going got tough. He'd said £50k would cover it. And already it was looking like £100k – even with my back-up cash, it simply wasn't enough. Ed wanted to take me up to Dragon Helicopters where he'd learned to fly. I wasn't stupid, I knew I was about to get the full stakeholder treatment. I was looking forward to going up with him all the same.

18

When we arrived at Dragon Helicopters, I was impressed with how Ed went about setting up the aircraft and opening the hangar. He'd completed his flying lessons with Dragon and knew the owner, who had permitted Ed to bring me up on a Sunday to take me flying. I could see Ed was in his element, I didn't talk to him as I didn't want to interrupt his train of thought. He was going through checks in his head. I just soaked it all up. My boyfriend – the helicopter pilot. Not everyone could say that could they? After he'd wheeled our transport out onto the airfield, I was invited to sit inside. Although I'd flown in a helicopter before, I'd never sat in the front. So many dials and switches. And Ed knew them all. He handed me some earphones and I placed them on my head. I could hear Ed through them talking to the tower.

He stopped and turned to me. "Just getting permission from the tower honey, then we can talk."

"No, it's ok, you do what you need to do, I'm happy to take it all in."

When we started moving, it was strange, we kinda coasted forwards slightly above the ground while Ed took the aircraft to the correct place to take off on the strip. A Cessna landed and then air traffic gave permission for us to take off. After we'd gained altitude, we headed off to the left. The sun shone down on the fields below, I looked over at Ed, the headset suited him. He looked hot! He continued talking to the tower for a bit and then asked, "So what do you think of my office?"

"It's beautiful, I love it, so free and peaceful."

He pointed to a forest below. "You see over there?"

"Yeah."

"Another time I'll take you there, it's secluded, but there's an open field where we can land, I thought we could have a picnic."

"Yeah, that'd be awesome."

"Today though, I'm taking you to Bristol."

"Oh, wow, so we're going to fly over Bristol!"

"Well, yes and no." He grinned. "I'll need your help to land when we get there. Telephone wires are a hazard for helicopters. I'll need all eyes in the sky to make sure we're clear."

I wondered where we were going, I wasn't expecting to land.

There was something about his face profile that captivated me while he flew us around. He was so calm, controlled, collected and concentrated. I felt so unbelievably safe up here in the clouds with him.

I could see the Clifton suspension bridge on the horizon.

Ed pointed to the right of it. "That's where we're heading."

"Ok."

"There's a pub, The White Lion – they do a great roast, I thought we could have Sunday lunch."

"Wow! Talk about arrive in style! Where do we land?"

"In the car park. The owner has given us permission – I called ahead, they're expecting us."

As Ed circled above the car park, I looked down and he'd attracted a fair bit of attention. People gathered below to watch.

"Right – where I need your help is to look for cables. Any you see point them out to me – we don't want to get tangled up. It never hurts to have an extra set of eyes."

"To the right and dead ahead – at the rear of the car park."

Ed landed in the centre of the car park, then lined up the chopper inside two car spaces. He manoeuvred it in like I would my car. It made me smile.

He turned off the rotors and powered down the craft. I looked at him.

"There are so many people out there looking – do you think they think we are famous?"

"LOL probably! Come on."

I took my headset off, unbuckled my belt and Ed had already walked round to open the door and help me out of the aircraft.

I felt a little embarrassed at everyone watching. I remembered something Dan had said: "Walk in like you own the place – no one knows who you are". Ed took my hand and led me inside, I smiled at people as we walked on into the pub When we were seated at the table, our drinks ordered, Ed said.

"That was bloody awesome, right?"

"Oh my God, so awesome. The way you parked up, properly – like a car. I'm in awe of you."

"It was cool wasn't it."

"Very cool. Five minutes ago, we're flying, and now we're sat at the table awaiting Sunday lunch. I mean how many people arrive at a pub by helicopter Ed?"

His face was smug, pleased with his execution.

I raised my glass. "Here's to the best date ever. I'll never forget today, Ed."

"The day isn't over yet honey." He smiled with that devilish look of his.

People in the pub were still looking over at us. I could see they wondered who we were.

"Seven o'clock – incoming," I said to Ed raising my glass to take a sip.

"Hi, how is everything?"

I could see from the name badge that this was Rosie the manager.

I smiled. Ed replied, "Wonderful. We've wanted to come here for a while, a lot of my friends have complimented you on your roast."

"That's excellent to hear. Have you come far?"

"Hereford, I think I may have spoken to you on the phone. I'm from Dragon Helicopters."

"Ah yes, so you're the one causing all the discussing in the car park." She laughed.

"Guilty as charged. There's not many places you can park a helicopter so it's brilliant to be able to bring my girlfriend out for lunch like this."

My girlfriend. My smile widened. He'd never introduced me like that before. It warmed me and provided me with an assurance I craved.

We finished our lunch and headed back out to the chopper.

I looked at Ed. "Here you go Ed, no pressure but all eyes will be on you."

He laughed – he loved the attention. It wasn't his helicopter – but no one knew that and he totally owned the perception.

When we reached it, an elderly gentleman came over to us.

"No one has touched it sir, I've been watching it for you."

"That is most kind of you, and very appreciated. I'm Ed and this is my girlfriend Izzy."

There it was again – *girlfriend.*

"My name is Gus and I've been a coastguard for 48 years. She can turn pretty quickly round 'ere. Cause I've never seen her from your view, I'm more of a land and sea dweller."

"How would you like to catch a glimpse of my view?" Ed said

"Sir?" Gus looked confused.

"I'll take you up, give you a quick tour from the sky, my way of saying thank you for keeping an eye on her,' he said, nodding to the helicopter.

Gus looked made up like he hadn't ever flown before let alone had a ride in a helicopter. I elected to stay on the ground so that Ed could give him the full experience. He was in his element up there, showboating across the sky. I took plenty of photos for Gus to share in the pub later – this would have to make him a celebrity at least for a week.

When Gus stepped out from his joyride, he had tears of joy in his eyes.

He turned to Ed. "You've made an old man very happy."

"Any time. Next time we come back, I'll take you up again – and you'll have to have lunch with us of course."

"I would like that very much."

"What's your number Gus, I've taken loads of photos to send you."

"There you go Gus, one trip up and you've pulled already!" laughed Ed. "You can't have this one though – she's mine!"

Gus gave an embarrassed laugh. "Ow, I don't have a phone – I've got one of those electric mail thingies though."

"An email address – great, give me that and I'll send you the pictures." I'd even taken one of him with Ed in the cockpit with the headset on – a standard and must have picture.

"It's been a pleasure to meet you sir," Ed said to Gus shaking his hand "We'll see you again soon."

Gus held the door open for me, and I stepped up to get in. I looked back. "See you soon Gus – keep looking after those waters."

He saluted and I gestured back to him.

As we lifted off, the locals had already started gathering around him.

"That was the amazing act of kindness Ed. You've made his day – truly." I couldn't stop beaming. "I'm so proud of you."

Back at the base Ed put the helicopter to bed and locked up the hangar. I could see why he liked it here. This is where he'd first learned to fly, I could see the appeal in sticking with what he knew to get him through his instructor training. Was I being selfish expecting him to start somewhere new just so he would be closer to me? In the grand scheme of things what was another six months? And he'd promised to come down every other weekend. It was still a far cry from what I wanted, but this wasn't about me. This was about Ed completing his dream.

Ed appeared, "What do you think of it here then?"

"I can see what you like about it."

"Bill is really supportive too, he'd be giving me a great discount, anywhere else and we'd be struggling for cash."

"Relax Ed. I'm sold. I want you to train where you think you have your best chance – and if that's here then I'm in."

"You're amazing – thank you! I'll be with you every other weekend, I promise."

"And call, Facetime, text – I want to be in communication with my boyfriend, not just thought about every other weekend!" I laughed, whilst meaning every sound beat.

"Are you crazy? How could I only think about you every other weekend ya loon! You are the only person that has ever believed in me – I won't ever forget what you are doing for me. I love you."

"I love you too. And it's only for six months right, then you'll have your wings and we'll live wherever we need to for you to fly."

"Have I told you you're awesome?" He kissed me on the head.

"You may have mentioned it once or twice," I said as he wrapped his arms around me from my back as we looked out from the office at the sunset over the airfield.

19

Having Ed home with me was short lived. He was right though, the quicker he started his training the quicker he'd finish. That wouldn't make me miss him any less though.

"I'll call you when I get there," he said, embracing me one last time before getting in the car. He was full of excitement and adventure.

"Drive safe, you're going to be great!"

"I always do!" he said, putting his sunglasses on and smiling at me – window down, arm out the window, music on. He blew me a kiss as he drove off down the road.

It always hurts when he drives away. The feeling pulls me down, it's like each time he goes, I lose him. Like I'm stuck on pause waiting for him to return. There is a physical pain that collects around my stomach. My body feels like it is trudging through treacle. With it comes the tears. That's the moment when my real life starts. The one without him. It's such a long life on my own. Every day feels like two. The wait for a text or a call feels like eternity. The anxiety – *what is he doing that he can't reply to me?* It all starts up when we are apart. I know he is going to complete his training and he'll be back every other weekend, and he'll call me when he can and that this is for the short term. Yet still nagging doubt is at me already, festering in my thoughts, waking up from dormancy. I have to be strong, it will all be all right. He'll be back in eleven days for our weekend. I'll focus on that. For now, I'll paint the fence – it needs to be done and it'll give me something else to think about.

As I topped up my creosote pot, my phone started ringing. I put it on speaker.

"Hey honey, I'm here."

"You had a good run up then?"

"Yeah, traffic was good. I've found my digs, the landlady is nice. It's just her, her son and his girlfriend. So, it seems a quiet place to allow me to study."

"That's good – glad they are nice people."

"I need to get my stuff in, but I wanted to let you know I got here ok honey, talk later ok."

"Ok, you go and get settled in, speak soon."

Well, that was that – he was all moved up to Leominster. At least it meant he could see his kids. Must be hard to be apart from them – I wouldn't be able to cope with seeing Maddy as and when. I went back to painting the fence – I wanted to get halfway around before Maddy ran through the door.

Later that night, with Mads asleep, I reviewed the spreadsheet for Ed's training. I'd already paid out for some it before he'd started, and there was his rent and living expenses I needed to manage from the loan. Flying was expensive, already I'd paid out £18k. Still, it would be worth it and I knew Ed would pay me back as soon as he started working.

Beep beep.

Hi honey – just going out for a walk and look around the area. The car barely made it here. I think it'll be on the way out soon. Do you think the budget would stretch to cover a new car?

Why do you need a new car?

This thing is knackered. I don't want to be stuck on the motorway somewhere and waste my time when I could be with you.

It's funny – I was just going through the budget. £18k is spent already Ed – we just can't afford a car that was never part of the deal.

I've seen something in the garage up here, it's only 8 grand.

That may be, but that's 8 grand you won't have to finish your helicopter instructor training – once you've passed and have a job, then we can think about a car.

Hm. Ok. It was just a thought.

Could a text sound disappointed?!

And don't worry, if you break down you are covered by Green Flag remember.

Thanks. Men really can be like little boys sometimes. I started to feel that feeling in my throat again, like it was closing in. Maybe I should book an appointment to see the doctor? I could feel a lump or something that I couldn't seem to get rid of. I ought to check it out.

My phone rang.

God. It was Ella! I knew she'd once had my number, but we'd kept our distance – for obvious reasons.

"Hello Ella."

"I hear you've been slating me."

"No... not that I can recall. What makes you say that?"

"Ed's been over this afternoon, and he said you weren't happy with me because I wouldn't let you meet the kids yet."

He'd spent the afternoon with Ella? He hadn't mentioned that.

"Ella, I'm not a bad person. I have a child too, one I've had to share since she was born, and Dan and I do that very amicably. It's hard when your children meet their dad's new girlfriend, I've had to go through it myself – it sucks – but I don't deny Dan that."

"Ed couldn't cope with the children on his own. There's no way I'd let you take them."

"Take them? I don't want to take them from you Ella – they're your children! Just to meet them one day would be nice."

"If you're still around in a year, then maybe. Ed and I are always going to be in each other's lives, and our kids will always come first."

"Just as Dan and I will always be in each other's lives, and Maddy will always come first.... And despite what you seem to think Ella, I don't come first in Ed's life... I don't know what he's telling you. But I don't."

"He's always with you when he should be here with his kids."

I laughed, but it felt bitter. "Really? Is that what he tells you? At the moment I'll be seeing him once a fortnight. Up to now it's been almost never. So I don't know why you think that!"

"Well, wherever he is, he isn't with his kids."

"And he's not with me all the time. I can promise you that. I hardly ever see him."

There was a pause. Then, "What's wrong with you Izzy? Open your eyes!"

"Open my eyes to what Ella?"

"I just wish he'd put the kids first, and nothing else."

"Do you mean that what you want is for him to *only* have the kids, and no one else in his life? But that's not realistic, is it?"

Another pause.

"Be careful with Ed, he'll say what you want to hear. I've learned the hard way, and he lies all the time, I don't think he can help himself."

Well, she was right there. He did say what I wanted to hear –

sometimes. And his actions didn't always marry up.

I plucked up the courage to ask her a direct question. "Do you still love him, Ella? Do you still want him? If there's a chance for your family to be together I won't get in the way of that."

"I love him and always will, but I'll never ever trust him."

"Look, we used to like each other before. I don't see why that has to change. Surely you'd rather Ed was with someone you liked. The only reason I could understand you hating me is if for you it wasn't over, and you wanted him back. But if you don't, he'll always be with *someone* Ella – why not me? Am I really that bad?"

"I'll talk to you later, I have to go, Ed is calling me."

Bitch.

I texted Ed.

Hey, where are you?

Out on my walk.

Who with?

No one – I'm alone.

Right. I called his number, it rang, he didn't answer.

Why aren't you picking up your phone?

I just wanted some peace, some me time, stop being so pressurising.

Are you with Ella?

With that he went silent. The text was read – but no reply. Who do I believe? His twisted ex or him? When he ignored me like this, not answering my calls, it was hard to think he was being honest.

Just remember which side your bread is buttered! I typed in outrage.

An hour later he called.

"Hey. You ok?"

"Have you been with Ella?"

"Why would you think that? I've been for a walk – which was relaxing until you started on at me!"

"You sound like you are in a car."

"I needed to get some fuel for the morning."

Convenient. I wasn't sure if I wanted him to know I'd been talking to Ella yet. Keep your enemies close and all that.

"I just wanted some time to myself, to think and prepare. It's a big day tomorrow and I wanted to be in the right frame of mind. I'm worried about money, worried about the car, it's my boy's birthday next week and she expects me to buy a bike. You accusing me of seeing Ella doesn't help – I've done nothing wrong. I know where my bread is buttered thank you. I know it's hard for you but I'll be back soon – you just need to hang on in there and be strong for us Izzy. I love you, come on, be on my side."

Maybe he hadn't been with Ella. Maybe she was just a stirring old shrew attempting to plant seeds in my mind and destroy my relationship. I had no evidence to say he was or wasn't with her. I decided I'd believe in Ed, we had so much invested together, he'd be a fool to jeopardise that.

"I am on your side, of course I am – hence I've re-mortgaged my house to support you Ed. It's tough being apart."

"I know – it won't be forever, by October we'll be living together again, I promise. I just need to find a way to get more money in. I thought I'd start gigging again."

"I don't understand, your flying is paid for and out of the loan you receive £1,800 per month to live on. Why is money an issue?"

"My family expect money from me, they think I'm rolling in it."

"Well put them straight – tell them you aren't!"

"It's my mum and sister – I have to look after them."

"What do they need?"

"Mum's heating has packed up, and Lucy needs a new washing machine."

"Well how much is that?"

"I don't know, probably a few grand."

"And how much is the boy's bike?"

"£100."

"Let me check the finances and see what we can do. It's pointless you taking six months out to study if you are going to start gigging at the weekends – that means you'll lose study time and I won't see you at all."

"It was just a thought."

"Keep focused. Six months to study and get your wings – don't let anything get in the way."

"She wants me to have the youngest next week, he's sick and she needs to go to work."

"What would she do if you were abroad?"

"Ask her sister."

"Well then! If he's sick – then you get sick and it delays your training – focus Ed, focus! You have time up there to see your kids – but you're not up there to play happy families, are you?"

"No. It's hard, she has expectations."

"Well re-set them."

"It's complicated."

"Why? Are you still together, are you playing me?"

"No, of course not – she just has this way of messing with my mind."

Now that I could relate to.

"Ed, if you want to see your kids – see your kids – but bottom line you have six months to get your wings and the money runs out. You need to focus to get what you want. You can do both – you have to be strong with Ella though or else you'll waste this opportunity."

"I'm not going to do that – I've come too far."

"Don't let her mess with your head."

"You're right, I won't, I deserve this, I'm going to make it work."

He sounded happier, less burdened.

"Good! Because I'm looking forward to 'the splash' when you crack that champagne open after passing your exams and becoming a flight instructor."

"Yeah – me too. Thanks, Iz. I'm going to go and relax and have a hot bath and get a good night's sleep."

"That sounds a good idea – I think I'll join you!"

"I wish you could baby"

"Well – I will in spirt. I love you Ed."

"I know you do baby."

"Good luck tomorrow!"

"Thanks, honey."

I returned to the spreadsheet – where could I find two grand from to help him out of this money issue? Every penny from the loan was accounted for. I looked to my bank account. I was saving to take Maddy to Disney. I've fooled myself it doesn't matter she went there first with Daniel and his girlfriend, what would matter was the experience we had when we went. Mummy and daughter time in the house of Mickey. I didn't want Ed to start gigging again, it'd delay his chances of everything he needed to do in the next six months. We couldn't afford for him to be away longer either. I transferred the money to him and sent him a text.

"Enjoy your bath and stop worrying about money. I've sent you over £2,100. Sort out your mum's heating, Lucy's washing machine and buy your boy a bike. Then stop worrying and concentrate on flying."

I then decided a long soak in a hot bath sounded just the ticket. Maybe it'd help soothe my throat – the lump was becoming more noticeable and swallowing was starting to make me gag sometimes. I'd have to sort that out.

20

For five months Ed had been doing his training. Most of the time I was empty. All I seemed to do was wait for him to come home. There was always something in the way of it. It wasn't flying weather in the week and he needed to catch up at the weekend; or it was one of the kid's birthdays; or he needed to help Ella with something for the kids; he'd promised the kids something or he had to go to Manchester to see his family – and, my favourite, he had to go to Ella's sister's wedding with her... Which was instantly followed by Ella posting a picture of them all on Facebook – the perfect family. There was always a reason to not see me. It made me doubt if it was me Ed loved or my money. Had I tried to buy him? By re-mortgaging my house so he didn't have to work abroad any more? Had I offered him what no one else could in a bid to keep him? Either way I didn't feel like you should feel when you are in a relationship. I didn't feel like I mattered, I didn't feel like he cared about me, I didn't feel loved. All I felt was used, and an idiot for allowing myself to get in this position. He wouldn't answer my calls and he'd rarely call me or make any other kind of contact. I could feel him slipping away from me, and I didn't know what to do to save us. I knew he wanted a new car, but I really couldn't afford another loan. He had his heart set on a Range Rover. If I took out a car loan, that would be all my wages tied up. There would be nothing for day trips with Maddy or savings. He would have had everything from me. I wasn't going to let that happen. I couldn't put myself into further financial hardship. I could feel a battle starting inside me. Part of me was giving up on him. The other part was hanging on.

Five months into his training, and he still hadn't passed the basics. It didn't take a genius to work out that he wouldn't be completed in six months. The money was running out and I couldn't re-mortgage the re-mortgage to supply him with more. Well – I could – but I didn't want to. He'd have to start working to start paying for what was left and supporting the loan I'd been carrying. I felt sick, like the inevitable was about to happen.

I'd confided in Liv about the loan. Her response was, "Well that's £70k you won't see again!"

The money had been a sacrifice, but what really made my head spin was not really knowing what he was doing up there. Was he living two lives? Ella up there and me when he fancied it down here?

Beep beep.

Thanks for today Ed – it was just what I needed! It was from Ella. How delightfully obvious – the old 'text the girlfriend "by mistake" with a note meant for her boyfriend' trick.

I replied with: *LOL – I think you meant to send that to Ed.*

I wasn't going to let her know she'd got to me.

She had got to me though. I was going crazy, like I didn't know which way was up. I decided to call Ed – just so that he could ignore my call again. To my surprise he picked up.

Hey baby!

I wondered if he called Ella baby too.

Hey. Ella sent me a text meant for you.

Oh – what did it say?

Thank you for this afternoon, it was just what she needed. What's that about?

Oh, I just helped her move some panels.

Some panels? It sounded like she was thanking you for more than panels.

Here you go again, I've done nothing wrong! Why do you keep on?

Why do you not care? Why do you not ever call and ask how I am? Why are you up there moving her panels instead of coming to see me? You haven't been home in a month!

I'm busy.

Yeah - moving panels.

Just stop will you, is it any wonder I don't come home when all you do is complain. At least Ella listens.

Really? I don't listen to you? I don't support you? You believe that do you?

I don't know, it's easy with her.

Easy?

She's the mother of my babies.

And? I'm the mother of Dan's first born and we don't carry on like you two.

You just can't communicate properly, that's your trouble. With that he hung up.

I couldn't communicate?

Me?

He thought I couldn't communicate?

That didn't compute.

He was projecting his inability to communicate onto me. If I couldn't communicate how was it I had a job where communication was key? My colleagues even called me the Comms Queen.

What's he doing up there in Hereford? Have I been played? Is he even flying at all? Has he simply taken my money and been living a double life all along?

I could go up there, catch him by surprise. See for myself. It's a long drive though and that wouldn't be fair to Maddy. I could ask Mum to look after her but I shouldn't be sneaking around spying on Ed. That doesn't feel right in a relationship. I don't know what to think.

When I think about what he's just said to me it tears me apart. Ella listens… it's easy with her. So, he can't talk to me then – I'm not easy. The exact opposite of what he used to say to me! Maybe he did want to be with her. I mean actions speak louder than words – and he's not here with me.

The next morning, I decided to go for a swim to clear my head. I wasn't going to get around Blenheim if I didn't put the training hours in. I only had another six weeks and then I'd be doing it for real. Today I was going to attempt all three legs in the same day. Swim > Bike > Run. There was a lake near me where people were allowed to swim in the early morning. My plan was to tackle the open water swim, then do the bike ride, then run around the lake. Plenty of people did it so it was a supportive environment.

As I approached for my swim, it looked like a scene from any good crime thriller. The mist lifted off the top of the lake. There were at least fifteen swimmers already in. A group ran by me on my way in. "Is it cold?" I asked one of them. "By the time you hit the second marker you will be warm," came the reply. I looked for the second marker. It was about 100 yds out. I put my hat on and made my way into the water. As I put my foot in the words *bloooody hell!* escaped from my mouth. The life guard looked over at me from his canoe. "Sorry, it's rather cold," I said. He laughed, as did the swimmers going by. *They knew!*

I began an inner monologue. *Shit, Jesus, fuck me this is freezing, why am*

I out here for God's sake, this is madness, I'm gonna die! I threw myself into the water as soon as it was waist high, I decided better to die quick than by razor cut. I had a three-quarter wet suit. My arms and legs were instantly numb. My head went under the water, I took a breath – *come on Izzy you can do this* said my cheerleader. I looked ahead for that second marker – the big purple buoy. *Keep moving* I told myself. *You can swim – you can do it in the pool – you can do it out here.* I imagined the worst thing possible to keep me focused: I had to swim this lake in order to get to Maddy. She needed me to save her and the only way I could do that was to remain calm and get my arse around this ice-cold lake. Suddenly my head was in the zone. My body warmed – my brain understood and I was swimming. I momentarily wondered what lived beneath me… Eels? I hated eels. They looked too much like snakes to me – as a child, I was once at the water's edge while my dad was fishing, and someone pulled out an eel. I didn't see this coming and screamed in fear, and our German Shepherd Dog Squire dashed over, growling at the boy I was screaming at. My dad told us both to fucking shut up, we were disturbing the fish. Squire was my protector. I loved that dog. His memory warmed through my blood as I pulled myself through the water.

As I pulled myself from the water and went to my bike, I could here my phone ringing. It was Ed.

"Hey," I said out of breath.

"Where are you? You're not at home."

"I'm training, why, where are you?"

"At home, waiting for you."

"I didn't think you were coming home this weekend."

"I wanted to. I needed to see you. Come home."

This was a surprise.

"Ok, I'll be home in twenty minutes."

I wasn't expecting Ed home, he'd been putting me off for weeks. I wondered why he wanted to see me so suddenly. Yesterday he was all about Ella and how she was easy and he could talk to her.

I arrived home to find Ed waiting for me at the front door. He opened my car door, scooping me up in his arms.

"I've missed you Izzy."

"This is a surprise."

"Can't I come home?"

"Of course, but you haven't in a month and I wasn't expecting you. I thought you didn't want to."

"I'm here aren't I? I needed to see you; it's been too long. I allowed myself to get swept up with everyone else and what they wanted, and didn't do what I wanted."

"Have you not been flying?"

"Yes, that's not what I meant. Ella confuses me, and makes me feel guilty – that I should be doing more for the kids. She gets in my head."

I had an uneasy feeling that he'd slept with her.

"Besides, I needed to do some washing!" he said laughing, washing bags in tow.

"Aw so that's what brought you home!" I laughed.

"No, this is…" He kissed me and held me tightly. "Come on."

"I've just swum in a scuzzy lake Ed; I need a wash first!"

"Ok, I'm flexible." He smiled.

21

Ed was with his kids this weekend, so I made the most of getting a few jobs done around the house while Maddy was with her dad. I decided to prioritise. I put the washing on. Dusting was a nice thing to do and I could usually swipe the dust off with the extension arm on the Dyson. I needed to do a food shop, so the weekly jaunt to Asda was on my list. I looked at my post-its. 'Finish painting the fence' – fortunately it was raining, so that was out for today anyway. I decided a deep clean of the bathroom was necessary – I'd ended up with so many bottles of I don't know what scattered all over the top by the sink. Ed liked tidiness. He was always complaining about how untidy Ella was. I tried to remind him once that she had three children to look after and probably feeding, cleaning and dressing them was a lot to handle let alone trying to keep a tidy house. It didn't go down well, from his point of view there were no excuses. He said he'd usually spend two hours cleaning the house when he returned from a tour just to make it liveable – he wouldn't live in shit. So, this was my chance to make sure he had a tidy home to return to next week.

Beep beep. How's your day hunny?

Hey, it's been good thanks, I've been having a tidy and a clear out. Just off to Asda soon, is there anything you want?

Ooh can you get me some red wine – Casa Diablo, and if you get us some steak, I'll cook us a nice meal Friday night. I could do with some razor blades too. Thank you, baby.

Ok will do. How's your day going?

Good thank you, I'm taking the kids flying – they're so excited.

Aw I bet they are – not every kid has a dad that can fly helicopters – now there's bragging rights in the playground. Have a great time baby! Let me know when you are safely back on the ground.

Will do hunny – taking off in an hour – should be back by 4 – the kids will be starving by then so I'll need to feed them.

I went off to Asda to do the weekly shop. Tomorrow Maddy and I would head off to the beach, I decided – it might be good kite-flying weather and it'd be nice to get outside and have some fun together, just us. I selected some steak and decided on runner beans, carrots and broccoli. It made me happy to think of Ed having a day with his kids. That's how it should be, they needed their daddy time. Odd as well, as usually Ella wouldn't let him take out the youngest, not without her anyway... He just said the kids. He didn't mention Ella. I wondered if she'd gone. That'd take the biscuit if I was paying for her to go fucking joy riding! I could feel my trolley rage as I neared the corner by the razors. I reached for my phone and my fingers started frantically texting.

So, when you say you're taking the kids flying, is that all 3 of them?

Yeah baby they're all coming flying.

That's great so Ella has finally let you take Robert! Thirty seconds felt like an hour and I couldn't control the rage inside me telling me Ella was out flying too.

Is Ella going with you too?

Look, I'm just taking the kids flying, we're gonna have a nice family day.

A nice family day? WTF? So, Ella was going — and it's now a family day — like you could fucking jump in and out of that. What a cunt. I couldn't believe it — I was enraged. After everything we had discussed about boundaries and setting expectations and now he was 'being the man', taking her on expensive days out that I'm fucking financing while I stay home keeping it all clean and ready for him. Fuck me. I was the cunt in this situation. Razor blades? He could fucking buy his own. Why should I also finance his looking good for other women?

I don't fucking believe you Ed — you've bloody well taken her flying haven't you after everything you promised!

Oi — where's my kisses?

240

Fuck your kisses arsehole!

Well that's not very nice is it – kiss your mother with that mouth?

Don't you dare fucking lecture me – I know what's right and what isn't – and what you're doing isn't right Mr and it's not on.

I just want to have a nice day with my kids and I don't know why you have to get all bent out of shape about it. I'm taking my kids flying and that's that. Go and have a nice day.

You're such a fucking cunt!

He hadn't admitted it – but I damn well knew he'd taken that bitch flying with them. I wasn't even allowed to meet his precious fucking kids, but he takes her flying – on a 'family day' – and I'm the mug fucking financing it. Breathless with rage I marched to the yogurt aisle and picked up Maddy's favourite yogurts. Tossed a loaf in from the bakery and picked up a pizza for tonight. Images kept floating through my head of them all on a happy, jolly family day out. Her smiling at him, stealing hugs and kisses that were supposed to be mine. I couldn't really give a shit about meeting his kids, since they'd have been primed to hate me anyway – what was the point in that conflict? It'd be another wedge between us. But Ella attending whenever he took the kids out, free loading, getting what she could – that I objected to. He was carrying on like they were still together! It also made me think – did Ella think they were still in a relationship? What the fuck was going on here? The only way I'd know was if I asked her. Even then could I trust her? I knew I didn't trust Ed – he didn't see the wrong, the harm it caused. He knew nothing of faithfulness, of loyalty, of honour.

I threw the shopping onto the conveyor belt. The checkout operator asked, "Would you like help with your packing?"

I looked at her awoken from my anger. "No thanks," I replied in a tone that suggested any more conversation would not be well received at this time.

She got the hint; I paid and went out to the car. *Beep beep*. A text from Daniel.

Hey, be back in five minutes, are you home?

Just at Asda, will be back in 5.

I arrived home to find Maddy and Daniel on the doorstep.

"Mummy!" squealed Maddy running in for a cuddle as I stepped out the car. She thawed my rage.

"Hello sweetheart." My anger had melted to sadness.

"Are you ok?" asked Dan.

"I don't think I can trust Ed. I think he's out with Ella today. He acts like they are still one happy family. I don't think that's normal behaviour."

Dan looked quiet, like he knew something.

"What?" I asked as I opened the door clutching bags full of

shopping.

"Ella texted me the other night. She said she thought Ed was playing away again and seeing someone."

"But why would she say that? Ed said they were split up."

Dan gave me that look. The one you give people when you're waiting for them to work something out.

"Oh, I see." So, my gut instincts had been right.

"He always does this Iz. He's just not the faithful sort." The irony in that statement was that Dan had left me for someone ten years younger when Maddy was nine months old. So, it would seem they had that in common. I let it go though. My eyes fell to the floor and I remained quiet as Dan said goodbye to Maddy and she waved him off.

"Is Mummy ok?" asked my little angel, looking up at me.

I pulled her in for a cuddle, picking her up and carrying her into the lounge. "I'm all better now you're here darling, let's have a cuddle up, where's Tigger?"

"He's here," she said pulling a floppy Tigger out from under her arm. He was stuffed with tiny beans and where he'd been carried around so much the tiny beans had mostly sunk to his feet, so he had a very floppy neck and middle and great big dumpy feet. Tigger went everywhere with Maddy. (I prayed to God that we never lost him. If I'd known he was going to be the one for Maddy I'd have backed him up.) I put on *Jake and the Never Land Pirates* and we cuddled up. In this moment I was at peace.

It was only the calm before the storm that was slowly fermenting inside of me though.

After I'd put Maddy to bed I reached for my phone and rang Ed.

"Why is Dan telling me Ella texted him to say she thought you were seeing someone? Why would she say that Ed? I thought you two had split up."

"I don't know honey; I don't know why she'd say that. She's meddling – come on, we knew she would, just hang on, stay with me here." He sounded convincing, desperate.

"Why would she say that?" I screamed at him, tears rolling down my face.

"I don't know, I'll ask her… hang on." I could hear him pull his phone down to his neck and call out to her. She was there! He was with her!

"For fuck's sake Ed, is she with you? She's always bloody with you! Who is it you are actually in a relationship with, or are you screwing both of us you sick cunt?"

"Calm down woman, I've just dropped them home, I'd left the house and she was about to shut the door and I called her back. Stop going off on one and calm the fuck down."

I fell silent. But I was far from calm. It was 7.30pm. Why the fuck was he with her?

"Ella said she didn't say that to Dan and I believe her."

I now knew I didn't trust Ella or Ed. Those two twats deserved each other. "Well, Dan said she did and guess what, I believe Dan."

"Dan's never wanted us to be together. He always scowls at me when he sees me in your house. He didn't like it when I was play fighting with Maddy. He hates me. Of course he'd say that."

"Dan's a lot of things Ed, but he's no liar." I searched my feelings and my instinct knew that I trusted Dan. Ok not with other women – but I knew I could trust him with the important stuff. Maddy. Money. The truth. I couldn't say the same for Ed.

"Think about it though, why would she say that? She knows I'm with you."

She was a calculating, manipulative cow. I could see that she could be playing a double double here. If I were Ella, what outcome would I want? Me out of the picture. So, I call up Dan, knowing Dan knew me and Ed were together. Tell Dan she thinks Ed's cheating, so that Dan then thinks Ed's cheating, tells me, then I go ape shit jeopardising my relationship with Ed. Well played Ella. Well played. Oh, how I despised that woman! She'll never let him go. She'll always be there destroying his relationships. She doesn't want him, but she ain't gonna let anyone else have him either.

Could I live in a three-person relationship? If me and Ed had a row, he'd always call Ella and tell her everything. I didn't involve Dan in our business. I don't understand the reliance Ed and Ella have on each other. Sure, they have kids together. So do Dan and I. But I don't meddle in his relationships. I don't keep Maddy from him.

"I don't know what to believe."

"You need to relax. Go and have a nice bath and chill out."

"I'm not sure about us," I blurted out.

"What?"

"I don't think I have the stomach to ride this rollercoaster Ed. She's just too much of a burden to carry around. Look at her behaviour from your last relationship. And you allow it."

This time he fell silent. He'd heard me.

"I don't want to lose you."

"Then fight for me. Stop playing happy families with Ella and show her you are with me. Show her it's different this time and you won't be swayed. Don't bad mouth me to her, involving her in our problems – which incidentally are mainly caused by her anyway. Actions speak louder than words – and how you treat me will ultimately decide our future. So why don't *you* get a bath and think on that."

Then I hung up. My gut turned over. Did I just do that? I should call him back. I can't believe I just said that. What did I say? Did I just end it? Did I give him an ultimatum? No, no, I can't back down. I need him to show me I'm a priority to him. If he cares for me, he'll show me. I need to sit on this, as uncomfortable as this feels. I just need to sit on it.

22

I could feel my energy draining from me the closer I drove towards Leominster. I could see it blowing over the hills as the rain swept through the trees. I could feel it in every lyric the radio played – as if it was an SOS secret message, especially for me. *"Give up your heart left broken, and let that mistake pass on. Cos the love that you lost wasn't worth what it cost and in time you'll be glad it's gone."* My gut ached, as if I'd lost something that was never mine in the first place. It sickened me. All I wanted was Edward. Yet, I couldn't seem to escape this constant calling from inside me that he was a bad 'un. That I had to admit defeat somehow. I hoped in my heart as soon as I saw Ed I'd know what to do. I felt too defeated to even think any more. Every twist and turn in the road seemed to push me further away from him.

As I reached the airfield, Ed was packing up his car. He waved and gave me that smile – but it wasn't doing it for me today. Being together just felt too impossible. I got out the car and walked over to him. My smile was faint.

"How was your drive up honey?" he said staring into his car boot.

"It was ok, stopped raining as I reached the airfield." Small talk –
to distract from what I'd really come to say.

"Yeah, it's brightened up – I'll take you up after lunch."

I kicked at the dirt. "We'll see," I murmured.

"Have you driven all this way to dump me?"

"I'm not sure Ed."

I wasn't. I didn't want to let go of him. I wanted him to tell me it'd
all be all right. I wanted my happy ever after.

"Let's get a beer," he said indicating in the direction of the flying
club bar. I followed, holding back the tears. I didn't know what was about
to happen but I could feel myself starting to grieve for it already. I had a
splitting headache – my body was starting to check out of this relationship.
My voice started to dry up – not wanting to say the final words. I'd never
hold him again. Never kiss him again. Never see him walk through the
front door on a Friday night. My top lip started to tremble.

"Right, what you drinking?"

"Water please."

"Water?"

"My head is killing me."

Ed turned to the bartender. "Have you got any paracetamol please?

She's got a headache."

The barmaid chucked me a couple of capsules.

"Thank you." I said.

"You need to eat. I bet you haven't had anything all day, knowing you."

Ed ordered us two jacket potatoes with chilli and cheese. I didn't want it but I couldn't find the energy to speak the words.

"Let's sit outside," he said leading the way. I followed and we sat on a picnic table far over from the crowd. He drank half of his pint. I took a small sip of water.

"Have you come to end us Izzy?"

I took another sip of water. He waited.

"I'm not sure Ed. Everything feels so wrong. I can't see how we'll ever work out. I love you so much but it's like we're doomed."

"Look. When we see each other you're ok, then when you are back home and I'm here you get all doubtful and worried again. It's a stress for me too you know. I said we'd be all right – we'll be all right but you have to stop doubting us. I can't keep taking it."

"Ella doesn't exactly make it easy, does she? Sending me text messages to make me doubt you. Only allowing you to see the kids in her presence. Not allowing me to meet them."

"She barely lets me see the kids – she ain't gonna let you!"

"And that's acceptable to you is it? You don't want us to eventually be a blended family, take the kids on holiday together? Shall I just go round there and knock on her door and ask her what her problem is?"

"You'd do that?"

"Yes – I've had enough of this shit. You two are separated. You should be allowed to see your kids without having to keep taking her out as part of the deal for free food and cinema trips. Plus, what does this show your kids? As far as they are concerned, you're still a family – nothing has changed."

"Don't do that. I'll handle it. I've always taken the kids on holiday with Ella."

"Yes, but you say you've been split up with her for four years, Ed. When are you going to realise that it's not acceptable to carry on like that when you are in a relationship with someone else? When are you going to consider my feelings?"

"I wouldn't fuck her. And it's the only way I get to see my babies."

"You would fuck her Ed, because you did, the last time you went on holiday together."

"I had to – she was so fucking miserable."

"And you see nothing wrong with what you're saying, Ed? I don't say to Daniel he can only take Maddy on holiday if I go. He takes Maddy on holiday with his girlfriend. I don't dictate to him. He's Maddy's dad."

"Ella doesn't trust me like you and Dan do."

"That's the problem Ed. I don't trust you either."

"It's the distance. You need me with you. When I've passed this training, I'll be back home, we'll be together I promise. It's just another two months. I'm not losing you. It'll be ok," he said assertively.

I stepped up from the bench.

"Where are you going?" There was a nervousness in his voice I hadn't heard before.

"I need the loo. It was a long drive." I walked across the grass and entered the club. I didn't know what to think. Entering the cubicle, I sat down. Could I give it one last shot? Could I trust him? Flashes of that smile crept into my mind. The last time we made love. The last time we kissed. The way he laughed. The way I laughed back. My heart was devoted to him. My head was full of questions, doubt and misguided loyalty. I pulled my trousers up, flushed and washed my hands. As I headed back out to Ed, I could see the food was just arriving. He turned to see me and stood up – stepping over the bench. He held his arms out to me. I cushioned myself in his embrace, hugging my face into his chest.

"Please don't leave me," he said before pressing his lips to mine and awakening my desire for him.

"I'm not, I love you Ed."

"I love you too." He held me close, cradling my head with his right hand.

"Right – let's get this eaten, then I'm taking you up. The Cessna is ready to go out – you're gonna touch a cloud." He beamed at me.

I liked going up with him. I'd never touched a cloud before. Ed became full of excitement; I couldn't help but be infected by it. Every happy tone he spoke brought me back to him. He was right. When we were together it was all alright. I had to find a way to block the negativity. To not listen to Ella. To not listen to anyone. When we were together, it was how it should be. We laughed, we played, he'd take me flying. He was training for our future. I just had to get through the next two months.

Inside the cockpit, the sound of the engine was deafening. I struggled to hear Ed through the headphones. The sun had come out and the clouds were plentiful. I looked down at the country roads, the varying shades of green – the fields, the hedges, and the thick clumps of trees. It was all so peaceful from up here. So far removed from reality. As if we'd extracted ourselves from the truth of our lives at this altitude. I liked watching Ed while he flew. His hands on the controls. The way his headset speaker balanced in front of his lips. How his flight suit covered his crotch. His pronounced tone of voice with the tower. I was proud of him.

"Right – slide the window open," said Ed.

"Isn't opening a window in a plane a bad thing?"

"Not at this altitude honey – open the window, and stick your hand out – touch a cloud."

I slid the small window open, reaching my hand out into the sky. My fingers danced, rippling through the moist air. Clouds always looked so soft. But now I was touching one, it wasn't at all – it was moist – like fresh rain on a warm day.

"Honey – come here." Ed beckoned, he wanted to take a selfie together. I leaned in, resting my hand on his leg to move over as far as I could. This was a first. He didn't usually take photos of us on his phone. It was usually me taking pictures. Maybe he has started to feel more serious about us. My hand stroked his leg.

"Can you shut the window please baby?"

"Sure."

"You were turning me on doing that. I can't fly horny ya know." He stuck his tongue out and pulled a funny face.

"Maybe later then," I smirked.

"The make-up sex is always amazing – I'll look forward to that."

I was safe in his hands as we glided through the clouds, his chatter with air traffic was impressive. My boyfriend – the pilot. He always looks so happy when he's flying – at peace with himself and the world. It made me warm to be safe inside his control. I smiled feeling happy we were still

254

together. Then I remembered that post on Facebook where he'd tagged someone else, reminding her of the day they went flying. Saying how much he "loved this woman – she was amazing" and the nagging doubt crept back into my thoughts. I expect taking a woman up flying was just part of his courtship. We all got the same treatment. I wondered if any moment was ever special to him. Or just part of the usual routine. My problem was I loved him but I didn't trust him. If you trust someone – love is there. If you don't trust someone – how can that situation ever work? How can it be right? How can it be trusted?

I looked down on the lives held by the landscape below, the little cars, the farmers in the fields. I wondered what it would be like to be someone else, with different problems and worries. I guess we're all here fighting our own battles, creating our own scars. At the end of the day, when you can't shake off the feeling, you know you have to save yourself. The real question I had to ask myself was, how much more was I prepared to take?

"You're quiet honey."

"Just thinking, enjoying the flight."

"You see those dark clouds over there?" He pointed

"Yeah."

"It's a storm coming in, I'll have to turn back now – it's about thirty minutes away, should be able to get back before it starts."

I nodded to show I understood. It was rackety inside and made it hard to hear. A storm coming eh? Didn't I know it. All the signs were there, yet still I couldn't make sense of them, or I didn't want to yet – I wasn't sure.

After we'd landed Ed completed his post-flight checks and I went back to the car to wait. It was a three-hour drive from home so I'd assumed I'd stay at the B&B with Ed – after all I was paying for it. I couldn't help but wonder what kind of a life he was setting up there. Was he seeing anyone else? It was hard to shake the feeling, he'd never really seemed as committed to me as I was to him.

My car door opened making me jump. "That's all done honey, what's your plans?"

"I figured we'd stay at yours?"

"No – we can't do that; my landlady doesn't like us having people stay over."

"Well, it's too far for me to drive back – I'd assumed we'd be together."

"I've got to go and watch the boy play a match – I promised him."

"Ok, so shall we catch up afterwards?"

"Can do – I'm not sure what time I can meet you though."

"Ed – I've driven three hours to see you – and it wasn't just for a quick chat, I'm your girlfriend, I expect you to make some effort here."

"Well, I promised the boy."

"I'm not saying don't go to the match – but you can go to the match and then meet me afterwards, we can get dinner – I'll find a Premier Inn."

"I s'pose I could meet you at eight."

"Well… as long as it doesn't interfere with your busy schedule, I mean, don't put yourself out!"

"Don't be like that – it's Ella. She'll expect me to go round for tea."

"Why, Ed? You've told her about us, she knows we're together – obviously I'd visit you – we're in a relationship. Just tell her you're seeing your girlfriend – simple. You'd have gone to the match for your boy, you owe her nothing."

"Try and get in at the Premier Inn just outside of Hereford – they have a great steak restaurant there. Book us a table for 8pm – I'll be there." He leaned in to kiss me, then returned inside. I'd been dismissed.

I booked a room using the app on my phone and re-set the sat nav to take me there. As I drove away from him, I had the same feeling I'd had on the way up.

Nothing has changed. I'd resolved nothing. He still thinks it's ok to go and have tea with her and play happy families, for Christ's sake. I mean, what is wrong with him? I cannot understand his logic. It's almost as if 'a woman' is the same person to him. A female body with a cunt to fuck. Like he doesn't see personalities, consider feelings or recognise the differences between them. So I'll face this like I face any problem in my job. I'll create a risk register, and talk to Ed about what mitigation he needs to put in for us to work. If he isn't prepared to meet me half way then I have my answer. I have to try to control this madness.

I drove into the hotel and parked up. I was tired, I would check in, have a sleep and escape my head for a while.

When I woke up it was 7pm. I'd had a text from Ed. *I'm on my way – should be at the hotel by 19:30.*

Right Izzy – time to show him what he'll be missing out on.

Ok – I've left your room key at the front desk and gave your name and car registration details for parking. Don't keep me waiting – I'm ready for you…

I put on my black basque with the lace top stockings that he liked. I decided on no panties. It gave quick access without the fumbling. I hung a long trailing necklace around my neck – which sat inside my cleavage. My hair I tied half up and left the rest bouncing at my shoulders. My make-up was perfect – I looked hot. I positioned the room so that when he walked through the door, he'd see me sat on a low back chair, one leg bent up, the other resting on the bed. I wanted him to see I was commando. As the door opened, I took a breath and smiled at him.

"Welcome home honey," I smiled, twirling my necklace.

"Oh my God, you look great Iz – I want to ruin you."

He threw his bag down and moved across the room to me, kneeling between my legs to lick my clit. I spread my legs allowing him access. He looked up at me.

"You're always so ready for me Iz – I love that." He stood up, pulling me up with him and taking me in his arms, pushing his tongue into mine. He turned me around and pushed me face down onto the bed. He released his zipper on his jeans and pulled his trousers and boxers down. Then he was on me.

"Lift your bum up," he commanded. I complied. He took his cock and rammed it into my dripping wet vagina. My hands gripped the sheets as I gasped out in pleasure.

"You are mine Izzy – you will always be mine," he said as rode me into ecstasy. He pulled his cock out, taking my juice with it and smeared it around my hole before pushing gently into my arse, massaging my cheeks as he went further in. My middle finger found my clit and I rubbed myself into orgasm as he pumped me royally from behind. "I love giving you anal. Your tight hole feels amazing Iz." He reached his hand around to grasp my boob, and started to mould it to his rhythm. "We have the best make up sex – you're amazing baby," whispered Ed.

"I love how you feel as you slide in and out of my arse, it's so sensitive, so intimate, I'd do anything for you baby."

"Swallow me Iz – I'm gonna come, get back here and take me in your luscious lips." He pulled out of me and rolled over. I did a quick scan for any shit, spat in my hand and massaged his cock to wipe away any excess fluid before taking him between my lips. My finger slid round to his arse and massaged him inside his hole. I could feel my finger pushing inside him as I sucked his cock, he started to moan out loud and I knew I'd hit the spot. His cum slid down my throat, I looked up at him, licking my lips. He lay gasping. "You're amazing."

"I know." I opened my eyes wide as I said it. He was turned on by my confidence and I by his mass appreciation of my sexual skills.

"What time did you book the table for?"

"Eight-thirty – I wanted you first," I smiled.

"Come on – let's get dressed, I've built up an appetite." He winked while pulling on his boxers.

The steakhouse was like an old pub. We were led to a staircase which had various off routes to small table areas. We had a two-seater table at the back. There was a candle lit on the table, and the lighting was dimmed. Ed smiled at me from across the table. "I'm gonna have a sixteen-ounce T-bone steak, I think. What do you fancy honey?"

"I'll go for an eight-ounce sirloin I think with veg of the day and chips."

"Are you having a starter?"

"I'm not sure – I need to check the puddings out first!"

"You always say that!"

"Do I? Oh well – at least I'm consistent!" I laughed.

"Do you fancy sharing some calamari and some chicken wings?"

"Yeah, why not – let's go for it!"

The waitress came and Ed took care of our order. I saw him checking her out the whole time he was talking to her.

"Would you like to ask her to join us?"

"Eh? I was just being friendly," he protested.

"She's the waitress Ed – she's paid to take our order; she doesn't expect you to ask her about her day – she's not your mate ok? She's paid to ask what we want to eat."

"Jealous, are we?" He laughed.

"I'm all for being nice, but you seem to talk to all women like they are the same person – they're not. Quick re-cap for you. She's the waitress. Ella is the person you're legally married to – but not in a relationship with. I'm your girlfriend and the best sex you'll ever have – got it?"

"Yes. ma'am."

"Good. Right while we're talking, I have a list of things I need to discuss with you. They are unacceptable issues that need to be mitigated."

"What are you talking about?"

I pulled my laptop from my bag.

"What are you doing?"

"Negotiating Edward – and there are some things I won't move on."

"What things?"

"Allow me to show you." I pulled up an issues log of all the things he did I found unacceptable that needed to change.

"One – holidays with your children."

"What about them? You saying I can't take my kids on holiday now?"

"No, that's not what I am saying at all. I'm saying it's perfectly acceptable that you'd want to take your children on holiday. What is not acceptable is to also take Ella. You aren't a family any more and I don't trust you not to fuck her – you have a record remember?"

"So, what are you saying?"

"If you want to take the kids away, do – but Ella's not going. That's a deal breaker for me – our relationship will be over. So up to you – do you agree?"

"Ok fine – I won't take Ella."

"Good. Right point two. No more walking in the door at Ella's and hugging her like you've returned home to her. You aren't together now, stop sending her out the wrong message. You're my boyfriend – your loyalty should be to me – not her."

"But the kids like family cuddles."

"You're confusing your children – you aren't a family any more. Cuddle your kids – not Ella."

"Ok – I see your point."

"Three – Christmas."

"What about Christmas?"

"I understand you'd want to see your kids at Christmas – but it's not acceptable to me that you spend it with Ella at her sister's with the kids. While I stay at home alone. Again – you're my boyfriend. You should be able to come to an agreement with Ella about having the kids on Christmas Day or Boxing day and then we all do something together then."

"I like seeing my babies at Christmas."

"Of course you do, all parents do. But people not in relationships any more don't carry on like they used to. It's not normal. Yet again you don't consider my feelings. There are other options – we could stay in a hotel nearby and bring the kids to the hotel so we can be together in the morning or afternoon. I don't see why I have to be alone when I have a boyfriend."

"No, you're right, that's not fair to you. What else?"

"We're in a long-distance relationship and I like to talk to you, I like to see you on WhatsApp – get some facetime. But when you're away it's like you don't think about me – and you distance yourself until you are due to come home. I hate that. I want to feel connected with you even though you're away. I want to feel like I'm a priority. That you want to speak to me. That you make time for me."

"Well I get busy."

"I know – we're both busy, but I'm never too busy to talk to you. I enjoy talking to you – but it's like you find me a burden or something. I like to look forward to talking to you – to know when we'll chat next – not just feel ignored."

"Ok, we can talk daily. Maybe that'll stop you feeling like you need to end us all the time."

"It'd certainly make me feel like I wasn't in this relationship on my own."

"Anything else?"

"Well. Consider this an amnesty Ed. Is there anything else that has happened that Ella could call up and tell me about that would cause me upset? Anything you think I should know?"

He looked like there was. His hands fidgeted and his eyes looked uneasy.

"If you tell me – we'll work through it – I just want you to be honest with me. I don't need any more surprises from her."

"The other day, she texts me saying she felt hot. So, I told her to put a skirt on – being summer an all."

"Ok…"

"Next thing I know she sends me a picture of her pussy. She's never ever done anything like that! So, I said to her what are you doing? And she apologised and we had a laugh about it."

"Show me the texts."

"What?"

"Well, if it happened as you say you won't have a problem showing me the texts will you?"

"I deleted them."

"Show me the picture."

"You don't want to see that."

"Yes, I do – show me."

Reluctantly he got his phone out and showed me. She'd literally whipped her knickers off and lifted her skirt and taken a photo of her natural beaver. No sexy lingerie, no trimming of the beard, just this huge fat cunt.

"I can certainly see why you laughed at that. Anything else happen?"

"No."

"Right then – let's push all that to the side and enjoy the here and now, shall we?"

"That's it? That's all you're going to say?"

"Yep! Ow look the starter's here!" I bit into a chicken wing. "This was worth the wait!"

"So, you're really not bothered about her sending me that picture?"

"I can't stop her sending you pictures Ed – as long as you aren't acting on them."

"I'm not – I told her I was with you."

"Then I don't have a problem. Besides, the woman has one fat ugly cunt – not at all in my league. And I gush more than her, and squirt further than her – and you know I give it better than she does too."

He licked the ring of his calamari and gave me that smile.

"Besides I'll deal with her later."

"What do you mean?"

"I'll call her and ask her what she's playing at. She can back the fuck off."

"Please don't, she'll stop me seeing my babies."

"I'm sick of her games Ed. She pulls you in every time. She only seeks to destroy our relationship – she doesn't want you – and she doesn't want anyone else to have you either."

"I'll talk to her I promise. Please?"

"Ok. But sort it – or I will – I mean it."

23

The drive from Leominster to the hotel was full of trees and intertwining landscapes. I liked seeing the countryside. It relaxed me, somehow, made me more grounded. Big old oak trees lined the way, the hills and the valleys looked like they'd loved each other for years. We were on a road trip, I liked driving with my guy beside me. He was good at playing DJ and feeding the driver. We talked about our dreams. What we'd do when Ed had finished his flight instructor course. The dream was to move out to Florida. He'd get a job flying tourists around. I'd write my novel. Maddy would go to high school. We'd make the most of the summer on the Florida Keys. It all seemed so in our grasp.

"I've looked at house prices," said Ed, "and we'd get a massive place if we sold your place and brought out there, we could have a pool and everything."

"Do we get our own crocodile too?" I jested. I was in love with the idea of moving away from everyone and everything, but I didn't much fancy the idea of living in a country which had a gator problem, or where snakes were common. In England we only had adders and even then, you'd be pushed to see one. I had the biggest unexplainable fear of snakes. I couldn't stand it even if they came on the TV or if a photo suddenly popped up in a Google search – it'd make me scream. Ed said, "I'll protect you baby; you don't need to worry about that." He would too. Ed was a man's man. He'd likely get a rifle and keep it for such occasions as we had a croc or alligator loose in the garden. I liked he made me feel protected – Dan was as scared of snakes as I was; Ed was phased by nothing. He faced into everything. I liked that about him.

The hotel had a long approach, a windy road that led up to a hill with a small carpark. There was ivy running up the front facing wall and a delight of trees and gardens to explore. It inspired me to write here. The gardens gave me some character ideas,, my mind became a creative river. I could feel inspiration pouring into me as I got out the car and looked around. We'd come here to chill out, to escape the constant drama from Ella. This was 'us' time. We had massages and candlelit dinners booked, this was going to be a great weekend, we'd re-connect and feel all loved up. It was the romantic break I'd been dreaming of. Our hotel room was the honeymoon suite. It had two huge beds – a day bed and another bed, with a lace curtain wrapped around it. White and gold décor. A huge white bathtub lay at the end of the bed, there was a slight gap and another transparent curtain to seal it off.

We had time to dump our bags off before going for our massage. I was looking forward to this, to relaxing and feeling calm. I hadn't booked a couple's massage because Ed insists on talking to his therapist and I like to just zone out and snooze.

I got undressed leaving my briefs on and got underneath the warm towels. I wriggled about trying to get my head into position. The sound of nature filled the room, the scent of jasmine ran through my nostrils. I closed my eyes and waited for the masseuse to reappear. This was going to be just what I needed to relax and let go of all the worry. Her hands were soft as she applied the oil to my back and neck. I eased into relaxation as she soothed away my stress and anguish. I had a whole hour of this and I wasn't going to miss a moment of it.

I awoke to the sound of my own snoring.

"I'm sorry! Did I dose off?"

The masseuse was looking at me. "It's ok, it's the best compliment I can have. Take your time, there is some water on the side, get dressed, and come out when you are ready. There is no hurry."

"Ok... thank you." I wondered if anyone had ever just stayed and finished their snooze? Translated, that meant *don't take your time, get up, get dressed and get out.* But I'll sit and drink the water awhile.

I'd arranged to meet Ed in the spa waiting area. He looked as dazed as I was.

"How was yours?" I asked.

"Really good, I'm all relaxed now."

"Yeah, me too."

He reached out to me to hold my hand and pulled himself up out the chair. "Do you wanna go back to the room and order room service?"

People seemed to eat in their robes here, but more than anything I was tired, I could do with a snooze. "That sounds great."

The hotel had these little lanterns scattered around the roof top; they were brown with a golden light inside that looked like a little fairy trapped inside. They made me feel warm yet sad. We walked back to our room; the sunshine glistened across the ivy leaves. Ed held my hand and we walked in contentment.

"That's the helicopter landing pad over there." Ed pointed. "One day I'll fly us here, I'll bring you for lunch." The thought made me smile and I caressed his hand with my finger.

We returned to our room. Ed lay on the bed in his robe. He patted the bed.

"Come here, come lie with me."

I slipped under the covers and nuzzled up next to him under his arm. I liked lying with him like this, safe and protected. His robe had come slightly undone, his chest hair poking through. My fingers circled his chest, feeling his skin, skimming his nipples, I kissed his neck, pushing myself closer to him, his hands held my sides drawing me near, my lips moved to kiss his face, he pulled me up on top of him, our bodies started to rock and grind into each other. His hand held the back of my neck forcing me down to kiss him. I could feel his dick stabbing at my clit, I wanted him inside me. I eased up and onto him, he let go of my neck, allowing me to straddle him, his hands moved behind his head, his arms folded. He was sitting back to watch the show. My brown hair hung down over my face, I looked through it shyly at him. My gasps came with every rocking movement. As I came down onto him, I squeezed my vagina around his cock, tightening the sensation, pushing down deeper onto him.

Five years I'd been waiting for this. He was finally my boyfriend and we were on a weekend break together and I was fucking him. I couldn't believe it was happening. We were going to be ok; we'd work through the problems with Ella and the kids. In a few years from now we'd have a happy lifestyle together. Finally, my life was starting and I felt like I had the man of my dreams. He moved his hand down to my clit and started rubbing me, the sensation of moving down on him combined with his fingers caressing me made me squirt. I looked down; he had worked out how to play me. Stopping rubbing me, to allow my clit to ejaculate over his dick. He brought me to climax then released me to squirt on him five or six times. I didn't want it to stop

"Bend over," he said randomly.

"Huh?"

"Get off me and get on all fours," he demanded. I liked a bit of doggy style; it went in deeper and made me gush. Obediently I did as I was asked. There's a vulnerability involved when your arse is exposed in the air like that, but the anticipation of his cock about to enter my dripping wet cunt was worth it. He placed his palms either side of my hips – my breathing deepened – it was about to go in…

I lowered my upper body pushing my buttocks up to meet his thrust, but instead of the expected fanny fuck, he pushed his cock straight into my arse. He didn't lube it up, he didn't go in gently and tease in and out for a while - he just went straight in there.

"Arrgh! You're hurting me! Stop it Ed!" I screamed.

"Shut up and take it."

What?

He kept going, kept fucking me – hard.

"Ed! Please stop! You're hurting me!" Tears were streaming down my face.

"Shut up and stop ruining my fun. Bite down on that fucking pillow and silence yourself!" he hollered.

His fun? Stop ruining his fun?

I tried to pull away, to escape his grasp.

"No, you don't, you're not going anywhere." He pulled me back into alignment with his cock, smacking me on the bum firmly before doing so.

"Please stop Ed. You're hurting me. I don't want this!"

He struck me again.

"I don't care what you want – this is what I want and you'll do as you're told."

This is what he wants? To hurt me?

My ring was on fire. With every thrust came a stinging agony. His cock sawing into me like glass, from the inside out.

"You're hurting me Edward!" I said, crying out loud now.

"Bite down on that fucking pillow and shut up woman!"

"Please Ed, stop." The thrusts came harder with every plea I made.

"I don't want to hear another word out of you – shut up Izzy!"

Another blow, this time to the back of my head. It was the first time I hated hearing him use my name. I'd become an object. He wasn't going to stop. This was going to play out. I had no choice; I couldn't stop him. I bit into the pillow, which drowned my screams and soaked up my tears. *How did I get here? We were having great sex which I'd consented to, yet now, in this moment, he's violating me. Who is this person? He's so cold. Cruel. It's as if the warmth has left his body and some Neanderthal instinct has taken over him. Shut up and stop ruining my fun… That's what he said to me. Like it's his right to take any hole he wanted under any terms. Is it his right? He's my boyfriend. It isn't like he's a* stranger *that has jumped me down a dark alley. How can he love me? He can't love me. He can't love me.*

He was treating me like his possession. I stayed on all fours, my face sunken into the pillow, waiting for him to stop. I wanted to scream out loud because of the pain in my arse but mostly for the betrayal in my heart, but I didn't much fancy another blow to the head. Best not to anger the beast. I tried to concentrate on my breath. Breathing would get me through this. My midwife's words came back to me. *Breathe in – then blow it away.* I concentrated hard on my breath, then fell into silent sobbing. He pulled out and came over my back. I stayed straddled on the bed. Waiting. My ankles trembling. He held my side with his left hand whilst shaking himself off over me with is right. My ring pulsated. I wasn't sure if I could stand up. My arse felt like – well like it was hanging out of my arse.

"That was amazing baby," he said, kissing me on my back as he lifted himself off the bed. I didn't respond, I was frozen like a stunned rodent caught in headlights. "I'll run us a bath." A warmth returned to his voice. He seemed normal. Did he realise what he'd just done. What had he just done? Had he done anything wrong? We've had anal sex before, I like anal sex, often it feels so much better than conventional sex. I'd begged him for anal in the past. Why was I feeling like this now? What was different? It really hurt. He hadn't stopped when I asked him to. Boyfriends in the past would have always stopped if I'd asked them too. Always. He didn't. I slowly tried to get up, it was painful to move. I noticed blood on the sheets. I wasn't on. I reached my finger round to touch my hole, I was bleeding from my arse and I could feel myself sagging out.

I winced as I walked towards the loo. Edward intercepted me. "Come and get in the bath honey, I'll clean you off." I was too scared to argue with him, so I quietly got into the bath in front of him. The warm water both soothed and stung at my wound. I tried to sit on my left side to give myself some relief.

"You're quiet, what's wrong?" he said surprised.

What's wrong? "My ring hurts," I said trying to mask the tears rolling from my eyes into the water.

"Well, I don't know why. You love anal sex; you love it when I ram it up there. You must have pushed into me too hard ya loon!" He laughed as he poured water over my hair and started to rub shampoo in. His fingers light and caring as if he loved me again.

"I asked you to stop and you didn't. Why didn't you stop?" I sat up, wrapping my arms round my knees.

"We were role playing, I knew you didn't want me to stop."

I started to rock myself. "I was crying and screaming."

"You were very convincing baby, it made me want to fuck you harder. You love it rough, and I got a couple of slaps in, thought you'd like that."

What? Role playing? We didn't discuss that. Did we? I've certainly never fantasied about anal rape. Oh my God. Rape. Was that rape? Is that possible with someone you love?

"I was thinking, once we've had our bath, we could go out for a nice walk in the gardens," he said excitedly.

I wanted out of this room.

"Ok," I said, sinking further into the bath, him lying behind me. I couldn't work out what had just happened.

Am I at fault? Am I too sensitive? Have we just had normal sex? Am I reacting to something that wasn't there? He's — well he's himself again. He doesn't think he's done anything he shouldn't. Yet, that didn't feel right. This isn't what I'd thought our weekend would be like together.

With every thought the tears kept running. I'd got silent crying to an art form now. I splashed water over my face, concealing my tears. I didn't think I should feel like this in a loving happy relationship. I felt so sad and confused but I didn't know why.

"Wash me baby," he said. I picked up the sponge and squeezed the soap into the centre, massaging his legs with it in gentle strokes. He liked it when I cleansed him. He used to say I treated him like a king. I sure didn't feel like his queen. His legs were stocky and strong. His arms like cannons. He could and did easily overpower me. What once I found a turn on, a demonstration of pure masculinity, now left me cold and frightened. He wrapped himself around me, constricting me like a boa constrictor would its prey. I stayed still, barely even breathing until he decided he'd get out the bath and get dressed for our walk. He climbed out from behind me and held out a towel for me – my cue to get out and get dressed too. I wrapped it around me and held it close. Walking back over to the bed I was reminded of the blood-stained sheets – my blood. He pulled the sheets from the bed quickly.

"I'll call housekeeping and have them re-make the bed while we're out," he said. "These sheets are sopping from where you've gushed all over them! I love how you gush." He pulled me into him, kissing me on the head. "Now, get dressed and we'll go for that walk."

I was stunned like after you've just had an accident and you aren't really sure what just happened. It was like I was looking in on myself, in on my own life. Only, I couldn't think of what to say to myself because I couldn't believe what I was allowing to play out here. *There's always a choice…* An old friend of mine had said that to me years ago at college.

I wasn't strong enough yet. I couldn't do it. Her words echoed through my mind. *Never feel you don't have a choice, there's always a choice.* Even if one of those choices is to do nothing. This wasn't right. I knew that. But I lacked the strength to make the right choice just now. I was scared. I'd got everything I thought I ever wanted and, where was I? In the realisation that maybe I didn't want it after all. So, for some reason I dutifully obeyed and pulled on my top and trousers. Looking into the mirror to do my make up, I stared back at myself. Who was I looking at? *Who was she – really?* But more importantly, where had I gone. Would I ever find myself?

As we walked around the beautiful hotel grounds, I saw the other couples. The way he'd gently touch her back as he brought her drink out and put it in front of her. The smile she'd give him in return. She didn't look like she'd get arse-fucked out of nowhere. A wedding was happening in the far field. A white gazebo decorated with pink carnations and gypsophila. White-covered chairs with pink bows. The guests waiting patiently for the bride to arrive. The groom looking slightly nervous. Page boys kicked at their heels, the desire to run like the wind into the nearby field poking at their every instinct. It made me smile to see life as it should be. People uniting, sharing their happiness with friends and loved ones. The bride appeared in a Rolls Royce. Her bridesmaids in tow. I couldn't imagine that scene in my own life.

"Shall we get a drink?" asked Ed.

"Yeah sure, I could do with a Pimm's." The one thing I could rely on with Pimm's was that it didn't take too many for me to be as pissed as a newt. Besides the alcohol might numb the stinging I was still feeling in my arse. It also occurred to me if I got Ed drunk, he wouldn't be able to get it up again today and I wouldn't have to worry about having to have sex with him again on this trip.

We found a nice spot in the garden and sat down in the sun. Ed took to reviewing his phone. After twenty minutes I asked, "Who you talking to?"

"Ella wants some help with the kids' homework."

This was supposed to be our time away from his crazy wife. I doubted very much she was wanting to discuss algebra. He carried on texting her. I wondered what they were really talking about. Then I pondered on if I cared. I finished my Pimm's and went to the bar to order another. Things were feeling out of place. I didn't know if I could put them back together again. I wasn't even sure if I wanted to. I took a deep suck on my £7.50 Pimm's and went back to the table.

"What are you really talking about with her?" I asked him.

"What? Homework, the kids need help."

"I see. So, the kids need help right now, at the precise moment we're on a break together? That stuff couldn't wait until tomorrow evening when you see them?"

"Why are you getting all funny, they're my kids, they need me."

"I just think Ella's timing, as usual, is pivotal. You do nothing but encourage it. You bring the drama Ed. You fuel it and allow it. This was our weekend. Tell your kids you'll see them tomorrow and help them with it then. There's no need to involve Ella."

"You're right, she just pulls information from me."

"Well don't give it, be respectful to me Edward, I'm the person in a relationship with you."

Ella was really straining our relationship. So much so it felt like there were three of us in it.

"You're right, it's a habit, that's all – I've always talked to her about everything."

"I get it, but you're not with her any more – you do that with the person you are in a relationship with. Sometimes I wonder if you see us as the same person, if you even know who you are dating."

"Of course, I do, you Izzy – I'm with you. I won't let her meddling come between us, come here." He pulled me in for a kiss.

I was still feeling so confused about what happened earlier. I decided to get another round in – it'd keep him at bay, from getting it up this evening at least.

When I returned with drinks Ed was talking to the hotel manager.

"I notice you have a heli-pad on the grounds – does it see much action?" asked Ed.

"Actually, we'd love to get a video of a helicopter coming in for our website – to advertise it."

"I reckon I could help you with that, I'm a helicopter pilot. I could arrange to fly in and you could shoot your video."

"Where are you based?"

"Shobdon, just a short flight from here. We're always looking for places to land when training – it'd help you – it'd help us."

"I tell you what – we'll even throw in lunch, if you and your good lady would like to fly back here so we can film you coming in." He smiled at me as I placed the drinks on the table.

"That'd be much appreciated, we've loved our stay here so far, I'm sure we'd come again."

The manager gave Ed his card. "Call me and we'll get it organised."

"I will – thanks," said Ed.

"That was nifty work Ed."

"I know, he just came by to see if everything was ok for us and I thought, well, why not ask about the landing pad."

"Don't ask, don't get! I'll look forward to coming back for luncheon and flying in with you. I've never landed on a big H before!"

"You and me both!" laughed Ed.

24

The drive back to Leominster was peaceful. I couldn't shake off how Ed had treated me. *Stop ruining my fun* echoed in my mind. Nagging doubt found a hook to hang onto. Did he really care about me? Was I just a fanny for him to fuck? How could he treat me with so little regard or respect? I was falling into this abyss of mistrust. I didn't know what it was exactly but things weren't adding up in my mind. It was as if he treated all women as the same woman. Was this how he'd treated Ella in their marriage? Was this why she didn't trust him? I didn't know what to say to him, so I let the Stereophonics do the talking as we found our way back to his digs.

"You've been quiet all the way back. You have doubts, don't you? Look, I have enough confidence for both of us, we're going to make it, we've come too far to give up now. Plus, Saturday night's roleplay was awesome." He kissed me on the head and held me.

I didn't know what to say to that, so I said nothing to acknowledge his words. "I best get going, I've still a three-hour drive and I have to get back to meet Dan to collect Maddy."

"Call me when you're home."

"Ok." With that I got in the car and just drove. I didn't know what to think any more. The one thing I did know was that how I was feeling right now, isn't how I should be feeling having had a romantic break away with my boyfriend.

My phone started ringing. It was Ed.

"Hey,"

"I don't like how you left; it feels like you have given up on us. I'm not letting you go Izzy. I love you. It's going to be ok, not long and I'll be home. Keep believing in me hunny – promise?"

"I'm tired, I don't know what to think, Ed."

"In that case, remember that you love me, why I'm doing this and that we'll be together soon and most of all remember I love you baby."

"I love you too." The words came out automatically.

"I've got a surprise for you too."

"What?"

"How would you like to go to the Wickham Festival in a few weeks?"

"I'd love that, I've never been, and it's not far from us."

"Great. I was thinking we could invite my sister and her husband and you could meet them. You'll like Lucy."

He wanted me to meet his family? Well, this was a first.

"I'd love that; it'd be great to meet your sis!"

"Brilliant, I'll call and check they can make it, then if you can go online and sort us the tickets – we'd want to go on the Friday – my favourite band is playing – you'll love it!"

"I can't wait – it sounds fun, I've never been to a music festival, and it will be really cool to meet Lucy."

"Great – I love you Iz – drive safe and let me know when you're home."

"I love you too, I will, I'll call you when I get back."

My mood lifted as I started to think about the next weekend we'd spend together.

I needed to get some more cycling and running in before then too. Blenheim would soon be here. My stomach sank at the thought of it. *You got this, me old cocker sparrow.* My granddad's voice massaged my mind as I drove down country lanes full of the warm, late summer breeze.

When I got home, I reached for the phone to let Ed know I'd made it back.

I had four text messages.

I opened them, expecting them to be from an excited Ed.

Instead they were from Ella.

What did she want?

I've been thinking about it, and I think it's only fair that you know Ed and I slept together when we went to my sister's wedding.

My heart stopped as I crumpled to the ground. He did what?

She went on. *Ed can't help himself. He needs the comfort of a woman.*

She made it sound like any woman would do.

You should get out now, while you can.

I should get out – or she wanted me out?

I don't mean to bring you hurt – you deserve the truth.

The truth? Could I believe that Ella was honourable enough to tell me the truth?

A picture came in. It was a selfie of Ella, Ed and their youngest in bed. Ed was asleep.

Beep beep.

Are you home yet baby? I'm popping to see the kids.

I called him instantly.

"Hey baby, good journey home? I'm just on my way to see my babies."

"Ella texted me."

"Oh? What does she want?"

"She said you two slept together at her sister's wedding."

"Yeah, we did but not like that."

"What? You're admitting it?"

"The hotel cost a fortune! We just shared a bed – nothing happened – I didn't tell you because I knew what you'd think – I promise nothing happened. It was just cheaper to share."

"Ella sent me a picture of you all in bed."

"Send it to me."

I sent it.

"I'm asleep, and she's obviously cuddled up next to me with the boy to make it look more than it is to make you jealous. Ignore her, Izzy, please. Nothing happened. I'll talk to her. And block her on your phone, she does you no good – she's just trying to get to you so that you leave me. She's doing what you said she'd do. You had her pegged from the start – don't let her win. Fight for me – please. I love you."

"I'm so confused, my head's spinning."

"No need for confusion, block Ella, delete her messages – she's stirring – she's trying to ruin us and we won't let her, will we?"

That all sounded feasible. Ella had said to me that she loved him but would never ever trust him. She had to have some deep-rooted anger that he was with someone else – it didn't matter that it was me.

"Ok – I'll forget about her and book those tickets."

"Oh, I spoke to Lucy – they can come – but Phill can't drive at the moment – so I said we'd book them a flight – I'll book it up for them. Can you send me some cash though?"

"How much is it?"

"£240 return for two – I got a deal."

"Ok, I'll send it over babe."

"I've got another surprise for you too."

"Do tell."

"What you doing Tuesday?"

"Working."

"Can you get the day off?"

"Yeah, I should be able to – why?"

"I'm going to fly down to Thruxton. I thought you could meet me and we could have the day together."

"I'd love that Ed."

"See – I told you – I'm fighting for us. I'm not letting Ella get in your head. I want to be with you Izzy – we're meant."

I sure did like hearing him say that.

But I couldn't help but wonder, was it possible, after all these years I've spent pining over and chasing after Edward, that now I've got him I don't want him?

I don't understand the chaos in my head. I don't know if I trust my own thoughts – somehow, they've gone crooked. At least I think they might be – I'm not sure. When I am with Ed everything is kind of ok. I feel ok. When we're apart my mind starts to wonder and I don't trust him. I am encompassed by this overwhelming feeling in the pit of my soul that I don't trust him with anything. One of my uni friends once said *you trust different people with different things. Very rarely do you trust one person with everything. For example, I have friends I'd trust with me bird, with money, with backing me up in a fight.*

Luke was one of my housemates when I was at uni. He was a cheeky London chappie that walked with the 'London bowl'. He always used to nick my Gap hoody. I didn't mind. He was like a little brother. He always said he'd like to see who'd stick around if he got in a fight in Southampton. One night the housemates were out (six of us) and a fight found Luke. I was the only one that didn't run away. Thankfully I didn't have to get in a physical fight – my gobby mouth stopped it. He'd already gone down by this point; I'll never forget his small frame bouncing off the pavement as he fell. My shouting every swear word under the sun at the guy attacking Luke and waving my phone in the air that I'd called the police made him stop. I often thought about Luke, and so far I hadn't met anyone I'd trust completely either.

I've often thought about that over the years – how we trust people with different things. It's probably a good thing to not have all your eggs in one basket, eh? With Ed though, I was starting to realise that I didn't trust him with anything. Not with my heart, not with my friends, not with other women, not with money. And not with what I treasured most of all – my Maddy. The only thing I was beginning to trust was the overwhelming sensation within me that screamed out to me *you can't trust him*. In the past my gut had kept me safe, so why was I finding it so hard to listen to it now? I'd wanted nothing but Ed for years. I'd believed in the hope that one day we'd be together and it'd all be all right. I'd hoped that Dan would come around to the idea of Ed and me being together. I'd believed Ed when he'd said he was separated from Ella. I'd bought into the idea that after Ed had completed his training we'd go out to America and work abroad. I'd allowed myself the daydream of living in Florida, writing my book while Ed worked flying helicopters for tourists. But something had put a dent in my belief system and the cracks were starting to spread, casting a foggy doubt over me. I just didn't know what to believe any more. I wasn't even sure if I could trust my own thoughts.

At work when I had a problem, I'd brainstorm it on post-its and move them all around until they made sense or I could structure the outcomes. I pulled over some post-its from across the kitchen table and started writing things down to remind myself of when I was feeling low. What did I want to remember? What did I want to hang onto? What wasn't I ready to let go of? Writing he first post-it was hard –I didn't know where to start. Did I love Ed? Yes – I did. I wrote down on the first post-it note, 'remember I love him.'

I then picked up the pace as the thoughts ran into my head.

- Be kind, be calm, be understanding

- Keep busy!

- X sleeps until Ed home (I used this as a countdown each day to keep me motivated)

- Control my emotions – don't let my emotions control me

- Keep showing him I care

- Meditate – every morning

- Things to talk to Ed about (festival tickets, diary dates, New Year's Eve – what fancy doing? Cadbury House? When was Lucy coming?)

- If Ella starts – remember she's a meddler! Don't believe her

I placed each post-it note on my kitchen cupboard door. Visible for me to remind myself every day that everything would be ok as long as I remembered and didn't let my mind wonder.

- I know he loves me – keep the faith

- House chores

- Finish painting the fence

- Hold in my inner chimp – chimp causes trouble! Be logical

- I'm better than that – I'm not throwing him away because of what others say

- Tell him every day "I love you"

- Talk about the future – plan little things for us to do

- Thursday 6 July – what would he like for dinner? How shall we spend Fri? Rest at home? Go into town? Cinema?

- Don't act on feeling

- Be understanding of his situation – it's hard for him too

- Show him you are there for him – be supportive not jealous

- Write a journal

I'd covered the bottom sections of three cupboards above the kettle. I'd have a reminder every morning when I made my cup of tea and every time I was in the kitchen. This would help me; this would keep me on track. Everything would be ok. It had to be.

I started to unpack and picked up the mail. I had a letter from my mum – that was odd. We spoke every day – she hadn't written to me in... well, I don't recall. I opened it, and started to read.

My dear Izzy,

I am writing to you today as a very concerned mother and I hope you will understand my reasons for doing this.

I spoke to a clairvoyant and she told me that Ed was using you for your money. She said if you let him, he'd take you for £105,000.

So, I want you to re-mortgage the house and pay me £150,000 so I can keep it safe for you.

With all my heart I hope Ed proves to be honourable and lives up to the expectations you are hoping for. But to me he is dangerous and I want to protect all of us, before he takes the lot and you are left with nothing.

I am speaking from my life's experiences. Pillow talk is cheap but reality is much more costly, believe me I lost my home and you are on the same road as I was, I do not want history to repeat itself.

So before he starts asking you to pay for things for him and re-mortgage your house to buy him a car (because of course the one he has is old and dangerous) and pay for his course (because he has run out of money and needs to finish his training, otherwise he will have to go abroad again and earn more money to pay for all of the above and also for Ella and the kids), I feel the time is right now to give me the money so he can't spend it.

You are a kind loving woman with a lot of love to give and I know you would give him the world if you could, but please be careful – you have so much to lose – whilst Ed has nothing to lose.

I hope you understand I only have your best interests at heart, you cannot see all the pitfalls when you are in love. I know – I have been there and I am paying the price now. Let's just hope he proves me wrong.

Love you

Mum

I could hardly swallow, my throat tight. I went to the cupboard to fetch a glass and filled it a quarter full with water. I'd hardly told my mum anything about what was going on with Ed – I'd tried to keep her from the truth. Yet here she was spouting off pretty accurately what I was doing financially to support him. Only she thought I hadn't done it yet. £105K. So far, I'd taken out £70K and was considering another £35K. That would make £105k if I succumbed to Ed's plea for a car.

But to say he was just after my money and that he'd take me for everything – I wouldn't allow myself to believe that. Why was everyone out to sabotage my happiness? I did love Ed, I still believed in our future together. We had plans. If anyone was being controlling it was Mum, expecting me to sign my house over to her Wasn't that the same as what she's accusing Ed of? And in any case, I offered to loan him the money so we could be together quicker.

I wouldn't mention this letter to Ed yet. We had plans in place and we were going to have a nice day on Tuesday. I wasn't going to let my mum's paranoia drip in my ear and destroy our happiness.

25

Tuesday couldn't come quick enough. Ed was flying down to see me and I couldn't wait to see him. When we were together the chaos in my head stopped and Ed was my safety blanket, bringing me the calmness I craved.

I arrived at Thruxton airport early enough to watch him fly in. He stepped out and walked over to me holding out his arms. All that swagger, all that sexiness – and it was coming for me! I cushioned myself into his embrace. He kissed me and I could feel the soothing in my soul.

"I missed you," I said cuddling in.

"I missed you too – we need today. Come on."

He led me towards the chopper.

"We're going up?" I asked.

"Yes, I want to take you somewhere."

I spotted a blanket and a hamper in the back seat. Pure romance at last.

I didn't ask where we were going, I just wanted to soak up and enjoy what was happening. Wait until I tell Liv about this!

Ed completed his flight checks and spoke to the tower, then we were off. I moved my hand to rest on his leg – I had to feel him.

"You're going to love where we're going," he said smiling away, all pleased with himself.

"I know."

"How do you know? You don't know where we're going? You might hate it!" He laughed.

"Will we be together?"

"Of course, that's the point!"

"Then I'll love it."

I loved looking down at the landscape as Ed flew. The twists and turns of the rivers, the altering shades of green and autumn in amongst the trees and fields. The view sure did give a different perspective. My mum's letter popped into my mind; this wasn't the moment though, or the place. This was our moment and I wasn't giving any air time to that here.

"Do you see over there?" Ed pointed.

"The coastline? There's a lighthouse."

"Yep – we've got permission to land – there's no one for miles – the lighthouse isn't manned. We've got the place to ourselves."

I loved the coast, the sea, the waves. This was what peace looked like. Just us, our blanket and whatever was in that hamper.

"It's perfect Ed." I smiled.

He set down, and we stretched our legs. Holding hands on a walk along the coast. This was my slice of normal. No one interrupting, no mother, no Ella, no deadlines or kids. Just us. Here. Now.

"When I've passed Iz, we can go anywhere. I can fly Maddy to see Daniel – he needn't lose his time with her. We can do anything."

"I like the sound of that."

"I brought some food – shall we eat?"

"Sure."

"Wait here, I'll go back to the chopper and get the stuff."

I stared out to sea. Who knew what was over the horizon? For now, I hoped he'd remembered I liked sausage rolls and chicken skewers.

Ed returned. "Come with me."

He put his hands over my eyes and walked me around to the other side of the lighthouse where he'd set up the picnic blanket with cushions and extra blankets to snuzzle up in the coastal breeze.

"Oh my gosh. That looks amazing – thank you! This is so lovely."

"I wanted to do something nice for us. Plus, I have something to ask you."

He got down on one knee.

Oh no. He wasn't going to, was he?

He took my hand. "Izzy – will you marry me?"

How could I marry him? He was already married.

"Don't be so silly!" I laughed. "You're already married – how can I?"

"I love you and I want to marry you Iz."

"Well. Sort out divorcing your current wife and then we can think about it, Ed."

"She won't divorce me unless I find someone that wants to marry me."

"Edward, if you were free and not married then I'd marry you in a heartbeat. You have things to sort out before we can officially make plans like that."

"Fair enough. But I'm committed to us Izzy – I want you – I mean it."

"Come here then and show me just how much you want me."

As we shed each other of our clothes there was something extra erotic about being naked outside. There was no one for miles, yet the feeling that someone might see was erotic. The sea air against my nipples added to the intensity of Ed's touch. He was gentle. He held me softly, and his penis lightly slid in and out of my sex. This was Edward showing me that he loved me.

"I wish we could stay here, just us, no interruption,." I whispered in his ear.

"We can come here anytime you like," he said ,holding me still as he gently rocked inside me.

Afterwards, we curled up under the blanket and had a light snooze. The sound of the ocean hitting up against the rocks soothed through me. I could lie here with Ed forever and never tire of it.

"What's in the hamper?" I enquired, the after-sex nibbles suddenly attacking me.

"Open it and see."

"Salmon sandwiches, scotch eggs, sausage rolls, crisps, Mr Kipling's Victoria sandwich cakes, grapes, cheese and crackers! What would you like first?" I said handing Ed the scotch eggs.

"You know me so well!" He smiled.

I wrapped the blanket around my shoulders and sat up to eat, basking in the moment. Ed wrapped his arms around me and munched his scotch egg.

"We'll have to get going in half an hour."

I lay back down and rested my head in Ed's lap. He stroked my hair and crumbs fell from his mouth onto my head. He brushed them away, laughing.

"When are you coming home then? Will you be there to collect Lucy and Phill from the airport?"

"I'll come home Thursday night, then I can get them from the airport while you're at work."

"Great Idea! Plus, I get to see you Thursday night!"

"I thought I could study at home Thursday – it's not like I'll be flying. Plus, I can have tea waiting for you when you get in."

"Careful – I could get used to that! What do you mean you won't be flying – why not?"

"The money is running out Iz – I'm trying to be careful on flying hours."

"How much more money do you need?"

"Realistically, it's going to be around another £35k to get through it all. If I'm going to finish inside six months. If not then I'll have to give up on it and get a job, I noticed there was a job going in Bristol."

"Bristol? But we live in Baddesley. When were you going to discuss this with me?"

"Now."

"How could this happen? We've been so careful with the money."

"It's my fault. I got the sums wrong in the beginning, I forgot about licence fees and miscalculated the number of hours I'll need to clock up."

"So, if we don't find another £35k it's all for nothing?"

"It won't be, I'll get a job, it'll just take a bit longer to get my wings is all."

"No! You're not working in Bristol, you promised you'd come

home and get a job near us. I've had enough of you being miles away and having a long-distance relationship. I want you home Ed."

"I have to go where the work is. don't I?"

"I'll speak to the bank about extending the re-mortgage. I want the plan we had. You pass your exams and then we can move and live wherever together – but we'll be together. And you can fly Maddy to see her dad at the weekend. Just like we said."

"That would mean I could finish my training sooner and give it my full concentration."

"Exactly – you've come too far – you're not losing focus now."

"You're awesome, thank you. Hey, whilst your re-mortgaging – maybe we could get enough for a new car too?"

"I'll see. I'm not promising anything – I have to pay this back to the bank you know."

"I know, and I'll pay you back every penny as soon as I'm working. Come on, let's get dressed and pack this lot up, as much as I hate to – we'll have to head back so I can get this bird back by 5pm."

"Ok. This has been just what we needed, Ed. Thank you."

"My pleasure, baby."

26

I arrived home eager to meet Lucy and get to know her better. As I walked

through the front door, I could hear Ed, Phill and Lucy talking. My heart

stopped. I could hear Ella's voice coming from my kitchen.

WTAF? I pushed the lounge door open, and Lucy smiled at me looking

up from the kitchen table where Ed's iPad was on speaker.

"Is that Izzy home?" I heard Ella say from the ipad.

"Yeah, she's back now," said Ed.

"I'll go then." *Yeah, your work is done here, well played, bitch!* My face

showed my disdain. I never could contain a poker face.

"I didn't wanna fucking talk to her," announced Lucy as soon as Ella

had rung off. "Why did you bloody ring her, Ed, if you didn't want to talk to

her, making me talk to that mad bitch?"

"I wanted to talk to my babies, I didn't wanna talk to her, "said Ed, who was cooking up steak for tea. I gave him 'the look'. Just hearing her voice. In my house. *Laughing.* With my boyfriend and his family. Them all acting like nothing has changed. In what world was that all right? What the hell else went on when I wasn't here? I could smell pot. Phill was up the garden smoking. Lucy smiled at me and gave me a hug. I noticed her crutches leaning against the table.

"We've got fajitas for tea," said Ed. "Oh, and I may have broken the washing up bowl."

I looked in the sink, it was completely cracked. "May have?" I replied looking at the hole, whilst not really being bothered by it.

"How was your trip?" I asked Lucy.

"Good thanks, way quicker than driving."

"Where's the pepper grinder?" asked Ed abruptly.

"You know I don't have one."

He looked annoyed.

"Can I help with anything?"

"Oh, now she asks!"

"What's up with you?"

"I'm trying to cook here, and all you've done is complain."

"Aw leave her alone Ed, you're well out of order," said Lucy.

"I'm going to the loo," I said, walking out of the kitchen.

Lucy called up after me. "Are you ok Izzy – has he upset you, love?"

"No, I just need the loo." What the fuck was that about? I walk into my own house and feel like a stranger, an outcast – his fucking wife's voice echoing through my personal space. He's broken my washing up bowl. I don't actually care but no apology, which would have been a common courtesy. I don't have a pepper grinder and he goes off on one. *What?* Interesting his sister put him in line, though.

We had company, I'd just ignore it – for now.

I went back downstairs. "Tea smells good."

"It'll be ready in five minutes."

Picking up on Ed's shitty mood I went outside to chat to Phill. "Hey, how are you doing?" Phill was taking a drag; he looked high and had that constant grin people have when doped up to the eyeballs. At least I could just sit here with him and didn't need to bother with small talk.

Lucy came out to join us. "Ed is well short with you, he's out of line. Does he always shout at you like that?"

It made me reflect. Did he? Had it become so normal I didn't notice it?

"I don't know," I replied.

"Don't let him get away with treating you like that," she said, taking a long puff of her roll up.

"Dinner's ready," shouted Ed from the kitchen.

We made our way in. "That smells great, I'm starving," said Phill.

"Help yourself, it's fajitas so you can just fill up with what you like."

"It looks great honey, thank you," I said, trying to get a smile out of him. He ignored me and filled his plate.

Lucy chatted through dinner, taking it in turns to talk between me and Ed who was still being shitty with me for some reason. I liked her, she was easy to talk to and it made a change to see someone stand up to Ed and not take any of his shit. Darkness came and we took to chatting outside while they all sparked up. Phill fell asleep on the sun lounger, Ed busied himself stacking the dishwasher and playing the role of the house husband in front of company. I became ever more confused as to his current state of mind.

"He'll be sucking up to you later, hun."

"Huh?"

"Ed – he'll start sucking up when we all turn in – he knows he was out of order."

"We'll see, I guess. I don't understand how he got like that so quick. It's over fuck all."

"Ed always did blow off quick – but he cools down quick too – he's just sulking at the moment like a little boy." She laughed. "Men are just little boys. You have to keep them in line or they'll walk all over you. You can be firm with him – he'll take it."

"Me – be firm with Ed? I don't think so – he wears the trousers in this relationship."

"Only cos you let him. Take control. Think about it." She nodded, taking another drag.

"Right you lot, we've got an early start tomorrow – time to turn in," said Ed from the patio doorway.

"Phill's already turned in!" said Lucy laughing.

"I'll make your bed up," I said, getting up to go and fetch the sheets.

Ed touched my hand lightly as I walked by. I smiled at him softly.

"I'll wake you all for 7am so we can get breakfast before we leave," I heard Ed say to Lucy.

"What shall we do with Phill?" Ed asked Lucy.

"Leave him there, he's happy – he'll come in when he wakes up."

I picked up another blanket to cover him with as he was staying outside and went to make up the sofa bed.

"I suppose you expect me to drive in the morning?" said Ed.

"No. It's my car – I'm happy to drive it, besides I won't be drinking anyway."

When we got into bed, I laid on my side and turned away from him. He reached over to scoop me up in his arms.

"What's been up with you since I got in?" I asked him.

"I didn't want to speak to Ella – I wanted to speak to the kids but Ella pushed her way in to a conversation. Nothing was happening," he said.

"I didn't appreciate her voice intruding into my home – she's not welcome here."

"I just wanted to talk to my kids."

"I get that, and you should be able to do that. You need to set expectations with her – show her she's not your priority – if she's not any more, of course."

"She's not."

"Actions speak louder than words Ed – show me, don't tell me."

I tried to wriggle from his grasp but he sucked me in deeper. Kissing my neck and slowly massaging my breasts.

"There's something else too. My mum sent me a letter the other day."

"What did it say?"

"She's worried about me, she saw a clairvoyant who told her I had re-mortgaged my house and had given you money. Now she wants me to sign my house over to her so that I can't lose it."

He looked shocked. "So, she thinks I'm after your money then?"

"Here," I said, sitting up and opening my bedside drawer. I passed him the letter. "You can read it."

"Well, this isn't true! What does a clairvoyant know about us?" He sounded angry. "Great – so now your mother hates me I suppose, and I'm some evil villain. What are you going to do?"

"Nothing. It's my house – I'm not signing it over to anyone."

"Good. Why does she think you would?"

"Because when my grandad died, she paid off my mortgage."

"Well – you can always say it was a gift – deny it."

"I wouldn't do that, Ed."

"Why not?"

"Because that's not honest."

"Make her prove it – what's she going to do, take you to court?"

"She's my mother, she's just trying to protect me."

"Enough of her, come here, where were we…?" He kissed my neck softly.

"Ed – your sister is downstairs – I don't think it's appropriate."

"She's knackered, doped up on weed – she'll be out of it. Come here – I want you."

He reached his fingers round to my clit and started rubbing me. His lips moved in to kiss mine as he pushed his fingers deep up into my gush zone. He stood up, and pulled me to the edge of the bed – my legs resting on the dresser, my bum just off the edge of the bed. He looked into my eyes as he pushed his fingers deeper into me. I gasped as he released my orgasm and a fountain flowed from me out over the floor – I could hear it as it hit the carpet.

"I love how I make you gush Izzy," he whispered with wonder as I lay there caught in this orgasm trap.

"Fuck me," I said.

"No – this is for you – not for me." He said as he pulled me back up into the bed into his arms, pulling me in as we drifted off to sleep.

The alarm went off at six o'clock. Ed bounced out of bed and went downstairs to make a fry up, waking Lucy and Phill as he whistled his way through the lounge. The smell of the bacon pulled us from our beds – there's something about crispy pork fat that stops me from going veggie.

After a good feed we bundled into the car and were on the road to Wickham.

I parked the car in the field we were ushered into. We each had a fold up chair, and I'd brought a picnic. I was glad I'd worn my wellies – the ground was already muddy and it'd only get worse once a thousand or so people had trailed through it. Lucy made it ok on her crutches. Ed said he'd carry her if it got too bad. We got in the queue to enter the festival. It was a warm day with a slight breeze – we were lucky.

"This is ridiculous. I'm not standing here," said Ed.

I watched him stomp off to one of the organisers and demand we be let in. He pointed at Lucy and her crutches and said she needed to get in and get settled. Oh my gosh – he was on one again. Why couldn't he ever ask nicely? I hung my head, concealing my embarrassment.

He emerged with a chair for Lucy to sit on. I didn't dare point out we already had four of those – I didn't want to poke the beast. Five minutes later they opened the gate and let us through.

"About time!" Ed shouted as he walked by the event staff.

As we walked in, Lucy noticed a woman struggling to push her husband in his wheelchair. "Aw, go and help her Ed," she said.

"Why have I got to go and do my back in?"

"Go on, Ed," she pleaded.

He went over and helped in a way only Ed would. He picked up the wheelchair with the woman's husband in it, and carried it over the mud to solid ground. It was reassuring to see he could be kind. Although a little taken aback by the approach I think they were grateful for his help.

"Right come on – through here, you lot." Ed commanded.

He was on a mission to find a good enough spot to watch his favourite band when they came out later. We all dutifully followed. I laid down our picnic blanket to stake out our pitch and set up the chairs. We were in!

"Phill, do you want to come with me and help get the drinks?" said Ed.

"Yeah, sure."

The guys went off for beer and Lucy and I sat in the sun.

"Did he apologise last night then?"

310

"Not really – but he came sniffing for sex! Ed doesn't really apologise as such."

"Did you give it to him?" she smirked.

"Well, he makes it hard to resist!" I laughed. "We're ok now."

"Good. You're good for him, I see why he likes you. I called Mum – she agreed you're not to take his nonsense and to put him in his place next time he treats you like that."

I could see Lucy meant it. I just laughed to pacify her. The boys returned with the drinks.

"I thought you could have one," said Ed, passing me a pint.

"Yeah, one will be ok if I have it now – by the time we leave I'll have pissed it away."

"Yeah, that's what I thought." He smiled at me and planted a kiss on my forehead.

"It's so relaxing here, isn't it?" said Phill.

"Next year we could camp and bring the kids – they'd love it," said Ed.

"That'd be great, ours would love that too," said Lucy.

"Do you think we'd be allowed to bring your kids Ed?" I asked.

"Who knows with that mad woman – hopefully she'll have calmed herself in a year. Maddy would like it here, there's loads to do."

"She would, we've never really had family days out together with other people – she tends to do those with Dan. It'd be great to do something all together."

"That's settled then – we're doing it," Ed said, downing half of his beer to toast the proposal. He smiled at me and pulled a funny face.

"What?" I asked.

"Nothing – just happy, honey." He had a massive grin on his face and reached out to hold my hand.

"Shall we go and have a look around?"

"Yeah, why not, sounds good."

"Are you two ok here if we do that?" Ed asked.

"Yeah sure – see if you can get me some more fags, eh, Ed," said Lucy.

As we walked around the different tents, I started to take in the variety in the music on offer here. It sure was a taste sensation. The stands sold flower hoops for girls to wear in their hair and big Stetson style hats for the men.

"Here Ed, the girls will like these," I said, stopping to look at the headbands looped with flowers and ribbons. I picked up three, one for Maddy, one for Ed's daughter and one for Lucy.

"I quite like this hat," said Ed, donning it and looking at me for approval.

"It suits you."

"It's £30 though – I shouldn't."

"If you like it, let's get it."

"Ner I'll keep looking."

"You sure?"

"Yeah."

I paid for the flower hoops and we walked on; we hadn't spotted anywhere selling fags. We found ourselves at the Fosters bar, and I noticed a lady smoking.

I turned to Ed. "Maybe she'll let you buy a few for Lucy?"

Ed went over and started chatting her up. I knew it was just so he could get some fags out of her so I wasn't particularly bothered, though I did note that talking to women sure did come easy to him. I picked up some more beers to take back while he flirted for fags.

We got back to the others and Ed threw the fags at Lucy. "Here you go, I had to flirt excessively in front of my missus to get those for you – make em last!"

"And I did no flirting at all to get you this." I offered her the hoop for her hair.

"Aw thank you – I love it!" She put it on instantly.

"It really suits you – you make a great hippy chick!" said Phill.

Ed pulled me to him and cuddled me from behind. "I love you Izzy," he whispered into my ear.

"I know."

He kissed me on the cheek and held me for a while.

Lucy and Phill went for a look around as we sat to mind the camp and listen to the music. Ed kept turning to look at me and smiling to himself. I smiled back – it was nice to see him so happy. He held my hand and we enjoyed the music together. This was so nice. Just being together, chilling out, soaking it all in. Another kiss planted itself on me – hitting my lips this time.

"Are you happy honey?" he asked.

"I am, this is a lovely day."

He looked deep into my eyes. "You'd never leave me, would you?"

"No," I said.

"You really love me, don't you?"

"Yes of course I do."

"You'd do anything for me wouldn't you."

"Yes Ed, I would."

"I know." He smiled with a grin wider than a Cheshire cat. Kissed my hand and kept it safe in his lap. We sat and enjoyed being a part of what was going on around us.

Phill and Lucy returned about an hour later with pizza and more beer. We scoffed that down and I opened up the picnic for business.

"I was in the queue at the bar and this guy talked to me – and then his girlfriend appeared – the way she looked at me – I wasn't interested in him for fuck's sake, I was just being polite! I've got no time for jealousy I tell ya."

"I guess we don't know why she might feel that way though Lucy," I said. If Edward was anything to go by, I could see how a girl might have cause to not entirely trust her fella.

"In my head it's easy – you either trust em or you don't and if you don't why bother hanging on?"

"I suppose." Wow – that was reality slapping me in the face!

"Right – I need a piss – who wants another beer whilst I'm up?"

"Well, if you're offering, like," said Phill.

"Thanks Ed," said Lucy, who was half cut already.

"He looks really relaxed with you," Lucy said.

"Yeah, he is today. He's very cuddly and appreciative for some reason."

"I told you! He's bloody creeping cos of yesterday!" she said taking a swig of her beer. "We should put a photo on Facebook of us!" she said excitedly.

"Oh, I don't know about that. Ed doesn't like tagging me in anything. I'm not even allowed to be his friend on Facebook."

"Why?"

"I think in case Ella sees it."

"Does she know about you?"

"Yeah."

"Fuck that mad bitch – she doesn't control you."

"I must admit – it does upset me that he'll not even be friends with me on Facebook, let alone announce me as his girlfriend. He's been telling me he's leaving her for years – he never will. I'm not sure why."

"No one in our family likes her. She's a miserable fuck. Mum would love to see the kids more but Ed hardly comes up to visit."

"I haven't met his kids yet – I'm not allowed."

"That's bullshit!"

"It is what it is. She's full of bitterness and hatred towards him and he's too scared he'll do or say something that will stop him from seeing his kids. He won't take her to court to sort out his access. He just lets her be in control. I don't get it."

Ed returned with beers and a Stetson.

"That looks good on you baby! I'm glad you went back for it," I said.

"I found one half the price at a stand further down – exactly the same."

I knew he was lying – but I didn't care, it looked good on him – if he wants to go through this charade so be it.

"Ed, get over here," said Lucy. She had her phone out. "It's selfie time!" She pulled us all in for a group photo, sent me a friend request then tagged me in it. *A lovely day at Wickham festival with Ed and Izzy*. "There – let the mad cow dare to say anything about that!" She laughed. "You're out of order letting Ella control who you're friends with on Facebook Ed – you shouldn't let her do that. It's disrespectful to Izzy."

My phone pinged. *You have a new friend request from Edward Coolidge.*

"Are you sure?" I looked at Ed, beaming.

"Yeah, I'm sure, Lucy's right. Come here." Ed got his phone out and took a selfie of us as he kissed me.

Edward Coolidge mentioned you in a post.

Great day out with my fabulous woman Izzy x

I couldn't believe it. He'd finally gone public with us. He's never done that in all these years. I was made up.

"Come here, I want to dance with my girlfriend."

He pulled me to my feet and we started dancing in the middle of the crowd. His hand held my lower back and the other held my left hand. He kissed me and we swayed from side to side in each other's embrace.

It meant the world to me that he'd come out about us. I was no longer his dirty little secret.

We all sat and chatted, the others drank beer and I turned to Coke Zero. I'd never needed alcohol to have fun – besides everyone around me was drunk – no one knew I wasn't – I could blend in.

I turned to Ed. "I need the loo – do you know where it is?"

"I'll come with you – I could do with another piss."

We walked through the mud which had become squishier by late afternoon. Ed managed to lose his step and stuck his foot into a massive mud hole. His left leg was covered. We laughed and walked through to the toilet block.

"Meet me back here," he said as we both went off to face the porta loos.

I was lucky – there was still some loo roll left and there was no wee on the seat. As I flushed and pushed the door open to exit, I could hear Ed's voice and the sound of a woman laughing. I looked over to where I could hear him, and there he was, flirting. She had blonde hair and wore a flowing red dress with wellingtons. They were nowhere near where he'd told me to meet him. Anger rose from the pit of my stomach.

In that instant I was struck by the obvious question. *How could I be so stupid as to think he'll ever be faithful to me?* I'd been gone – what? Two minutes? Literally the time it took to pee. I walked slowly over to the washbasins and started washing my hands. All the time I could hear her laughter. Hear his chat up lines. Telling her he liked her dress, she looked pretty. She swooshed the dress with her hands. Who the fuck wore a dress like that to a bloody festival anyway? A fucking tart, that's who! I dried my hands and walked past him. My face meant business – I didn't stop. I walked with purpose away from that girl and her stupid laughter.

He ran after me. "Where are you going? What's wrong?"

"Who the fuck is that?" I said as I stopped walking and pointed to the blonde idiot.

"She's just someone I was talking to in the queue."

"You were with me in the queue, Edward, we both went for a wee at the same time – she's nowhere near where you told me to meet you. You were flirting with her. Chatting her up."

"No, I wasn't. I was just talking to her – she was with her mum."

"I heard you Ed – I heard what you said, I saw how you looked at her. I know that look you had on your face. You've ruined everything, all our plans, our future – it's all gone. All because you just can't be faithful." Tears ran down my face. Inside, I imploded at his betrayal. He couldn't resist a pretty face. I'd never be enough for him. How could he do this *in front of me?* What the hell was he doing when I wasn't around?

Without warning he erupted like a volcano. No one has ever screamed at me with such intensity as his.

"Your jealousy is going to be the end of us Izzy – you're a fucking jealous cunt! All I was doing was talking to her. If you'd come over to me, I'd have introduced you to her."

"Introduced me? To some tart you just met in a toilet queue? Have you fucking heard yourself?" With that I walked away. I found my way back over to Lucy and Phill. We were with people. We both needed to calm down, and just sit, not speaking to each other. I sat next to Phill. But Ed appeared like some Neanderthal man, ranting and raving.

"She is a jealous fucking cunt!" he shouted for the whole festival to hear. He loomed over me.

"And you are a lying fucking bastard!"

His rage fed off me. "All I did was talk to someone in a queue and she thinks I'm being unfaithful. You're an ungrateful fucking twat! And one jealous cunt!" he hollered from above me at the top of his voice. I looked around. People were staring. I could see in their faces they were afraid for me, that he might swing at me.

"Jealous am I Ed? Or maybe it's a pattern of behaviour I've grown to recognise in you during the last five years of this toxic relationship!"

He silenced.

I turned to Lucy. "That's right – not four months – five years we've been seeing each other. Five years he's been telling me he's leaving Ella and wants to be with me. Then some other bit of skirt comes out the woodwork. Five years I've listened to your bullshit!"

He actually looked shocked. I'd crossed the threshold by outing him to his family.

"Who has supported you during all that time? Who finances you now so you can train to be a flight instructor? Who paid your debts off? Who bought your kid a bike? Who has always been there for you? Is it too much to expect loyalty in return?"

"Don't make it sound like you're innocent – you've caused all of this, not me. I was having a nice time until you started getting all jealous. You're insane. You will be the end of us. You're a right fucking cunt!"

Lucy stood up, leaning on her crutches. "Pull yourself together! You don't talk to a woman like that. Our dad would be turning in his grave – he'd put you on your back if he heard you talking like that. I'm out of here."

This was my chance. I followed Lucy and got away. If I went his fire would surely burn out.

"He's well out of order talking to you like that," said Lucy. "What happened?"

"I went to the toilet and when I came back, he wasn't where he said he'd be, he was chatting up some 18-year-old, blonde, in a red dress. I heard him Lucy. I heard the way he spoke to her, his tone, her giggly laughter at being noticed and a guy giving her attention. I saw his face – I know that face. It was disrespectful to our relationship. He'll never be able to love me like I love him, Lucy. I've always been one of two women he said he loved. I've given him everything I had to give and time and time again he just takes and I'm always left feeling like I wasn't a choice for him. I wasn't the woman he chose. I was just the last one left that hadn't walked away from his bullshit. Ed never made the conscious decision that it was me he wanted. Ella didn't want him and so

321

he came to me. I was never his choice though. I was never the woman he loved.

I guess I was just better for him to be with rather than for him to be alone. I

was the next cunt for him to fuck. But he never loved me. His love was cold.

That's the reason he never put thought or feeling into doing anything for me.

Simple things like finding out what flowers I liked, or what perfume I liked. Or

even running me a bath and putting out candles or rose petals. He never went

the extra mile for me like I did for him. Because he's never loved me – he's just

loved what I've provided. Trust has always been a serious issue for me with

Ed."

"Never let a man make you feel like that darling. You need to tell him

– there's the door, and don't let it hit you on the arse on the way out."

"But what if I do that and he leaves me, Lucy?"

"Do you really want someone that leaves that easily?"

We walked for a bit, and then made our way back towards the others.

Lucy went over and sat next to Ed and started talking to him. I sat some way

away, out of sight, and Phill saw me and wandered over. All I knew was I didn't

want to be there. I turned to Phill. "If Ed asks where I am – I've gone to call

my daughter to say good night."

"Ok love." He was stoned – but at least I'd told someone I was going

and given them a story.

I walked to the far field and called Liv.

"Hey Iz – how's the festival?"

"Awful."

"What's happened?"

"You know we made that pact, and I told you that if one more big thing happened you needed to tell me to pull the plug?"

"Yeah."

"I think now's that time. I think it's time to say enough is enough."

"Oh no – what's the cunt done now?"

"I was coming out of the toilet – and I could hear him – he was laughing and flirting and using that tone of voice he uses when he's turning on the charm. And as I looked over, he was chatting up some random blonde in a red dress. I was only gone two minutes Liv. I saw his face. I heard his words. He can't talk his way out of this one."

I could hear the realisation sweep through my voice. The feeling hung heavy within me. Although I'd thought it many times before, this time it was different. His rage had really scared me. I was grateful we hadn't been here with the children, that my Maddy hadn't borne witness to his uncontrollable anger. I thought back on it, and the memory came in slow motion. His face savage like a villain. His weight hanging over me as if to claim dominance and berate me. On my shoulder, I could feel the opinions of those I respected the most. Liv – my little rottweiler that wanted to swing at him and bite his nuts off. My boss at work, who simply looked at me with that knowing way of his which encouraged me to do what I knew I must.

This time Ed had impacted my very soul, and I knew his behaviour wasn't acceptable, and I knew, I really knew, he had to go.

"What a fucking cunt – get rid of that prick Izzy, he's taking the fucking piss! After everything you have done for him. Go home – now – and leave the cunt there!"

"I can't do that Liv!"

"Yes, you fucking can! It's no more than he deserves – he needs to remember what you've sacrificed for him. All he does is fucking take."

"I can't abandon Lucy and Phill, and if I leave him here – God knows what sort of rage he'll be in by the time he gets home. He'd probably destroy the place and me with it!"

Beep beep. Come back – please.

"Don't stand for it – the cunt's had his day – he's got to go now, Iz."

"I know – don't worry mate – he's going."

"Text me later, ok?"

"I will mate – thank you."

"I'm always here – take care – and don't take any more of his shit!"

"I won't Liv – take care too. Bye."

I'd been summoned. Had he calmed down? Or was this round two? I walked slowly back to the others. My feet sinking in the mud. I felt numb. Nothingness. I knew what I had to do – but how to do it without receiving his wrath? Or worse?

I could see Lucy ahead of me wobbling on her crutches. She was crying.

"Lucy! What's the matter?"

"When you went, he started on us, going on about how much money it cost him to bring us down here, and how we weren't grateful. Phill's gone off – he's a proud man, I don't know where he is."

"Lucy, it cost him nothing, I paid for your tickets – and honestly it was my pleasure. I'm sorry the day has turned so ugly. Have you got Phill's number?"

"He doesn't have a phone."

"Did he take anything with him?"

"A camping chair."

"He's probably gone back to the car. Wait here – I'll go and find Ed and tell him we've gone to look for Phill."

Just when I think Ed couldn't sink any lower and he goes and does that to his own sister.

Fucker.

I found a grown man that looked more like a stroppy little boy that had been told he couldn't have something.

"Where's Lucy and Phill?" I said.

"Well, where do you fucking think?" came the backlash. Round two it was then…

I knelt down in front of him, placing my hands on his knees, and started to rub them gently. Looking up into his eyes, I said, "I don't know Ed, that's why I'm asking. Where have they gone?"

"Well, it's your fault isn't it – you kicking off like you did made them feel uncomfortable, so they've fucked off back to the car."

"I made them feel uncomfortable? I haven't been here for the last thirty minutes, Ed."

"You and your fucking jealousy – that's what started all of this."

"What were you talking about then, before they left?"

"As usual I don't get to do anything I want to do! All I wanted was to watch my band and you've managed to fuck it all up. I didn't get to go to the air show, now I'm going to miss this – you're such a cunt Izzy."

"Ed." I spoke quietly – like you do when a toddler has a tantrum. "You asked me to come back here. I did. I'm being calm with you, please lower your voice to me."

His face flashed an awareness. He didn't like the realisation that maybe he was the cunt.

"I met Lucy on my way back here and she was in tears that you'd said they weren't grateful for you paying for their tickets. She's devastated at how you spoke to her and her husband. They don't have much Ed – and that's why I paid to get them here. Not you. How could you say that to them?"

"Well, they've been bleeding me dry – wanting beer, wanting fags."

"They've bought beers too, and food." I held my assertive look. "I'm going to help Lucy find Phill. You stay here and watch the band and I'll come back later, ok?"

He put his hands on my mine and pushed me away from him. I lost my balance and fell backwards, landing in the mud. I could feel the air gasp, like the crowd around us thought this was the physical fight that had been brewing. I sat up and started to pack up the picnic. He stood up and his rage smothered me again.

"You're pathetic, all of this is your fault, you've caused everything and now I don't get to see my band." He picked up his chair and walked off through the crowd.

If ever there was a time where I wanted the ground to swallow me up this was it. I'd never felt so humiliated in my entire life. I carried on packing up the stuff, picked up the two remaining chairs and started to look for Lucy. Groups of people parted for me to walk by. I could feel their eyes judging me as I passed. My body started shrinking with the shame of every step I took.

I found Lucy, and we headed back to the car.

"What happened?"

"He went off again. It's everyone's fault but his own."

Ed was walking 100 yards ahead of us. Lucy called out to him.

"Ah Ed, are you sulking?" she said in a soft and kind tone.

He turned back and glanced at her, his face still that stroppy little boy's.

Inwardly I laughed, I felt my mouth curl and then slapped myself back to reality. He'd punch me in the face for sure if he thought I was laughing at him.

Lucy turned to me. "He's just sulking – tomorrow he'll be all apologetic and won't be able to do enough for you."

"He's gone too far this time Lucy. This is it. I can't have someone so volatile in my life, I can't have him around Maddy. There's no coming back from this."

"Let's see – tomorrow is a new day – see how it is when everyone has calmed down."

I was calm. He was toxic. He had to go.

When we reached the car, Phill was sat on his chair, stoned, happy as Larry. He sprang up. "Are we going?"

"Fucking looks like it doesn't it!" snapped Ed.

"Do you want to go back and watch your band? We've got thirty minutes to get back there."

"No, fuck it, it's ruined now."

"Well, it doesn't have to be. If you want to see them, let's go see them."

"Yeah, go on Ed, Phill and I will wait here – go see your band."

"Nope."

I leaned in and said quietly to Ed, "It doesn't have to be like this, we can go see the band – but don't give me shit for it later when I'm telling you right here, right now, I'll go with you to see them."

"No, drive home, you've ruined everyone's fucking day – it's too late."

I turned to Phill and Lucy. "Have I ruined your day?"

They both shook their heads.

We piled the stuff into the boot and got in the car. I turned the ignition and pulled us out of this heavy situation.

When we got home, I slung some pizzas in the oven and made some tea. We all ate quietly, except for Ed who had found Show of Hands on his phone and was in the lounge tuning in live to the festival.

Phill turned to me. "Ignore him. He's sulking. He caused this. Do you think you'll get over it?"

"No, I don't. He's gone too far."

"That's a shame that, I like you, it'd be good to have seen you again."

"I like you guys too, you're a laugh. I'm sorry it's turned out to be such a crap day. I really was having a great day until – well you know."

"He'll be all over you tomorrow, making up for it, sucking up," smiled Lucy while taking a drag.

I knew he'd gone too far, and once I'd taken Lucy and Phill to the airport tomorrow, I'd be asking him to leave. As I lay in bed, I was haunted by the truth that the man I loved had never really loved me at all. He had treated me like nothing. When he came up to bed, I closed my eyes and played dead. I turned to face the window. He slipped into bed and cuddled up into my back. My body stiffened at his touch. He kissed the back of my head – I didn't move. My breath stopped. He stroked my arm before turning away to put in his ear plugs and going to sleep. Thank God. I was safe to sleep now. Tomorrow I'd need all of my strength. My heavy heart sank into the mattress. I shed no tears. There was just the daunting realisation of what I had to do next. The feeling clung to my soul and took me to my sleep.

27

I awoke at 4am to the sound of my alarm. Ed was in the foetal position, his side of the covers thrown over my side. The feeling from the day before hit me and with it an inner knowing that this would be the last time I saw him in my bed. There was nothing he could do to erase the events of yesterday. It saddened me to the depths of my soul. No amount of apologising could ever excuse the way he talked to me, and I knew in my heart of hearts I couldn't accept the way he'd treated me. He had to go.

I dressed and woke Phill and Lucy to take them to the airport. In the car Lucy said, "You wait, he'll be creeping all day today, trying to make it up to you."

"I don't think any amount of creeping can make up for what happened, Lucy."

"That's a shame that," said Phill from the back of the car. "I like you Izzy, you're good fun, he's a fool is our Ed. Do you think it's really over between you?"

"With regret Phill, yeah I do. How can I ever accept being treated like that? I just can't. I'm done."

"I'm sorry to hear that Izzy, I liked you too, I'd like to have seen you again."

"We can still be Facebook friends Lucy!" I said as we arrived at the drop off zone.

"Well, I hope you work it out, you're good for Ed. Even if he's too stupid to see it!" she said as she got slowly out of the car and reached back inside for her crutches. Phill got the cases out of the boot.

"Thanks Lucy. 'Bye Phill. You guys take care, safe flight home."

It was 5.30. I didn't want to go home to face him. Not yet. And anyway, I needed to kill time before I collected Maddy from Mum's and took her to Daniel. I decided to mull things over at the McDonald's at Rownham services.

Life kinda happened around me. Slow motion. Like I was taking myself out of the race for a while. I couldn't escape the feeling that I couldn't allow anyone to treat me like that – no matter who it was. To carry on as always, to say nothing, that was my accepting his behaviour was acceptable. And it wasn't – not by a long shot.

I drove on autopilot to collect Mads and take her to Daniel. I slapped on my best fake smile and they all bought it. I didn't have the energy to explain yet. I wasn't sure what was going to happen when I went back home. I dropped in at Asda. I didn't want anything. I sat on a rock in the car park and phoned Liv.

"Are you ok, hun?" she said.

"I don't know what to do, Liv," I said in a quiet voice.

"I think you do, Iz."

"Yeah, I do. I just don't know if I can. It's the thought of going home and him being there and then having to start the whole fuck off conversation. I'm scared he'll get violent."

"Has he hurt you before?"

Visions of our trip to Cadbury by Hilton and the arse rape I received shot through my head. I hadn't talked to anyone about it.

"No," I said. More lies.

"At the end of the day Iz, it's up to you. Either you find it acceptable or you don't."

"I don't. I know what I need to do, I'm just not looking forward to it."

Beep beep.

"Ed's just texted me."

"What does he have to say then?"

"He's asking where I am and when I'm coming home. I best go and deal with Liv, get it over with."

"Good luck hun, stay strong. I'm here for you – call me any time."

"Thanks mate. Speak to you later."

I texted Ed back. *On way home now – just dropped Maddy with her dad.*

Part of me hoped he'd realised what he had done was wrong, I was expecting an immediate apology when I came through the door, him begging for forgiveness. As I walked in, I caught a flash of Ed in his blue dressing gown.

"Smelt the bacon, did you?" he said from the kitchen. He was cooking up a fry up.

"I thought you'd still be in bed."

"Ner, I'm up, just going to eat this and catch up on Airwolf."

Unbelievable. He'd forgotten all about yesterday. He was carrying on like it didn't even happen. I felt so tired and weak. I decided I'd go back to bed and let him scoff his fry up.

"I'm tired, I'm going to catch up sleep."

"Ok," he said, sitting down in front of the TV.

I dragged myself up the stairs, feeling weak and defeated at not having just got it out the way. But I really didn't have the energy in that moment to start something. I went for a wee, and pulled my phone out, opening up his Facebook page. I decided to scroll back through and see what he'd been up too now that I had access. There were some nice pictures of his kids, a few updates from when he'd been flying. Then, Ed *and Amy's trip to Cadbury by Hilton.*

I looked through. Pictures of him with some girl called Amy at our spa. He'd taken Amy back there for the free lunch offered to us. He'd taken her in the helicopter. Who the fuck was Amy? I'd been asking him about that lunch and he said he was busy and probably wouldn't do it. Then he takes some other woman. A new release of energy swept through me. I walked slowly down the stairs, looked over the stair rail and said:

"Ed."

He looked round at me from the armchair.

"Who is Amy?"

"What?"

"On your Facebook page, there's a status update that says '*Ed and Amy's trip to Cadbury by Hilton.*' I was calm. Mainly because I felt so weak and defeated by him.

"You and your jealousy has to stop! This is crazy! I can't go on like this Izzy!" He bellowed.

I couldn't believe that he actually still thought he had a point here. He was going to go off on one again – I could see his face physically erupting before me. Time to nip this in the bud.

"Edward. I think you are under the misconception that I want to be in a relationship with you. I don't. You are despicable. Your behaviour and the way you reacted yesterday was awful. All you did was show me how much you didn't respect me yesterday." I held my thumb and forefinger half a centimetre apart. 'You made me feel that small. I was so embarrassed and humiliated. I want a man that loves and respects me enough to never speak to me the way you did. I'm done. Clear off."

With that I turned and walked slowly up the stairs to the bathroom, where I locked myself in. I didn't really know what would happen next. For some reason I didn't expect him to pack up and move out, but he did. I heard him open the front door, then his car, then going backwards and forwards from the house to the car. Loading. He came up the stairs and knocked on the door.

"Wash kit," he said.

I unlocked the door, my eyes looking at the floor and passed it to him. He moved into the bathroom and started taking other bits. All of it I'd paid for but I said nothing. I didn't look at him, I passed stuff to him and he rushed downstairs.

The last thing he said to me before he went was, "The key's on the side. I'll contact you about when I'll collect my stuff in the garage."

He was actually going.

I didn't know what I felt.

Disappointed.

Relieved.

Hurt.

Betrayed.

Sad.

Foolish.

Abandoned.

He didn't fight for me.

It would have been reasonable to have expected an apology at least for what he said to me yesterday, the way he treated me.

He should have been falling at my bloody feet!

But nothing. No realisation that I even deserved an apology. Nothing.

I couldn't believe it.

He just went! I mean I know I'd asked him to, but he didn't even try to apologise. He actually thought I was the one with a problem.

I couldn't cry. I wasn't there yet. I felt stunned. I didn't get it. I just sat on the loo, rocking myself, going over and over it in my mind.

28

As I sit here, I remember the time I felt safe in my house. All the things I did, didn't and was forced to do for him. I sicken myself. I don't know who I am today. I'm not sure I'll remember by tomorrow, or even the day after that. I'm not sure if it even matters if I remember. I've lost my sense of self. My friends have said I've lost my sparkle. I'm not sure what that means. I don't feel like me anymore. Only – I am here. Physically. So where did I go? How can I go anywhere without myself? It doesn't make sense. That's the trouble though. Sense. Things always seem to need to make sense, don't they? If something doesn't pan out the way we'd hoped, if another human acts in a way we did not see coming or would not act ourselves – then we declare *well that doesn't make sense.'* What is sense anyway? Who is it that can make sense of sense? Not me, that's for sure. Not today. And certainly not while I'm sat here on the loo in my dressing gown trying to work out if it's safe for me to leave the bathroom yet. I text Liv. She said it'd be ok. That I'd done the right thing. My head hurts. I'm not sure I could move if I wanted to. Something has left me. I've left me. I think I'll just sit here for a bit longer. I'm not really sure what just happened. Or if it was worth it. If taking the moral high ground is the right thing to do, the thing that makes so much sense to everyone – why do I feel so empty? I can't even cry. It hasn't sunk in yet. My fingers tremble as they catch up to the action. I feel cold. It's August, the heat of late summer pours through the window. But I'm cold. My phone flashes. A text from Liv. *Are you ok hun? What's happening?* I don't really know. But I don't want Liv to worry. If she thinks there's cause for concern, she'll pack up the kids in the car and be over here in a shot. I don't want to put her through all that upheaval. *I'm ok thanks mate. It's done now, it's over.* I should feel relieved. I should feel like I've done the right thing. Shouldn't I? If I've done the right thing – I should feel it! All I feel is emptiness. Disappointment. The silence of the house gets the better of me and slowly I unlock the bathroom door. Hesitantly I pull the handle down and push the door open. The air is still – chaos has departed. I can't even hear the neighbours through the walls. A breeze floats in from somewhere. I move down the stairs, holding onto the bannister. The front door is wide open. I walk towards it, looking out onto the street, I can see his car has gone. It's safe now. I close and lock the door. I glance out from the porch window. The street is empty today. No one in their gardens mowing the lawn. Number five isn't out washing his van. It's like they've all been sucked away somewhere. As I turn to walk into the lounge, I start to notice the things that are missing. His coat and trainers from the porch. The floral headband I bought for his daughter. From the kitchen, the printer, coffee machine, text books. In the bedroom all his clothes are gone. He's emptied his bedside cabinet. That's it this time, he is truly gone. I can't cry. I just sit. Sit and hold myself as I start to involuntarily rock. I notice a stain on the carpet from my mum's dogs. It reminds me that she owes me a new carpet. What a strange thing to think of at a time like this. But there it is. Reality. My reality anyway. I look at the clock. I have five hours before Maddy comes home. Five hours to sort my shit out and then I have to be Mum. At least that's five hours away. I feel so tired. I want to sleep to escape the torment. But the sheets still smell of him. I get into Maddy's bed and snuggle up next to Tigger. I'll be safe here.

An almighty knock at the door woke me. Oh God, was he back? I looked at the clock. 5pm – Maddy was home. I raced downstairs to unlock the door.

"You look awful – not well?" asked Daniel.

That felt fair, I'd take that. "Yeah, dodgy curry I think."

"Poor Mummy!" announced Maddy, rushing to give me a cuddle.

"Is Ed home?" asked Daniel. I realised the being sick lie wasn't going to work.

"Maddy, why don't you take your things up to your room" I said moving into the kitchen. I put the kettle on – I don't know why. Then I just collapsed onto the floor and started to cry.

"Izzy! What's the matter?" said Daniel.

"He's gone Dan," I said sobbing. I could tell Daniel thought my reaction was extreme. To Daniel's knowledge we'd only been together three months.

"Someone's slept in my bed!" shouted Maddy from her room. "Who's been in my bed? Why?" she demanded, running down the stairs. I sat on the floor, rocking.

"You need to sort yourself out," whispered Daniel sternly. "You don't want Maddy to see you like this."

I think what didn't compute with Dan was when we split up, he never saw me as upset as I was now. He'd never seen me so in despair.

So many lies. So much deceit, which I could bear no more.

"Daddy, someone slept in my bed!" said Maddy, stamping her foot down in disgust.

"It's ok Maddy, I think it was probably Mummy."

"Was it Mummy? Was it you?" she asked, walking towards me. I couldn't look up at her.

"Mummy's not feeling well, Maddy, I think you best come home with me tonight. We'll check in on Mummy tomorrow."

Maddy moved over and cuddled me. I held her back. "I'm sorry sweetheart. I'm sorry I'm not feeling myself at the moment," I whispered.

"That's ok Mummy – you can sleep in my bed, I don't mind." She paused. "I'm taking Tigger to Daddy's though." I hugged her tight. I looked up at Daniel and mouthed *thank you*. He took Maddy out to the car, then came back in. "I don't know what's gone on, but this isn't you. And what's with all these post-it notes? Sort yourself out and we'll talk tomorrow."

I nodded. He was right of course. I'd gone insane. Who the hell has to write a post-it to remind themselves they love someone?

I felt guilty that I was relieved he'd taken Maddy for the night. I heard the door close and the car drive off. Silence again. It felt hard on the kitchen floor. But I felt safe in the corner. I rocked a little more. The tears had arrived with a depth of feeling I hadn't anticipated. They felt every atom of rejection that surrounded me. I'm an ugly crier, as I've said. Especially when I first get going, add in the gasping and the double-sniff piggy snorts – well you get the picture – it's not a good look. I was grateful for no witnesses.

I scanned my cupboard door. It was all about Ed. Every reminder was to remind me everything was ok – but it wasn't ok, it was far from ok. Why had I been trying to convince myself otherwise? I hadn't wanted to conclude I needed to let go of the only man I thought I'd ever really wanted.

Had that really just been because of sex? If I had to write down what I liked about him? If I had to say what we had in common? If I were to say how good an influence/father figure he was for Maddy, for example… I'd have blank post-its. My heart yelped as this realisation came to mind. *The hardest thing to do is the right thing to do.* I could feel my heart dying. So, this must really be the right thing to do. I couldn't let Edward Coolidge back in my life. Back in Maddy's life. I'd allow myself a pity party for one night. But tomorrow I had to start re-building myself. I had to be a better mother. I had to get my life back on track.

I don't know how long I sat there. I only remember that it got dark. A voice in my head told me to get up and put the light on, but I didn't want to. It was small but persistent. *Get up. Put on the light.* I don't wanna, I told myself. *Do it.* In a minute. *Now.* I pulled myself up reluctantly and walked slowly to the light switch. I reached out my hand and then there was light. *That's better. Right, what you gonna eat?* I opened the fridge. Cheese, salad, and the small pork pies he liked. Closing the fridge door, I felt surprised he didn't take those. *You've got to have something.* It sounded like my mother. Another text from Liv beeped in. *Make sure you eat something Iz – you need to keep your strength up.* Told ya. For fuck's sake. I'll have some toast. And a cup of tea. *Good. Beep beep,* more from Liv. *And a bath – have a bath wash that cunt right off you!* I didn't want to, it didn't seem right with all that had happened, but I allowed myself to smile on the inside, which grew into a chuckle, providing a glimmer of hope and warmth that everything would be ok. I could always rely on Liv to make me laugh when it was most inappropriate.

29

Anxiety is a silent killer. It creeps up on you from behind like a blanket smothering the flames of your soul, wrapping and twisting itself around something deep inside you that you didn't know was there until the pain arrives. That twisting, gut-wrenching feeling that squeezes through my stomach, sickening me to the core. I'm helpless to think about anything except him. I can't function. Nothing else matters. I check my phone every few minutes to make sure the ringer is on and that silent mode hasn't crept on. The feeling is all consuming, a vacuum that pulls me in until all there is, is the anxiety of if/when I'll hear from him again. It's never timely. It could be hours or days. He had no pattern. Sometimes I could see from WhatsApp that my message had been delivered, but not read, then I'd keep checking to see if at least he'd read it yet. It added to my misery. Because my message wasn't even worthy of being read by him. It was parked in a queue. He'd deal with me later... When

I receive a message from anyone, my phone alerts and I read it and reply straight away. Not him. He liked to add to my misery. To heighten my emotions, make me so anxious that by the time he replied, I was so happy and grateful to have heard from him, I didn't even notice or acknowledge the torment and pain he put me through.

Let me be clear – hear me right now – no one that loves you – friend or lover – would ever put you through that kind of torture. NO ONE. And anyone that did would always start their reply with *I'm so sorry for the delay…*, then proceed to tell you what held up their being able to respond. Until Eds reply the anxiousness grew. Then when he did reply, a slight wave of relief comes with it. *He did read it, he did care, I do mean something because he's replied!* I then respond straight away and the whole cycle starts again. Squeezing at my guts, wringing them out like a mangle. It drained me, making me reliant, making me weak.

Mixed with sleep deprivation, anxiety made me feel like I was losing my mind. You can crave people and you can fear being around them. The opinions of others only kept the chaos burning. So, I learned to distance myself from the people I once trusted, because I couldn't take their questions. I didn't appreciate they pointed out Eds flaws. You start to think they are jealous of you, because you found this great love. No one was happy for me. Everyone pointed out the failures in my relationship. I tried to rationalise in my head what the truth is. What is right? What is wrong? What did I even believe myself? Now that's the real question. I craved peace. I wanted to distance myself from the drama, but I distanced myself from the wrong people. Bringing Ed ever closer. Anxiety took my life from me. It took my energy. Time. Mind. It was hard to cling onto myself. Traces of myself screamed out in my mind, challenging the chaos, reminding me of what's right and what I believe.

Reason sits heavy in the forefront. Logic is hard to argue with. When something is so – it simply is so. It's the one thing he never took from me. He stripped me of many beliefs and things I thought to be true. He took my love, my time, my money. But he could never take my logic. Or rather, the logic of those I respected and looked up to. My work surrounded me with highly intelligent people (don't get me wrong – there were some real idiots too). Edward made a mistake one day – one I couldn't forget. He started to say I didn't know how to communicate. It was my fault that our relationship was in the state it was in. Now, the moment he said that he started to lose me. My logic awoke to the situation and I said, "If I couldn't communicate – Jon wouldn't employ you." It echoed in my mind like a wish in a well. Jon is the SVP & CIO. He is a highly intelligent man. If I wasn't up to the job - I wouldn't be his communications manager – it was that simple. Maybe I didn't quite know it at the time, but it was the turning point I needed to start doubting Ed. I remember looking at Edward and saying, "but Jon wouldn't employ me if I couldn't communicate." I said it with such innocence and looked him right in the eyes. His face knew he'd been beaten. Then I walked away to soothe my mind, to make sense of the chaos. If I was to believe I didn't know how to communicate – then I had to believe that Jon couldn't recognise a communicator – I simply couldn't do that. I couldn't doubt him – I never have. Which left me for the first time with a logical doubt over Ed, that couldn't be disputed. He couldn't talk his way out of this one – which is why he didn't even try.

And my friends' words came back to me in my mind. "What's the line? When is enough, enough?" "How much longer are you going to let him do this to you?" "When are you going to cut it?" But when they spoke those words to me it was like it was a foreign language. It didn't compute. I didn't know what to do with what they said. So, subconsciously, I stored their words. At the right moment, one day, they would make sense to me. I hadn't caught up with my friends' thinking – I wasn't there yet. They didn't understand. I loved him. He was the love of my life. I couldn't function without him. That love was a shield that blinded me to the doorway to truth. Never a truer saying than love is blind. Somehow, I'd managed to block off all of his misdemeanours, infidelities, disloyalties, unfaithfulness, selfish acts, unkind gestures, hurtfulness… and somehow, I'd managed to justify it all. Enabling him to add life to this world he was creating, going along with it, enabling it, permitting it – losing myself.

But I couldn't go along with this for ever. I couldn't doubt the intelligence of a man I respected and looked up to. Sometimes people can be so motivational to you that all they need do is be present in your life for you to think to yourself, *what would they do in this situation?* There doesn't always need to be some long, life changing conversation. They can just be present in your mind. That's what Jon was for me. I guess he was a bit of a father figure really. In my mind's ear Jon spoke to me. *You don't need me to tell you what's happening here Izzy. You know.* And I did know. I knew it was the beginning of the end. I knew I was being played but I didn't understand it yet. I couldn't see how Ed controlled me. I couldn't see how he was using me. I wanted to believe that he loved me. I wanted to believe that I meant something to him. I'd spent most of my adult life alone. Finally, I thought it was my time to experience a full loving relationship with someone who'd love me as much as I loved them. I was wrong though. The disappointment of realising that stung. It stung worse than losing fifty grand. I didn't even care about the money really.

It had all been fake. You couldn't measure that much loss. I couldn't anyway. It felt like a death. Most of the day I had to carry on. I had to pretend that life was happy, and slap a smile on my face. I had Maddy to look after, a job to do, bills to pay – his debt to clear. But in those moments where I could grieve, I've never felt so lost and in such utter turmoil. Sometimes I'd just cry, uncontrollably, like a child, with snorts and everything. Others I'd just sit with my thoughts and there could be no tears – I was all dried up. I'd just sit and think. Then I'd think some more. I'd think about all that we did and all that we'd planned to do. I'd think about the tomorrows that would no longer be for us. But mostly, the thought that raced around my head is – *he just left.*

In my search for closure, for peace, I scoured the internet looking for answers. I came across a blog which described a personality I began to recognise. As I carried on reading, it could easily have been Ed that the author was writing about. It discussed narcissistic partners.

As I read through the blog, I understood more and more why things had gone the way they had and ended the way they did. Ed was a ***narcissist***. He was sick, he needed help. My first instinct was to want to save him, to help him. But every bit of advice you'll ever read will tell you a narcissist can't be helped. The best you can do is save yourself and have no contact with them. Considering most narcissists are attracted to kind, compassionate people – empaths – this was particularly hard for me to do.

I knew I also needed help. I approached my doctor and he arranged for some counselling for me. I had always felt that Ed and I were destined to be, it felt right, like I'd known him from a previous life. I'd not seen a counsellor before. The thought of talking to one made me feel I must be sick. That something was wrong with me. But the experience of it wasn't like that at all.

I was asked about my childhood.

"How would you describe your mother and father's relationship?" Bex asked.

"My dad was away a lot. When he was home, he shouted a lot. He used to throw things at my mum. His dinner, hot coffee, forks."

"And how would your mum react to that?"

"Like there was nothing to see here. She never stood up for herself. She just took it. I think she was afraid Dad might turn on me or my brother."

"How did that make you feel?"

"Scared. I preferred it when Dad wasn't home. I didn't like how he treated my mum. How he treated me." My voice started to tremble and my tears started to fall.

"Do you want to talk about that?"

"No," I sobbed.

"How your dad treated your mum wasn't right, Izzy. It wasn't how it should have been. Is it possible that the reason Ed felt so familiar to you – is that it reminded you of your family dynamic?"

I thought about it in silence. Maybe it was. Ed was a torrent of emotions. He'd go from happy to angry in seconds. From kind to cruel. He left a trail of hurt people behind him. He didn't care about how his actions affected others.

Eventually, the words stumbled from my mouth. "Yeah, I think you're right."

In that one meeting, I'd opened Pandora's box. My childhood wasn't normal. It had given me the wrong core beliefs. I needed to confront my past to have the hope of a peaceful future. Bex was going to help me to do that.

Find acceptance.

30

1970s Disney. Truth? Myth? Or an outright fucking lie? My dad always used to say, in the absence of the truth, create a myth. When the myth becomes more believable than the truth – believe the myth. That's what Disney did to my five-year-old self. It did me no solid. Setting the foundations for my impending doomed relationships. My expectations of love set by age five. One day my prince would come – all I had to do as a female was wait… I'm now forty and I can say with the utmost certainty – what a crock of shit! There is no 'love's true kiss' or 'happily ever after'. Not in my story anyway. All my life I've been conditioned to believe that I needed a man to save me. Not just by film makers, by other women – victims of the same charade. Past behaviour indicates future behaviour. What I've learned from that, is when I've needed saving – the only person who stepped up and did what was right by me – was me. I didn't need to wait for a hero because I'd been there all along.

Each time I rebuild myself, some other guy comes along and knocks me down again. And I'm left thinking – what's the point? I mean why bother? Why leave myself wide open to being hurt again? At least I can say this. As a singleton, I don't have the fear of the heartbreak of losing the man I love. I've already gone through that. I don't need to fear losing him to death. He's already dead to me. If you ain't got nothing, you've got nothing to lose, right? I don't have to worry about my guy's head being turned by the next pretty thing that walks by. Because I don't have a guy for his head to be turned. I don't have to worry if my love has a car accident late at night and is never coming home to me – because I have no guy to be coming home to me. I don't have to worry about the £100 I spent shopping because it's my debt to pay and no one else's. Life is simple now. I look after Maddy, I look after me and I pay the bills. This is my life. I don't need another person to get me through it. Love isn't coming home to me because I'm taking love home. I am enough. I am my own hero. When I needed saving, there was no mystical man on a white horse riding in to rescue me. I found my voice and I saved myself. Only I could save me – because only I knew that I needed saving. Screw you Disney. Life isn't a 1970s production of happy endings playing out on repeat. Happiness is not a destination – it's a way of life – how many times have I seen that on *Fakebook*? Never a truer word said though. I've learned that to be happy means understanding what makes me happy and making that my focus. The myth 'and they all lived happily ever after…' That very line assumes you need 'a person' to be happy ever after. The only person that can be responsible for my happiness is me. It's an unfair expectation to burden that load on another. I know that now. From now on, I'm in the front seat of my life, I'm the driver, the navigator, I'm in control. Here's to the open road ahead, the bumps along the way and the journey we call life.

Beep beep. Ah! Who the fuck's that? Here I am giving myself the inspirational speech of my life in my head and someone has to text and interrupt my flow... I slide my phone from my pocket. **'TWAT – do not respond'** has sent me a message.

How's things, it's been a while...

Yes, it has and you know why that is cuntus don't you!

I hit delete and slide my phone back into my pocket.

For the first time I can breathe the open air. I don't need his words – I let them float away with the rest of his unkept promises. I'm no longer his puppet. I don't need his white horse, or the ride to nowhere it offers me.

I step out to take my place at the starting line at Blenheim lake. The sun is shining, I place my goggles over my eyes. Maddy is waving from the stands with my mum.

Come on girl, this is what you trained for – you've got this.

'Fight Song' plays in my head as the starting pistol fires and I run into the water. The coldness hits my body, as I hit the water, I take a deep breath, pushing my head under and then rising up to breathe out. For the first time in a long time, I feel alive – reborn; about to start the first day of the rest of my life. Eat dust my ex-narcissist – this lover has evolved.

Afterword

What is it that I want to do? I'm a writer – I want to help other women that may be in this situation now and not recognise it. There is a way out. There is hope. There is life. You can be free of the narcissist. Only women who have been on or are on this journey will understand the turmoil in this book. Those who have not met the narcissist – may judge, condemn, think us stupid. I think unless you've walked the life – you'll never understand its pitfalls and vulnerabilities. I pray you don't walk this road. It can find you trapped, lost and alone with fear of no way out. So, if you haven't walked it – well done I congratulate you – but I also ask that you do not judge those who have. They were once strong, confident women who fell pray to one who is very sick and could never be helped. They tried to help – they thought they were the one to change this person. That's because they are kind, caring souls who would do anything for anyone. The last thing they are is stupid, or deserving of the treatment they received. In a world where no one knows what's around the corner – the one thing we can all be is kind. Not only in our actions but our thoughts of each other to each other. After all we are all human. We have the same flaws, insecurities and battles – and we're all on a one-way ticket to the same place.

THE AUTHOR

N. I. Lockwood is a single parent living in England. She has 4 dogs who are great for those long walks and dreaming moments every good writer thrives from.

Growing up in the South during the 1970's, where she was raised to believe you don't cry, especially in front of others, you shouldn't bring everybody down with your worries. And absolutely you never ever speak of anything untoward – like watching your dad throw things at your mum, yell at her or abuse the pair of you. These things were never to be spoken of.

Lockwood lived within the normality of an abused family, watching her mum suffer it daily, and being victim to it herself, she felt compelled to write this book in the hope it would provide strength for those suffering to take life into their own hands and break free.

This is 2022 - abuse isn't part of a normal way of life. It never has been.

Printed in Great Britain
by Amazon

84936633R00206